Sleeping Dogs *Lie*

WILLIAM TELFORD

Sleeping Dogs Lie
Copyright © 2021 by William Telford

All rights reserved. No part of this publication may be reproduced, distributed, or transmitted in any form or by any means, including photocopying, recording, or other electronic or mechanical methods, without the prior written permission of the author, except in the case of brief quotations embodied in critical reviews and certain other non-commercial uses permitted by copyright law.

Tellwell Talent
www.tellwell.ca

ISBN
978-0-2288-6728-9 (Paperback)
978-0-2288-6729-6 (eBook)

For Vince,
If there is to be any peace, it will come through being... on the fairway.
Hit it straight!
Bill

For Cheryl

1969

"Let me be, why don't you babe?" The singer's plea escapes the crush of a seven-minute intro, while the guitar's last note lingers like lightning on a distant plain. For an instant, all thoughts are still; all eyes focused, captured in time by singer and stage. The spell, however, is quickly broken by the crash of a cymbal and performer and audience go their separate ways. The ensuing clamor crescendos under an umbrella of a hundred frantic conversations and the momentum of a Friday night in the 'Peg' resumes. Bartenders render glass after glass of draft beer while waitresses weave among tables far too close for comfort, in a desperate attempt to quell the insatiable thirst of the overflowing throng. November has been generous this year, in defiance of seasonal tradition, and the local denizens are out in numbers.

They sit at a table near the band, which Andrew thought might inhibit conversation, but the two young ladies opposite merely yell a little louder. Almost identical in appearance, save for the leather headband favored by one, their long straight hair cascades down over their shoulders and nestles upon their tie-dyed T shirts. He thinks to himself that the only thing missing is a daisy behind an ear or maybe painted on one cheek. The summer of love is a distant memory but these flower children are living proof of the adage that fashion finds Winnipeg only when there are no other places to be discovered.

Smoke rises from every table and hovers menacingly overhead like a coiling serpent. Meanwhile all lungs labor collectively in a vain attempt to filter the air. A commotion has erupted near the door and a large behemoth suggests that the potential combatants 'take it outside.'

"I said, you sound just like Mic Jagger. You know…of the Stones." The girl with the headband spews smoke as she shouts across the space between them.

"Never heard of him," Andrew answers sarcastically. "I'm a Beatles fan. I'd rather you said that I look like Paul McCartney."

She smiles. "Well," she pauses and then brightens, "Dave Clark, maybe. Will that do?"

He shakes his head and takes a pull on a Rothman's. She turns to her sister and they share a laugh. Back to Andrew she says, "Allie wants to know if Noah is coming tonight."

He shakes his head once again, "Finishing up a paper. I suppose you think that *he* looks like McCartney." Neither girl offers a denial and he changes the subject. "Who's that band?"

"They're called *'The Fifth'*. They are going to be bigger than *'The Guess Who'*." Taking the cigarette from her sister, she lights a fresh one from the glowing ember. She exhales and her words follow the smoke across the table. "The Fifth. Strange name, eh? What do you think it means?"

Andrew fingers the question absently. His thoughts are elsewhere. "Maybe it represents the fifth note in the scale…. symbolism is popular among musicians," He sips at his beer, "like Beatles, for instance…it's not the insect, it's the *beat*."

The girls share a blank stare. He reasons that they are not of a musical disposition. What, then, gives them the confidence to anoint this particular band as one verging on the brink of stardom? He tests another theory. "Maybe it is a reference to the amount of alcohol they consume prior to their performance? A fifth of Scotch, perhaps?" This at least draws a response.

"Yeah. Maybe they get loaded backstage. I guess we'll just have to find out some time, eh Millie?" They giggle and Andrew wonders if beer is not the only thing they have consumed this evening. He glances around before continuing.

"S'pose it could have a dimensional component. As if they were trying to break free to another world, say. Like the Doors." He drums on the table and sings, "*break on through to the other side, yeah.*" He punctuates this with an imaginary stick to the high-hat. "I would even venture to suggest…" He looks across at his tablemates and suddenly realizes that, not only have they lost interest, they are gazing dreamily through him in the direction of the band. The strobe light has been set ablaze and all things white are illuminated. Its syncopated rhythm and the hypnotic guitar of the band's cover of *The Wind Cried Mary* holds them firmly in thrall where nothing, particularly his inane blather, can penetrate. He leans back and drains his glass and as he does so he fingers the bills in his pocket. He hopes that forty dollars Canadian will be enough.

The set screams to a climax and the buzz of conversation explodes. The girls are reinvigorated, and their enthusiasm returns. It has been six months since they arrived in the city and, having spent most of the summer living out of a tent in Memorial Park, they are still looking for a more permanent arrangement. Andrew and his friend Noah represent their best prospect with their spacious apartment in the heart of Osborne Village. The *village* is the Haight-Ashbury of the Canadian prairies and the place to be for any neophyte artist, musician or writer. The term 'hippy' is still in vogue and nomadic youth gravitate here in large numbers. Still, accommodations are at a premium, particularly as this city is cryptically known as '*Winterpeg*' and December is just around the corner. The girl with the headband is about to begin her pitch. Her words, however, are cut short.

Hovering over them is an imposing figure. He pulls back the empty chair and sits, eyes roaming the crowd, searching the faces of those nearby. Satisfied that all is safe, he nods to the waitress as she passes, and he leans forward. His imposing presence pollutes the space and anxious looks are exchanged around the table. His gaze comes to rest on Andrew and the girl with the headband, sensing trouble, speaks up bravely.

"I'm sorry but we are saving that seat for our friend. Maybe you could…"

"Fuck off!" He skewers her with a glare and then returns his attention to the only other male present.

"Well, I don't think you have to be so rude about it…we…" She does not finish. Her sister takes hold of her arm and cups a hand to her ear.

"He means that we should leave. C'mon, let's go."

Both girls reluctantly push away from the table and take a step backward. "Let's go Andy. We can find space at the bar." The headband tries to sound defiant, but fear overshadows the attempt.

"It's ok. I'll stay for awhile." Andrew's voice is calm and although the girls don't get it, they begin to move away.

"We'll order you a beer. See you in a few minutes, eh?" They push their way through the crowd leaving their friend to save face in his own way. After all, guys have their pride.

Andrew appraises the figure opposite with a writer's eye. His dark locks flow randomly from under a bandana, and it is impossible to distinguish the point where they cease and his beard begins. Rheumy eyes peer out suspiciously from behind this great mass and remain fixed on Andrew's. His frame is thick and powerful and covered by a denim shirt and leather vest. His sleeves are rolled up and his forearms, a disparate array of tattoos, suggest that their owner has been involved in more than a few bar brawls. Andrew has no doubt that the *'Harley'* parked under the overhang at the front of the hotel belongs to him. Finally, the intruder speaks.

"You a cop?" A deep voice escapes from its cage.

Andrew has anticipated this question and, although his response is at the ready, he finds that he is not feeling as self assured as he thought he might. "Definitely not. Matter of fact, I'm not even Canadian."

The stranger maintains his stare. Whether drama or uncertainty slows him, a few uncomfortable moments pass. Finally, he seems satisfied. He glances in the direction of the waitress and a beer appears. He pays with a two-dollar bill and gestures imperceptibly. The waitress pockets the change, and her hand lingers briefly on his shoulder. Then she is gone. "Forty," he spits. This is pronounced in such a way as to leave no question of negotiation.

"How does it work?"

The band starts up once again. *"Let me take you down, because I'm going to Strawberry Fields…nothing is real…and nothing to get hung about…"* The individual in front of Andrew is oblivious to music or lyric. He is a salesman, and the *Menagerie* is simply his workplace.

"Bitch at the bar. Blue jean jacket. Walk up to her. Give her a hug like you're old pals. Put the money in her pocket. Then go to the can."

"Ok. Then what?" This is all new to Andrew and common sense tells him that it could be a complete rip off. Still, what else can he do but go through with it.

"That's it. Go to the fuckin' can and then get the fuck out of here."

Andrew doesn't ask again. The less time spent in the company of this guy, the better. He rises and wends his way through the tables. The girl watches his approach and when he gets closer, she grabs him and pulls him to her. Andrew does as he is bid and slips the money into her jacket pocket. She steps back briefly and looks him in the eye. He is about to walk away when, suddenly, she pulls him back and kisses him passionately on the lips. She smiles at him and then glances over his shoulder at the man observing from the table. She tosses him a look that says, 'you don't own me', and then she kisses Andrew once again. Finally, she releases him and returns defiantly to her drink.

    Andrew fights through the mass of sweaty bodies toward the washroom. As he does so, he is jostled to and fro and, occasionally, someone offers a mumbled 'sorry bud'. When he is finally through the door, he finds that all the urinals and stalls have line ups. He maneuvers toward a sink and begins to wash his hands. The diminutive neighbor adjacent to him splashes water on his face. He turns and smiles and then says politely, "Check your back pocket." He gestures vaguely with his head. "And like the man said…get the fuck outta here." He then runs his wet hands through his hair and disappears into the din.

⚘

The Roslyn Road apartment is not only spacious but modern as well. Noah pushes back from a kitchen table cluttered with reference books and a small portable typewriter and stretches his legs. He rubs his forehead with both hands and tries to ease the tension building behind his eyes. The only light in the space comes, not from overhead but, rather, from a single lamp which he has strategically placed amidst the clutter. He has always preferred to work from within what he calls this 'finite circle of inspiration'. He sniffs the air and smiles. Taylor, the lawyer who lives next door, is smoking up. Noah isn't sure if it's a sign of celebration or defeat, but he makes a mental note to inquire tomorrow. He glances back to the sheet of paper protruding insistently from the machine and decides that it can wait. It's time for a break.

    He rises and takes up a glass from the counter. He wipes it with the front of his flannel shirt and examines it cursorily. Clean enough. A partially empty bottle of Mateus, leftover from his birthday the previous weekend, stands in wait on the counter and he scoops it up. A moment later he is stretched out on the sofa. His thoughts turn to Andrew, and he mutters out loud. "Hope it's going ok."

He sips the wine and settles deeply into the plush cushion behind his head and as he does, he allows his mind to wander. What a difference the passage of time can make. At this time two years ago, he was crammed into a single- room dorm next to a downtown university finishing up his undergrad degree. Tonight, he is living decadently in the lap of luxury, his scholarship money collecting interest in the bank around the corner. Grad School had never promised to be so comfortable. And it is all due to a chance meeting or as John Fowles, a favorite author, might say, *'hazard'*.

He had been in line for what seemed to be hours, waiting to pay his fees. The young man in front of Noah turned and offered sarcastically, "You'd think that they would be a little more amenable to the procurement of our money. Particularly at such exorbitant rates." His posh British accent had drawn a number of quizzical glances.

Noah smiled but said nothing. His thoughts were elsewhere engaged and the dialogue between two of the characters in his most recent story almost always supercede conversations set in real time. The stranger continued. "Oh, and by the way, I really love *Blackbird*" There was no doubt that he was speaking directly to Noah.

"I'm sorry?"

"*Blackbird.* Love the guitar. You are Paul McCartney, aren't you?" He offered up a genuine smile.

The reference was not new to Noah. Ever since the Beatles had exploded onto the North American musical scene, he had been reminded of his likeness to the famed member of the Fab Four.

"Sorry to disappoint. I'm just a guy waiting in line to pay tuition."

"Andrew Sutton. Pleasure." He offered his hand and their conversation had continued. They had gone for coffee afterward and the inevitable exchange of interests and backgrounds had ensued. One thing was certain. Both students had a keen interest in writing and Noah soon added an unfamiliar term to his vocabulary. His new acquaintance had been 'sent down' from Oxford, the British equivalent to expulsion. No particular reasons were offered but it seemed that his only recourse was to come to the 'provinces' to continue his education. Moreover, his father, the Earl, was footing the bill. "You must see my flat sometime," he had stated.

A few weeks later, Noah had not only checked out the place but soon had accepted an offer to move in. It had been decided that his contribution would be light on the financial side, a situation which was much appreciated, and heavier on the cleanliness side. This, again, he found agreeable as his new roommate preferred not to lift a finger in that regard. Thus had begun their friendship.

Noah pulls back the drapes, inviting a magnificent panorama into the room. Just beyond the balcony, the Assiniboine River lingers past and from its opposite bank, the exquisitely domed structure of the Legislative Assembly Building rises majestically. Bathed in the soft glow of a thousand lights, it radiates outward from the centre of a vast greenspace. Above, a host of stars provide the supporting cast to this brilliant centerpiece. Andrew has often referred to it as the St. Paul's Cathedral of the prairies. Noah has never tired of this vista and he and Andrew have spent countless hours sitting on the balcony gazing out across the river while discussing their individual works. Both have several manuscripts in varying stages of completion and even a few which they consider ready for publication. Bouncing ideas has become normal discourse between the two and the architectural wonder just beyond their reach always seems to add to the glorious possibilities of youth.

Although Noah has not heard the door open or close, there is no mistaking the owner of the voice who has just stepped inside.

"You really don't want me...you just keep me hanging on..." He exaggerates the vibrato on the last note until he is out of breath.

Noah does not turn but throws over his shoulder, "If you had one, I'd encourage you not to give up your day job." Then more tentatively, he asks, "Did you get it?"

Andrew kicks off his desert boots and flops down on a chair. He catches Noah's eye and says directly, "I did."

A moment passes and then Noah offers, "Great."

Andrew can't suppress a smile. "It was a scene right out of a cheap novel. I'll tell you all about it later. How's the paper coming?"

Noah looks up, "I don't think I have added anything new to the collective understanding of the romantic poets, but it's pretty much done." He returns to the sofa and sinks in, trying to be casual. Meanwhile Andrew has scooped up a crumpled piece of paper from the floor and is smoothing it out.

"What's this?" He holds it up to the light.

"Noah thinks for a moment and then it comes to him. "Just some doodling. Fingers were tired of banging keys."

"It's a poem."

"I can't draw."

Andrew examines it more closely and laughs. Then he clears his throat dramatically and reads aloud.

"Lord Byron's was a fertile mind
And of his wife, his words were kind
His readers tho' are soon to find
His thoughts were fixed on her behind"

He laughs again. "That horny bastard. What do you think Professor Jacobs might say about this?" He crumples the scrap and tosses it toward his friend. It lands at his feet.

Noah cleans imaginary glasses and places them on the bridge of his nose. "Well, Stafford...meter and cadence are passable...

rhyme pattern is simplistic to say the least, but I suppose it will do. But the sentiment, Stafford….it's completely juvenile. Unacceptable, really. Still…I suppose you make your point… in the *end*." He gestures rudely.

As their laughter subsides, they realize that the volume next door has been cranked to the max and a familiar refrain reaches their ears. '*and although I'll never lose affection…for people and things that went before…I know I'll often stop and think about them…in my life, I've loved you more*'.

"Melancholia," says Andrew, "must have lost this one." More laughter and then, seemingly out of left field. "I met him you know."

Noah gives him a quizzical glance. "Taylor…no kidding."

"Lennon."

It takes Noah a moment to process. Eyes roll dramatically and he lowers his tone.

"Ya right. You met John Lennon. Was that before or after your tour with the Stones?"

"He showed up at a party hosted by my father. He was with Epstein, his manager. My old man and Epstein's knew each other socially. Brits and their clubs, right? Think it was just after they filmed '*Help*' because Lennon had a suntan. Anyway, there he was…black turtleneck and tight leather pants. Boots, of course."

Noah shifts his weight. With Andrew, you never knew. Especially given his privileged background. "So…tell me."

"Curious thing." Andrew draws himself up. "There he was…John Lennon…one of the most famous celebrities of our time…getting sloshed on scotch and cokes…and finding himself completely ignored by the rest of the guests. I mean really…you've seen '*A Hard Day's Night*'. Here's a guy who can't take a step outside without getting his freakin' clothes torn off…and yet, in my house…with that crowd…he was bloody invisible. So, I guess I was it…we struck up a conversation. I was the only one who knew or at least cared who the hell he was."

"Well....what did you find to talk about?" Noah has taken an interest.

"Music, mostly. Told him I was a big fan...should've tried to play it cool but I was seventeen bloody years old and my fuckin' idol was sitting across from me offering me sips from his fuckin' drink." Andrew's arms are extended, as if he were testing for rain. "Finally, he notices my guitar and he picks it up. For a minute I thought he was going to play but he suddenly thrust it at me. Looked me right in the eye and asked me if I did any bleedin' writing."

Andrew pauses to light up a cigarette before continuing.

"You see how clever he was?" Still no rain. "Most people would ask if I played, right? Not John Lennon. He saw the guitar and he had already made that obvious assumption, so he skipped the bullshit and got straight to the point."

"So, what did you say?"

"Well, keep in mind that I'd never actually played in front of anyone before, let alone sung my own songs for them, but I thought, what the hell...and I squeaked out a yes. It must have been the intimacy I felt between us. Kind of like we were kindred spirits or something. So, I took up the guitar and strummed an E minor cord. Then right there, for the first time in my life, I allowed someone else to hear my inner thoughts. And that someone was John fuckin' Lennon. Think about it."

He fingers an imaginary chord as he summons the scene from his memory.

"So, what did he think?" Noah knows all too well his roommate's private nature and he appreciates how difficult it would have been for him to open up.

"Well, he was silent for a moment. Never took his eyes from me. I could feel his humanity. In seventeen years prior to that moment, I have never felt so close to another being." Andrew draws deeply on the Rothmans and then exhales with a flourish.

"He belched and said, 'it's fuckin' shite, man', and he staggered off. I never saw him again."

Neither speaks. Noah doesn't know whether to laugh or offer words of consolation so instead, he stares at his glass. After a few moments, he downs the last of the wine. Casually he asks, "So when do you want to do it?"

"No time like the present." Andrew takes out the envelope from his back pocket and opens it. He lays the contents on the table. Two sugar cubes rest innocently in front of them, holding them enthralled.

"How do we know its acid?" Noah asks quietly.

"What else could it be? It cost forty bucks."

"So…what do we do?"

"Eat it, I guess."

"Ok…"

CHAPTER

2002

They are to meet at Claridge's, and David is late. Claridge's, the Mayfair hotel in the heart of London, where one's fantasies need only to be articulated in order to be fulfilled. The hotel where Winston Churchill once had room 211 declared Yugoslavian territory so that the Crown Prince Alexander II could be born on his own country's soil. Claridge's… the hotel of Hepburn and Garbo; of Crosby and Grant. The very hotel which prompted Spencer Tracey to once declare, 'When I die, I'd rather go to Claridge's than heaven'. Claridge's, where David is to meet the man who may offer him a way out. A man who's extended hand he will either choose to grasp or, once and for all, slip beneath the surface of his own self pity.

David Whittier has, of course, heard all the stories. You don't grow up in London without an appreciation of the local landmarks. And Claridge's is certainly that. His favorite story is one told by a previous manager. 'People used to ring up the telephone operator and ask to speak to the King. The operator was always quick to reply, 'which one?' It never failed to bring a smile to his face. That said, he has never set foot beyond her gilded doors.

He is led through the foyer by a gentleman who, in another time, would undoubtedly have commanded the service staff of a fine country estate, and then is left, momentarily, to his own devise. He is surprised that he is not feeling hung over. After all, it is only noon. He catches a glimpse of his own reflection in the glass of a French door. Maybe he should have shaved. His attendant returns and, with not a hint of condescension, says, "Your host will see you shortly, sir. This way please." He turns away and as he walks offers, "you may call me Benson, sir."

David's assumption that he is being escorted into the main dining room is short lived. Instead, he is guided to a small anteroom. "Forty-two regular, is it sir?" Benson slides open a panel revealing a row of dark business suits. He then stands aside. "Shall I select one for you, sir, or would you prefer to choose your own?"

David is not offended, merely surprised. Then again, why should he be? In fact, in his previous life, he would likely have anticipated this. It is just another reminder of how far he has fallen. He gathers himself. "Thank you, Benson, I think I can take it from here."

"You will find a full array of toiletries in the lavatory, sir. Razors, aftershaves and bracers. I shall return shortly." He turns and, without further comment, departs, leaving David to shave, shower and dress for his lunch with the Earl of Derbyshire.

The dining room is even more lavish than David could have imagined. He follows Benson's lead, and they stop before a table near a window. He is formally announced. "David Whittier, your lordship." And with this, Benson disappears.

"Whittier, my dear boy. What a pleasure it is to meet you. You will forgive me if I don't get up. Please." He gestures to the adjacent seat.

David sits and they shake hands. "The honor is mine, Lord Derbyshire."

"It's Andrew, please. I will tell you, this 'your lordship' nonsense is something that I will never quite get used to." He shakes his head. "And, if you will permit me, I will call you David." He pauses and takes a deep pull of the oxygen through the tubes which invade both nostrils. David glances at the tank which rests upon the floor beside his host's chair.

"Emphysema," offers the Earl noticing the look. "Bloody pain in the ass, I can assure you."

A moment passes. David wavers between some form of inadequate consolation and a new direction of conversation altogether but neither finds his lips.

"Entirely of my own doing, though I am proud to say that I have finally kicked the habit. Smoke, do you?"

"Only as a kid. Gave it up when my old man caught me. He showed me a better way."

"Good for him. You owe him a debt of gratitude. Drink?"

David is about to launch into the story of how he came to make the acquaintance of alcohol when he suddenly realizes that a waiter is standing, silently, at his shoulder. He quickly recovers, "tea, please."

"A sensible choice." The Earl nods and the server disappears. David waits patiently as his host adjusts the modulator on his breathing devise and although quiet conversations are taking place all around them, he finds the momentary lapse of dialogue unsettling. That isn't to say that he is unfamiliar in a situation such as the one in which he currently finds himself. In point of fact, in his previous life, he has interviewed a plethora of people from all walks of life. From celebrity to clergy, countess to cook, he has probed the depths of their innermost thoughts, and, from their stories, he has carved out a comfortable niche for himself in the print media. At least he *had* done so. Today, however, has a much different feel as it is he who finds himself under the microscope.

"I wonder, David, if we might dispense with the pleasantries and get to the heart of the matter. My stamina isn't what it once was." Each sentence is punctuated by a wheeze as the Earl gulps in precious oxygen.

"Of course, your lordship. But I must tell you that your invitation was a little vague. To be perfectly blunt, I'm not certain just why I'm here." He takes a moment to observe his host. Though he looks much older, David knows that he is only in his mid fifties. Wisps of silver hair flow dramatically down across his forehead in the fashion of an aging film star and clear blue eyes gaze outwardly from across the table without the aid of glasses. His thin frame supports a navy blazer which appears, to David, to be cut to fit a larger man, indicating that he has recently lost weight. His most distinguishing feature, however, is his voice. It is both deep and rich and when he speaks, each word comes out perfectly formed and set apart in time and space from the last. It is a voice spawned from an intimate knowledge of tobacco and alcohol. And its owner is a man who has learned patience. He knows that those things which he desires will transpire, inevitably, in their own time. They always have.

"It's Andrew, please," that voice replies. "*His lordship* belongs to the previous owner. And I spent a lifetime never knowing whether I was expected to use that offensive term or simply *father*. I finally did neither." He shakes his head. "But enough. This is about you. Please accept my heartfelt condolences on the loss of your wife."

David is nonplussed. He recovers just enough to reply, "Ex-wife," and after a moment he manages, "Thank you."

"Terrible thing." His look is genuine. "I'm very sorry that it has become such a part of the public domain. But then, I suppose you knew what you were getting into. After all, you *are* in the business."

"Look, your lordship…Andrew…what is your interest in all of this? I would think that…"

"What are your thoughts about the lawsuit? Do you really have the resources to take on an establishment so formidable as the medical profession?"

David is suddenly weary. His instinct urges him to tell this bastard to sod off and just walk out. That it's none of his bloody business. Instead, he sighs and says nothing at all.

"Look, David. I've read your articles. Those are very inflammatory allegations you've leveled. It's the bloody medical profession, David, psychiatrists for God's sake, not the Women's Temperance League. They have power, man…and influence."

"They can all go to hell!" Brave words but spoken in a tone which acknowledges defeat.

"Do you at least have the backing of *The Times?*"

David shakes his head absently. "They've hung me out to dry. Issued their own apology just after they cut me loose. I'm on my own."

Andrew Sutton, The Thirteenth Earl of Derbyshire, looks sympathetically across the table at his guest. He breathes deeply from the tank resting at his side and then says finally, "On your own, David…on your own?" His look is both gracious and determined. "No, David, you are not. Not anymore."

"And so, you see, ladies…and *gentleman*…," The speaker turns and acknowledges the single male member of his audience, the retired Anglican priest who lives on the eighth floor, "that the solving of a homicide, unlike the suspense novels that you have all undoubtedly read, is fairly routine. We act on tips from the public and we ask ourselves one overriding question. *Who benefits from this crime?*" He pauses. "And when we know the answer to that question, we have our man." Again, he glances at the priest and smiles, "or woman." The priest winks dramatically. "After that," he continues, "the hard task of assembling the evidence begins and, if we are good enough at our job, the courts have an easy time with theirs."

Zelig Belinski stands awkwardly behind his podium; a teetering music stand left behind by the violinist from the previous week. His robust appearance and square features seem greatly at odds with those of the frail members of his audience. The kid from the north end of Winnipeg, although he has just passed the half century mark, still retains the rugged look of the defenseman who managed to turn his physical talents into a degree in criminology. He has reluctantly agreed to address the members of the Nassau Street *chit chat* group for one reason only. His mother is its chairperson, and she beams at him proudly from the front row.

"Are there any questions?" The stand finally gives way, and he puts it gently aside. There is a lull, and several members begin to shuffle in their chairs. It is, after all, nearing the lunch hour. Finally, one audience member speaks up.

"Detective Belinski. In your opinion, could what happened in New York to those poor people at the World Trade Centre ever happen here in Canada?"

It has been more than a year since the terrorist attack on the United States shook the world but here, in the senior's block, it is still a great issue of concern.

"Well…mom…we should never be complacent about such things but, to the best of my knowledge, we are not in any danger at this time."

"This is a very tall building, dear."

"Even so…I think we should all feel grateful to live in a country as safe and secure as Canada." He smiles patiently and prays that he has summed things up.

"Well then thank you very much, Detective Belinski, for speaking to us today and giving us your valuable insight." A smattering of applause indicates that the session has reached its conclusion and that lunch is served. Belinski hugs his mom and slips, unnoticed, out the side door.

"Not even one of them little sandwiches? Are you kidding me? I been sitting out here for a friggin hour." Jean-Guy Lemaire is working up his usual lather. Small in stature, he has learned that *attitude* is his greatest asset. Having come up through the ranks, he has chosen to deal with adversity by invoking his sharp tongue and by showing an enthusiasm to mix it up with much larger opponents. This tenacity has earned him the moniker, *Grunt*, though never to his face.

"You were sleeping."

"Like hell…I've been sitting out here wondering how you were making out with the old fogies. *Worrying* for you, for Chrissakes. And you don't even bring me a friggin piece of cake."

"Let's go." Belinski's even temperament has been tested enough for one day and they have several more hours to get through.

"So, what'd you tell em'?"

Belinski settles in. "Kept it simple. Figured they didn't want to hear all about routines and procedures. Hell, *I* don't even want to hear about them. So I said we try to answer the question of who might benefit the most by someone's murder. I think that was sufficient."

His junior is beside himself. "That's it? That's what the great homicide detective comes up with? Geeze, Zel. These codgers are watching CSI every other night, for Chrissakes. They know more about how to solve a crime than we do." He shakes his head in disbelief.

"Seniors."

"What?"

"They're senior citizens. They deserve our respect."

"OK, fine. But picture this. Every bloody *senior* in the block is gonna be comin' up to your mom and sayin', "Nice boy you have there, Mrs. Belinski, but he doesn't know shit about detective work." He shakes his head again, "And not even a friggin cookie."

As the unmarked car pulls out from the curb, Belinski's only response is, "find a Tim's."

⁂

The locker area at the Princess Street station is abuzz with conversation as bodies come and go from the showers and preen in front of steamed up mirrors. Shift change is a time of congregation and congestion. Though Belinski and Lemaire are relative strangers here, they have come in the hope of catching up with a patrol officer who had assisted them on a recent case. They feel that they owe him a debt of gratitude and Grunt has decided that it should come in the form of a twenty-six of Polish Vodka. They endure the inevitable jibes from their fellow officers with good humor and Lemaire gives back as good as he gets. Their bantering subsides as their attention is drawn in the direction of the outer hallway.

The door opens and two uniformed officers enter. As their presence is acknowledged, all conversation comes to a halt. Each walks slowly toward his locker in silence, though neither looks up. Finally, someone in the crowd can contain himself no longer and bursts into an uncontrollable fit of hilarity. The entire room erupts, and a few tears find their way onto the cheeks of grizzled men. The two unfortunates at the centre of *'Speaker gate'* are in the building.

Late into a shift on the previous day, the two officers in question had pulled over in front of a deli on Portage Avenue, the main artery through the downtown district. After picking up a bite to eat, they were content to sit and chat. One thing had led to another and, before long, Constable Ginelli had launched into the intimate details of his date the previous evening. Prompted by the expert questioning of his partner, he had spared no details. They chewed their bagels and sipped their coffee, seemingly unaware that a crowd was gathering around their black and white. Even the CBC news crew, complete with camera and soundman, which had just wrapped up a story down the block, had failed to catch their attention…or to interrupt the telling of the tale. What they had not realized at the time, but were soon to discover to their deep mortification, was that they had somehow tripped the switch to their outside speaker.

The crowd, not to mention the media, had heard every word. Finally, whether out of a sense of civic duty or simply pity for the young officer, a bystander had tapped on the window. The irritated driver had scowled momentarily and then, as the realization of what he had just been told began to sink in, he had returned the window quickly to the closed position. Ginelli's nocturnal adventure was now part of the greater public domain, and, though neither had yet been called on the carpet, the embarrassment they are to suffer at the hands of their fellow officers might just be punishment enough.

As the laughter subsides, Lemaire turns to his partner and reflects, "I think we should come here more often. Best laugh I've had in a long time." He adds, straight faced, "Then again, I didn't get to hear your speech to the old fogies." He is scorched by a look from Belinski and then adds, "Ok, ok, seniors."

CHAPTER Two

Their lunch has been an abbreviated one as David's host had required medical attention. Nothing serious, he had been assured, but nevertheless their meeting had ended abruptly, and, although Andrew had insisted that he remain and enjoy his lunch, David has made a hasty exit. He walks absently along the walkways, wondering what to make of things.

Of course, he has heard of Andrew Sutton, the latest Earl of Derbyshire. In fact, he had tried to interview him on a number of occasions over the years. A celebrated writer by the time he was twenty-seven, his first novel had been acclaimed 'brilliant' by the *'Times'* long before David had ever dreamed of becoming a journalist. The sequel was held in even higher regard and had propelled him into the public spotlight. Never shy with the media, Sutton had always shown a readiness for commentary and was considered to be a prized quote by the newshounds of the day. Even after his posting to the literary department at Cambridge, where dons have traditionally retired to the sanctuary of their ivory towers, he had continued to remain a very public figure. That did not, however, explain his interest in David.

A horn blares as a London cabbie tosses a few choice words out of his window at a jaywalker and David is wrenched out of his reverie. His wanderings have taken him into the heart of his old haunts, which doesn't surprise him. He often finds himself here, where bittersweet memories linger around every corner and where the scents and sounds of its restaurants and bars, so familiar, remind him that he is no longer welcome. After a moment he forces himself to look up. There, behind the corner window on the third floor was where she had lived…where *they* had lived.

An auspicious beginning, it had certainly not been. David had arrived early at the Wood Street Bar and was awaiting, uneasily, the arrival of his former classmates. The 'Wood' had been a favourite watering hole for he and his mates from City University London and the promise of a ten-year reunion had seemed a good idea at the time. Tonight, however, he had hopes that he, alone, would be the only member of the group to remember the pledge. And as it turned out, he was.

His third pint had been less palatable than the others and, as each minute passed, he felt more and more foolish. A final swig and he was ready to go. As he turned, however, he was jostled by the punter next to him and the remainder of his bitter was airborne. But not for long, and the recipient, a woman of about his own age, had turned in disbelief. She began several times but could not find the words to express her outrage. Nor was there any need. Her look proved to be sufficient, and David had been scorched by her fury. He had blathered out an apology and his offer to pay for the cleaning had been churlishly declined. He left quietly.

Weeks later, while attending a performance of the London Symphony Orchestra at the Barbican Centre, David had made an astonishing discovery. There, amidst her fellow violinists, in the second row of the string section, sat the same woman with whom he had unintentionally shared his pint. Six months later, they were engaged.

He wanders through the old mansion, stopping here and there to straighten a picture or to adjust the angle of a table, his constant companion trailing behind. With each new exertion, he takes a pull of the precious oxygen which remains his lifeline and, as the evening turns to night, he is cognizant that sleep will be, once more, elusive.

The music room has changed little over the years and, as he takes up the old guitar, a tear glistens in the corner of one eye. His fingers fumble uneasily about its neck and, after a moment of uncertainty, he strums a muffled chord. E minor. Just for an instant, the distant echoes of another time play about his memory and all the promise of youth seems to stretch out in front of him. "It's fuckin' shite," he whispers to no one and lays the guitar gently against the ottoman.

David reclines wearily into the only decent chair in the small flat and propels his feet through the pile of letters, most of which remain unopened, cluttering the surface of the coffee table. He has long since given up acknowledging any correspondence received from Bartlett, Bartlett and Hind, solicitors for The British Medical Association. He's become immune to their threats and to their bullying tactics. If they had any sense at all, they would have realized that they had beaten him into submission weeks ago. Yet they continue to supplicate him.

Though he has lived here for the better part of three years, he has given no thought to the room's dreary décor. And why should he. It has merely come to represent a place of temporary shelter, a purgatory. He remains here while he awaits the inevitable, though he cannot articulate, even to himself, just what that will be. Nor does he care. All that he had, and all that he had been has been taken from him, and he knows that life outside these walls will carry on without his participation. He pours from the bottle.

Three years. To David, it seems like thirty. No documents were proffered, none were signed. She merely asked him to leave, and the seven happiest years of his life had come to an end. He left quietly.

They had been enthralled with each other. Of this, David was certain. And Christiane had told him often enough. Their contrasting personalities complimented each other in a way which surprised them both. Her passion for the arts inspired him to embrace novel experiences; to take on new attitudes. His practicality had provided the counterpoint to her impulsive nature in a way that allowed for each to find joy. They were a perfect fit. Theirs was a perfect love. And then her depression had begun.

At first, the episodes were mild and infrequent, a vague sadness which seemed to come on from nowhere in particular. Gradually, over time, they had intensified and finally, when the medication began to lose its effectiveness, periods of hospitalization were necessary. Through it all, neither of them lost hope and, as she relied more and more on him for support, David had remained certain that they would find a way. The events of one evening, however, were to render that impossible.

The celebration had been a riotous one, a friend's fortieth birthday dinner, and they had stayed afterward for a few drinks. Deciding that the walk would do them both good, they had set off arm in arm, and had taken a circuitous route back to their flat. Turning a corner, engrossed in each others company, they failed to notice him. But he saw them. A hooded thug, brandishing a knife, had jumped from the shadows, blocking their path. It was a shock unlike any David had ever experienced before and he was momentarily rooted to the ground. The stranger demanded his billfold and wrenched the small clutch purse from Christiane's possession. He growled something about not giving him a reason to hurt them as David searched desperately for his nerve. He even took a few steps forward. Christiane pleaded with David to comply and to do nothing that would put himself in danger. The knife glinted in the dim light of the lamppost as its owner waved it menacingly in front of David's face. He grabbed the billfold angrily and then, before dashing off into the night, he ran his hand across Christiane's breast, all the while maintaining his eyes on David's. Then he was gone.

David knows, without question that, from that moment on, everything had changed. Although Christiane had told him repeatedly that she was relieved that he had acted with restraint; that neither of them had been hurt, the feeling between them; that indefinable chemistry that had fueled their love, had been stolen along with their money. What's more, David had discovered that he was a coward, and more importantly, he knew that she had as well. Their time together, like her passion for him, slipped gradually away with each day's passing. Before long, he was gone.

CHAPTER
Three

Police vehicles block the alley at either end, and the small group of onlookers has been cordoned off. Belinski and Lemaire wend their way through the crowd led by a uniformed officer, taking care not to step in the garbage which has escaped from the overflowing bins.

"Friggin' stinks back here." Lemaire dodges an empty pizza box. "Why don't they clean this shit up?"

The senior officer has grown immune to the endless ranting of his partner. He knows that most of the commentary is rhetorical, and it serves to fill the vocal gaps in their relationship. Belinski knows that he, himself, is not exactly loquacious. In the cavity between two buildings, they spot the forensics team which is just completing their procedures and Sgt. Johnson, the Forensic Identification Unit manager waves them over.

"This one yours, Belinski? Sure do draw the important assignments, don't you?"

Lemaire takes a few steps forward.

"Shut the frig up, Johnson," he spits, "they give us these shit jobs because we get results."

"Relax, detective. We're just wrapping up." He turns back to Belinski. "Maybe you should keep him on a leash. Be outta here in just a moment. I should have the report for you later today."

"That's fine, Johnnie, what do we have?"

"Another bum. No ID but he had a card in his shirt pocket." Johnson checks his notebook. "Freedom Mission." He nods in the direction of the victim. "Blow to the head. Want to take a look?"

Belinski advances and kneels down beside the corpse. Though he has been in this situation more times than he would like to acknowledge, he still feels the same abhorrence. It isn't the carnage, the blood and tissue. It's the sheer senselessness of it all. The loss of a human being. "Can I move this?" He motions toward the filthy wheelchair.

"Go ahead. We're finished with it."

"Did you dust it?" Belinski gently shifts it away from the victim.

"A few prints…It'll be in the report."

The body which lies in a heap in the back of an alley is jammed awkwardly against the brick wall of the building. Small in stature, one of his legs has been amputated and the pant leg which has been sewn closed is frayed and tattered. His clothes are soiled, and his baseball cap rests in his lap. His arms are raised, and twist defensively over his face, the fingerless gloves clenched tight. A single bruise, purple in hue, protrudes from the side of his head and his wispy beard is covered in spittle. Belinski offers a silent prayer and then retreats. "I want a clear photo before you take him." Then he turns and walks away.

"You heard the detective. Get that friggin' picture to us pronto, *jonnie*." The grunt spits and hurries after his partner.

⁂

Freedom Mission occupies the corner of the block in one of the poorest districts of the city. This section of Main Street is dominated by cheap hotels and pawn shops. Its denizens represent the down and out of Winnipeg society and most are on one form of social assistance or another. If not for the shelters and food banks which proliferate here, many of the inhabitants would go homeless and hungry. It is a constant struggle to meet the needs of these people and those who work or volunteer in the area know that they are losing ground with each passing year.

The car comes to a halt and the two detectives immerge. A chain of bodies, some leaning against the building, some stretched out on the sidewalk, points the way to the entrance. The evening meal is being prepared inside and, with nothing else on their agenda, hopeful diners have arrived early.

"Belinski and Lemaire." They hold out their badges for inspection and are led to an office at the rear of the building. An elderly gentleman, looking as if he should have retired long ago, nods to his assistant and bids them welcome.

"Hello, detectives. How can I be of assistance?" He rises and, grasping a cane, limps toward them, hand extended. "Klaus Sigfisson." He smiles. "I don't suppose you are here to help with the dinner prep?"

"Not today, I'm afraid." Belinski holds out the photo. "Can you identify this man?"

Sigfisson's jovial mood disappears. "Oh, my lord." His shoulders slump and he takes a moment. It's obvious to him that the man in the picture is deceased.

"It's Murray." He leans back against the edge of his desk. "He's a regular here." He exhales heavily and then adds, "God bless him."

"Would you know his last name?"

Sigfisson ponders for a moment and sighs. "It pains me to say that I don't."

"Live here, does he, Mr. Sigfisson?" Lemaire is generally the note taker of the two and flips to a blank page in his book.

"We have a dormitory on the second floor. We don't assign bunks. It's on a first come, first served basis. Murray is almost always one of the frontrunners through the door. I think the others cut him some slack because of the chair."

"Would he keep his belongings upstairs, sir?" Belinski this time.

"Belongings?" Sigfisson's tone is not sarcastic, merely surprised. "As far as I know he doesn't have any. Just the clothes on his back…and his wheelchair. He goes out to solicit after breakfast and returns for his dinner in the evening." He pauses and then adds, "at least that was his routine."

"Sorry, I didn't mean to be insensitive. Can you think of anyone who might know his last name?"

"It's hard to guess, detective. But if I had to, I would say not likely. They're mostly transients. They come and go and don't really socialize much with each other." Sigfisson slides back into his chair. "I suppose it wouldn't hurt if I asked around at dinner. I'll contact you if anything comes of it."

Belinski places a card on the table. "Thank you. Call at any time." He reaches out and they shake hands. Lemaire nods and begins to retreat.

"One moment please, Detective Belinski." Sigfisson hesitates. "What will happen to Murray…that is… what will happen to the body?"

The two officers look blankly at each other. "Well, if there is no next of kin…"

"We have a small fund set aside." This time it is Sigfisson who provides his card. "If you're unable to locate Murray's family, please let me know and I will make all the arrangements. It's the least we can do."

"Let's stay in touch, then. And thank you for your help."

"What a friggin' way to live." The two detectives sip coffee and watch through the window of their vehicle as the raggedly clothed army of vagrants patrol the city centre. A few are passive, sitting against a building while holding a cup or their hat on their laps. Some are overtly aggressive and badger those who must, of necessity, cross their path. Others, still, employ an altogether different strategy. Smiling and gregarious, they charm potential benefactors with their playfulness, and only when rejected do they explode with profanity and derision.

"Let's go." Belinski places his cup in the holder and shifts his bulk to the sidewalk and, although there is no doubt that they are peace officers, they are paid no heed. It's business as usual on the downtown streets of Winnipeg. They begin their search in front of the local hockey arena. One of the modern jewels of this multicultural center, the glass and steel structure glitters in the afternoon sunshine. A street crew is busy washing the interlocking stone at its entrance. Lemaire beckons to one of them while Belinski wanders down the block.

"Ever seen this guy?" He turns to shield the sun and produces the picture.

"Who wants to know?" His response is noncommittal.

"A friggin' cop wants to know." He rips out his badge and thrusts it forward.

The cleaner starts backward and then recovers. "Sorry, officer." He hesitates, as if a part of him cannot really believe that the man standing opposite him is actually a representative of the law, and says finally, "Ya, I know who he is. It's Murray." Then, as it finally dawns on him that the man in the picture is deceased, he says, "Ah shit."

"Last name?"

"Couldn't tell you. Just Murray."

"Not his, numnuts…yours. I gotta keep records." He slips out his notebook.

Lemaire jots down the man's personal information and then asks, "So what can you tell me about Murray?"

The cleaner thinks for a moment. "Not much…see him around all the time but…well he doesn't talk to me, and I don't talk to him. Look around…he's a bum…city's full of 'em." Some of his cockiness is returning and he will want to tell the boys that no cop pushes him around. Then he decides to add, "Why don't you ask Darrell." He nods to the hot dog vendor across the street. "That guy's here every day. He probably knows every bum around."

Lemaire offers no thanks and heads to the opposite side of the street, waving his partner over as he goes.

Belinski catches up. "Anything?"

"Nothing we don't already know. He's a beggar and this was his area. Cleaner says we should ask the hot dog guy." Lemaire nods toward the barbecue cart on the city sidewalk a few meters away. "Shouldn't have had that bagel. I friggin' love smokies. Maybe we should come back a little later."

"Give me the picture. I'll take this one."

Belinski walks toward the hot dog cart. A group of patrons wait patiently for their orders while others load condiments on surprisingly palatable looking fare. He steps between them and the cart and reaches for his badge.

"Back of the line, buddy. Plenty of food to go round."

"Detective Belinski, homicide."

The clamor of rush hour traffic continues behind them but all conversation beneath the cart's awning comes to a halt. Darrell puts aside his tongs and looks up from his grill. His look is hard to read.

"What can I do for you, detective?" He motions to his customers to stand back and give them a moment.

Belinski holds out the picture for inspection. "Know this man?"

The vendor goes silent as though measuring his response. His customers, feigning disinterest, remain a respectable distance away but strain to take in whatever part of the conversation they can. Finally, Darrell offers his answer loudly and clearly. "No, detective. I have no idea who that is. Sorry that I can't help."

"Sure about that?" Belinski is no rookie.

"Never seen him before in my life. Now, if you could excuse me…" He takes up his set of tongs. "Smokie with cheese," he shouts and business resumes.

Belinski returns the picture to his pocket and he and Lemaire move on down the street. They stop passers by and even a few street people, but no one seems to recognize the photo. They are about to leave when a youngster scoots by on a bike. He bumps into Belinski and hops off. Before Lemaire can launch into a rant, the boy makes his apologies. He then hands Belinski a note and flies off down the sidewalk. The detective uncrumples the paper and examines it.

320 Cranston Street Any time after 8. Darrell.

CHAPTER Four

"Ah there you are, Mrs. Stafford. May I present Dr. Pierre Belanger?" They shake and their elderly host continues on. "Since your last visit we have made a few changes here. Dr. Belanger has taken over your husband's care. I suppose that I should brag a little about his brilliance, but I think I will leave that to him. I'm sure he can speak for himself. After all, he is a psychiatrist." It isn't clear if his self-satisfied smile is meant to hide his pride at this new addition to his staff or his own appreciation of the cleverness of his introduction. "At any rate, I am very happy to have him. I will leave you in his capable hands." With this, he is off.

"Please," Belanger nods in the direction of his office door, "this way if you would be so kind." They enter and sit. The desk between them is bare, save for the laptop which sits, neatly to one side. No pictures adorn the walls. The room is clinical, both literally and figuratively.

Belanger notices her glance. "Please forgive the surroundings. I've yet to find the time to settle in. I have been more anxious to begin the work."

She does not respond. Ever since the invitation to meet had arrived, she has been filled with anxiety and has run the gamut from hope to dread. The less small talk that better as far as she is concerned. The only thought in her mind is *get to the bloody point.*

Belanger senses that he should begin. "You will forgive me, but I have been over Mr. Stafford's file many times but …well… there is no mention of a wife."

She is not surprised. "It's Miss Stafford, doctor. Terri, if you like. Noah is my brother, not my husband."

Belanger nods his head slightly and smiles. "Well, I am pleased to clear up the misunderstanding."

"Doctor McKenzie is not much of a listener. I've cleared up that misunderstanding with him several times." She pauses to allow for a change of subject. "Doctor Belanger, if you don't mind…why am I here?"

He leans forward and his tone is confessional. "There has been a change in your brother's condition."

They are the words she has prepared to hear and, although she is no nearer an understanding of what they herald, she steadies herself. If he is ill then it will break her heart but at least it may ease his suffering for that is what she perceives his state to be. And if it isn't health related, then what. Psychological? In his near catatonic state, she cannot imagine how his condition might worsen. He is completely oblivious to his surroundings. But what if neither of these scenarios apply? What if, in fact, there is a change for the better. She can barely bring herself to consider this option. Positive change…after all these years. She allows her question to escape her lips. "What kind of change?"

"Please." He reaches for his laptop, places it between them and inserts a cd. After a few clicks an image appears. It is a video of Noah. He sits in his familiar straight-backed chair and stairs blankly out the window in front of him. His slender build and placid state are suggestive of a Buddhist monk deep in meditation. After a moment an attendant approaches, and appears to engage him in conversation. Noah's eyes remain fixed beyond the glass and the woman's comments go unheeded. The screen goes black.

"These images were taken six weeks ago, Miss Stafford. They were taken just after my arrival. I'm certain that you have seen Noah in this manner many times. The file indicates that since his arrival in 1969 he has been uncommunicative. Would you agree that this is the case?"

Tears come to her eyes. Of course, she has seen Noah this way. It's always been this way. Still, to hear the words spoken; to have his pain framed in time is too much to bear. *Since his arrival in 1969.* She can only nod. She wants to add her usual argument which she has made so many times to Dr. McKenzie. What about the push ups; the arm pulls. He jogs around the bloody compound for God's sake. That's got to mean something. He's still Noah. He's still my big brother. He's still in there. Please get him out!

"Now this. Please." Belanger replaces the disk. Again, it is Noah. This time he is in the sitting area. Other patients come and go. Some sit about together while a few watch television. He is in his chair, but he is not alone. Dr. Belanger sits at his side and appears to be speaking. Occasionally he is animated and punctuates his conversation with gestures. He produces a book and reads a passage from it.

"Ah. Please. Watch intently" Belanger moves the screen closer. Terri leans in. It is a moment unlike she has ever experienced in her life and when she tries to recount it later, she will find no words. But there it was. The image from the laptop is grainy but clear enough. Belanger closes the book from which he has been reading and places it on Noah's lap. He rests his hand on Noah's shoulder and whispers something in his ear. Then he takes a step back. It is unmistakable. Noah turns his head and his lips curl upward. Then he places both hands on the book and he bows his head forward. A tear trickles from the edge of his eye and lingers momentarily on his cheek. The screen goes dark.

They sit in silence. A clock ticks off the seconds rhythmically from its hidden location while a few murmured conversations invade from the hallway without. Terri's eyes remain fixed on the blank screen. Finally, she summons her voice. "I don't know what to say. I can't…I just…" She looks up. "What does it mean, Doctor?"

"Of course, it's too early to say and recovery can take many forms. Noah has severe brain damage. How much he can achieve… if anything at all…well there is much work to be done. We shall see. I have many ideas which I would like to try but I will need your permission, of course. I would like to explain my…"

"Can I see him?"

"Of course. We will talk after your visit. But please, Miss Stafford, do not set your hopes too high. These changes take time. I will take you in."

They exit the office and wend their way down the hallway. Terri turns and takes a last look at the laptop and asks, "May I have a copy of the cd, Doctor Belanger?"

He ponders the ethics for a moment before replying and says, "Do you know that I have never been asked that before. Certainly, you can."

She is not finished. "The book, doctor. What were you reading to Noah?"

He smiles. "It's the only book I brought with me to this country. A compilation of poems by the French poet, *Paul Eluard*. I think that Noah most liked this line. *Love is more beautiful than the world in which I live so…I close my eyes.*"

They arrive and she taps on his door.

CHAPTER *Five*

The house sits, midblock, amidst a collection of similar structures in an affluent section of town. Two stories high, its white siding is adorned with hunter green shutters and large picture windows. Halfway up the paving stone walkway Lemaire comes to a halt. "Geez Zel...this place is as nice as your..." He doesn't finish his sentence. "I mean your old..." The usually quick-witted Grunt is suddenly lost for words and wishes he hadn't used the ones he did.

"Nice place," offers Belinski. The two detectives hurry up the steps in silence. The bell is answered by a woman, mid forties, whose pleasant demeanor makes them feel immediately at home. "Welcome officers. I'm Cynthia. Darrell is round back. Would you like to come through?"

"We'll use the side gate, maam." Lemaire is quick to respond. There is no way he's taking off his shoes at the door.

They find Darrell standing over the swimming pool, net in hand, reaching forward to scoop up some leaves. He turns as they enter. "Hi, fellas. Be right with you."

His offer of refreshments is declined, and they sit under a patio umbrella. While Lemaire takes down the hot dog vendor's particulars, Belinski looks around absently. Finally, he says, "Change your mind about what you told me earlier?"

Darrell clears his throat. "Not exactly...it's like this. I work down there. It's a different world. Say the wrong thing to someone and there's bound to be trouble. Look around...I'm just like you...I have bills to pay. I have to be careful."

"But you did recognize the man in the picture."

"Name's Murray. I gather from the photo that he's dead. He sighs.

"What can you tell us about it?

Darrell shakes his head slowly. Belinski knows people and he can see that the vendor is genuinely upset.

"Murray was a good guy. A regular. Smokie with mustard and hot sauce. Sometimes he had money, sometimes he didn't. I told him he always had credit with me. I'll say this...the man had integrity. Kept a tab in his head. He'd come by and say, Darrell, I'm working...that's what he called it...*working*...down the block today. I'll be able to pay you later. And he always did." He pauses, caught between his memory and his disbelief.

Both detectives remain silent. They understand that questions will only get in the way.

"It's a dangerous area. Gangs, street people high on sniff or drugs, criminals. The vendors just blend into the surroundings. We're kind of invisible." He exhales audibly, and the officers take it that he sees far more than he would like. "So anyway, Murray is on the corner by my cart. He's eating his meal when this guy in a suit comes up to him. They talk for a minute and then the guy pulls out a twenty and gives it to him." Darrell looks at the officers. "It happens. There are some decent people around." He thinks for a moment trying to regain his train of thought. "Only thing is, I wasn't the only one who saw it. One of the bums... sorry, Cynthia doesn't like me to call them that...street guy named Romeo saw it too. Last thing I saw was Murray going into the alley and a moment after that Romeo followed him in." He looks at the officers, wondering if they can read his feelings of guilt, and says, "That's about all I can tell you."

Lemaire has neither the time nor the patience for feelings. "This Romeo got a last name?"

"Couldn't tell you. But he'll be easy to find. Dark greasy hair, wears a leather jacket whether it's cold or not. Haven't a clue how old he is but he's got this thing…a wart maybe…right under one nostril. Hard to look the guy in the face."

Belinski looks at his watch and then at his partner. Lemaire is quick to follow.

"Why not," he answers, "let's go.

Belinski heads for their vehicle but Lemaire lags behind. He looks at the pool and then at Darrell. Glancing back again at the backyard he asks, "You pay for all this by selling friggin' hot dogs?" The question is not a new one to Darrell and he gives his stock reply. "Course not, officer," he pauses for effect, "I offer smokies and burgers too." And with that, he returns to his battle with the leaves.

Prairie light lingers til ten in the middle of summer as do the armies of the street. Belinski and Lemaire return to the same corner where, only a few hours earlier, shoppers and office workers bustled to and fro, driving the commercial engine of the thriving city. Now, in their wake, the pace is slowed, the denizens are in no particular hurry. The officers tread cautiously past extended legs and small groups huddled on the sidewalk.

"Somebody outta do something about this, Zel. It's a friggin' embarrassment." Lemaire steps over a passed-out body leaning against a trash can. "I'm friggin' serious."

Belinski reaches out and stops his partner short. He nods at a figure holding court with a group of younger males. "You walk past so we have him between us. I'll take him down."

Lemaire does as he is bid and Belinski moves in. He holds his badge in the face of the older man and the kids scatter. "Got some questions for you, Romeo."

The man in the black leather jacket looks down the pavement, gauging his options. Lemaire closes the distance between them. Romeo sags and slurs, "Whassup officer?"

He stinks of cheap booze and gasoline. Belinski knows that, though he can arrest on suspicion, he will have to wait until tomorrow to question him legally.

"Let's go Romeo. You're under arrest as a person of interest in a murder investigation. Anything you say…" Belinski finishes reading him his rights and his partner grabs hold of one arm. Minutes later Romeo is asleep in the back of their car on his way to the lock up.

"That's one friggin' ugly human being." Belinski is at the wheel while his partner regards their passenger intently. "Bet no self-respecting woman would go near him with a ten-foot pole. Even if it was his." He smiles at his own lewdness. "God, he stinks. How we getting that stench out of the back seat?"

"Tommy'll get it out. Always does."

"Who the hell is Tommy?"

"The guy who cleans the squads. Who'd you think does it?"

Lemaire thinks for a moment. "You?"

Belinski goes silent. His mind is suddenly elsewhere.

"Think bedbugs can jump?" Lemaire is scratching the back of his neck.

"Sure. A few feet at the very least. How else would they get around?" Belinski suppresses a smile.

Lemaire slides forward in his seat. "Why didn't we get a couple of uniforms to bring this guy in?"

Belinski isn't finished. "It's the fleas and lice I worry about?"

"What the hell do you mean by that?"

"They jump up to twenty meters. It's pretty well documented."

Lemaire goes silent. The only sounds in the car are the snores coming from the back seat and the scratching and squirming from the man riding shotgun.

⁂

It's past eleven on a moonless night. Belinski is halfway through the pot of coffee and the sounds of apartment life have fallen silent save for the distant hiss of running water. A late shower maybe. The evening is warm, and he reclines on the single patio chair tucked into the corner of his balcony. Even the few stars that he half believes he can identify are absent. He is alone.

Whether by choice or chance, he has opted for a block facing the river. Slightly downstream and on the opposite bank, he thinks he can just make out his own backyard. He built that fence himself. He closes his eyes and visualizes the house of his dreams. Although the north end of his city is a rough place in which to grow up, Scotia Street, with its tree lined canopy, is a rose among thorns. Large two- and three-story homes nestle luxuriously on expansive properties, which recline regally down the bank to the rivers edge. They hearken back to a time when this area held all the promise of the future. And Belinski's house stands as proudly as any.

I'll get over to cut the grass tomorrow, he thinks to himself. He glances at his phone, thinking that maybe he should call Anne and confirm, but he knows it is only an excuse. He misses her voice. It's been almost a year, and nothing has changed. They talk, they plan but he's still here and she's there. He dumps the dregs of his cup into a potted plant. He figures there's a word for it, but he couldn't care less what it is. All he knows is that the job brought them together and the job is keeping them apart. The job. He fights the urge to toss his mug out into the night sky. Instead, he places it on the concrete and closes his eyes. It's late and sleep may as well come right here.

CHAPTER *Six*

The call had come without fanfare and Andrew's invitation had been simple. "Why don't we get together and discuss this ridiculous lawsuit. We can dine together in my home." Time and place fixed, Andrew had rung off. Unlike his novels, which unveil their layers of love and longing, heartbreak and loss, in a leisurely unfolding of sentiment and style, Andrew's demeanor on the phone had been succinct and to the point. David is reminded that each sentence comes with an effort which he himself cannot fully appreciate. He arranges for a cab.

"Of course, I know it, Mate," responds the cabbie as Andrew hops in. "It's not Buckingham Palace but it isn't far off now is it." The London residence of the fourteenth Earl of Derbyshire, though not a common destination for the vast majority of cab fares in the city, is certainly well known to those who ply their trade in the transportation industry. "Good friends with the Earl, are you sir?" Conversation is second nature for the driver, and this is as good an opening as any.

"No." David isn't in the mood. He turns his attention to the evening ahead. It's one thing to go over and over the depressing events of one's life alone, something he has done continually in his waking hours, his sleep, even in his drunken stupors. It's quite another to discuss it with someone else, especially when that someone is a complete stranger. Why on earth does he feel so bloody compelled to go through with it? He knows that it isn't too late to change his mind. He also knows that he won't.

He slips reluctantly into his memory. She had called, as she so often had done in the final days, in tears. Having been asked to take a temporary leave from her position with the symphony and, although she had seen it coming; had even welcomed it, she was overcome with melancholy. She vacillated between hopelessness and anger, one minute lashing out, the next going silent. Most importantly, on this particular night, she could not promise David that she would be able to keep herself safe.

He had called emergency services and raced across the city, dreading all the while what he might find. She was alive and sitting up, talking with members of the crisis response team. Seeing the tears on his face, she smiled, "Only a few pills, David. I think I'll be fine. Talking to you helped." She half turned back to one of emt's and said, "It always does."

She was taken to a nearby hospital and admitted to Psych Services for observation. David had made the trip in the ambulance, holding her hand the entire way. He found it impossible to read her mood. She seemed oblivious to the events around her, choosing instead to focus on him and to reassure him that everything would be fine. It was after one a.m. when he had finally arrived back at his flat.

The call had come just before dawn. The distant ringing finally invading his sleep, he answered it groggily.

"David." Her voice was soft, just above a whisper. "Everything is going to be fine, David." He could hear her breathing. "David… I'm sorry…I love you."

"Sixteen quid mate. Nice round figure."

David is wrenched from his thoughts. He wipes the tears from his cheeks and hands the cabbie a twenty. He is standing on the steps before the cab can begin its return to the manor gates. He feels the anger, his constant companion over the past few months, rising within him and he needs a drink.

Andrew meets him at the door and, pleasantries dispensed with, they find themselves in a large reception room where armchairs surround a great hearth. Above an elaborate mantle the portrait of an ancient family member glares disparagingly down at them, standing watch over his empire. David notices that an electric insert has enclosed the space where once prodigious logs had blazed gloriously.

"Smoke is hazardous to my current state of health." Andrew manages to blend mirth and sincerity into a single sentiment. "Drink?" He motions toward a tea wagon, which serves as a portable bar, nestled off to one side. "Would you mind playing *mother*? I'll have a scotch and coke. Do make it a stiff one."

David pours and they take their places opposite the fire, the ever-present tank resting indifferently at the chair's edge. While his host decides upon an embarkation point, David takes in the surroundings. Twenty-foot ceilings provide the anchor for scattered chandeliers while their supporting walls are adorned with originals by Degas and Remiallard. Landscapes and still lifes, even a nude, provide a backdrop of opulence which neither brags nor blusters. Though neither is it understated. Instead, its singular statement is that those within these walls are the chosen. It's simply understood.

"Harold McMillan once sat in that very chair." He wheezes and nods at David. "It was just after he made his famous *Wind of Change* speech." He clears his throat. "The wind of change is blowing through this continent...blah blah blah. The old man called him a bloody idiot right to his face."

David is struck by the fact that, the events that every schoolboy is required to learn from a book take on a separate significance within these walls.

"I'm not an historian," he replies, "but, in retrospect, you'd have to say that McMillan was right. Independence was a question of inevitability."

"Well, it's all behind us now," Andrew exhales, "like so many things." He takes a pull from his glass and then raises it, examining it like a crystal ball. "What prompted it, David? What made you think you could criticize the bloody establishment?"

David is startled somewhat by this sudden veer in the conversation.

He wonders for a minute if he even has the energy for it and says, finally, "Where do I start?" He takes a gulp of the liquor and begins in the only place that makes any sense; the day they met.

His host is patient, as though he is reliving the experience alongside his guest and does not interrupt. David unburdens himself, reluctantly at first, and then more readily, cathartically, as he re-immerses himself into the events of his past. Finally, he reaches the night of Christiane's suicide.

"They sent her home," he whispers, and then indignantly, "they sent her bloody home." He drains his glass and rises for more. The interruption allows for a question from Andrew.

"There was an assessment, I presume?"

"I did some digging...well after the fact. A few of the staff were eager to speak with a promise of anonymity. The psychiatrist had to be summoned...Dr. bloody Fitzpatrick, his pager had been turned off but somehow they got hold of him...at home presumably."

"I suppose that could be the routine," Andrew interjects.

"I was told that when he arrived, he was in a foul mood. Smelled of drink. Snapping at everyone like it was their fault that he had been disturbed. Then he met..." David sighs and collapses forward. He tries to collect himself. "Then he interviewed Christiane. Gave her five minutes of his valuable time. Pronounced her fit to leave...and then he beat her out the door."

"And of course, you saw his attitude as unprofessional." Andrew puts down his glass and breaths deeply.

"It was bloody incompetent!" David thrashes down with his free hand.

"So, you employed the only weapon you had at your disposal."

"Short of killing him myself. I wrote the article. I called him out for his negligence…"

"You called it murder, David." Andrew's tone is conciliatory.

"And I bloody well stand by it!" He half rises out of his chair before falling back again spilling his drink.

"I don't disagree with you. But let me ask you this. What did you hope to achieve? What *can* you possibly achieve?" He sips. "You're the object of a libel suit. It won't end well." He looks him in the eye, "Why not just walk away…give it up?"

Naturally David has asked himself this question a hundred times. He has never been able to come anywhere near a satisfactory answer. "I want to hurt him. I want him to suffer the way we have…ok, the way I have. I don't bloody know. Maybe I want the public to know what a bastard he is…what a useless, pompous, ass faced, incompetent…" he pauses, catching himself in the rant that he reserves for his private drunken rages. "I want revenge if you must bloody well know." He rises to refill is glass.

As David returns to his chair some of his vehemence dissipates. An attendant, waiting silently in the shadows, takes the opportunity to replace the oxygen tank and disappears as quietly as he has come. Andrew maintains his focus on his guest.

"Would you agree with me, David, that you have been able to inflict some measure of damage on this Dr. Fitzpatrick? Now that the article has come out? I believe, and you must surely know this, that it was picked up by *Reuters*. It has been widely circulated."

David has never given this question a moment's thought, and its posing provides him with a slightly different perspective. Reluctantly he answers, "Some I imagine."

"Then why don't you let it go. Issue an apology."

David chews on Andrew's last suggestion like rotting fish and then blurts, "What the hell is going on here? He rises. "He's one of your bloody friends, for Chrissakes. This is a bloody setup." He drops the glass on the carpet and vacillates between grabbing Andrew by the lapels of his jacket and bolting for the door. The look on the face of his host, however, holds him firm and something assures him that this is not the case. Andrew shakes his head slowly and speaks calmly.

"No, David. It isn't so."

And somehow David knows that he speaks the truth. Andrew has another agenda entirely and David recognizes that patience is his only option if he is to discover what it is. He sags into his chair and mumbles something about being sorry for the outburst.

Andrew fixes him directly with his gaze. "Alright, David. No apology then. Can you let it go… give up the vendetta?

The anger and the anguish, which, for so many months have preyed upon him, weighed him down, are suddenly too much to bear. He returns Andrew's gaze with an intensity that they both recognize as desperation and says, finally, "Why the hell not." Blood rushes from his head and he collapses deeper into the chair. He fails to notice the signal given to the attendant and is surprised to see the telephone appear. Andrew takes up the receiver and waits a moment. Then he speaks.

"Good evening, Charles. Yes, yes, all is well. The matter we discussed earlier," he listens a moment, "that's right…let's go ahead as I have requested, shall we." Another pause and then, "excellent, Charles. And thank you once again."

The phone and the attendant vanish. Andrew turns his attention back to David and says, simply. "The matter is closed. The libel suit against you will be withdrawn."

David stares blankly. He understands neither how nor why. Thoughts race tangentially through his mind in a random barrage. Who is this man? Why is he helping? What the hell is going on here? They are interrupted by his host.

"In this country, privilege is still power, my boy." He smiles reassuringly.

David can only offer a bewildered, "I don't know what to say. How can I thank you, Andrew?"

His host has his reply at the ready. "We shall come to that over dinner, David." He breathes deeply from the tank. "And by the way, it may please you to know that Dr. Fitzpatrick, formerly of the Psychiatric Services of London General, has been relieved of his duties." He regards David over the rim of his glass for a moment. "Hungry?"

The elongated table would accommodate thirty or so guests with ease but on this occasion, it is set for two. The light is dim, and a candelabra envelops them within a circle of intimacy. They sit at the far end, Andrew at the table's head and his guest to his right. This symbolism is not lost on David, and he cannot but wonder what might be asked of him. Andrew pours from a crystal decanter.

"I hope you will excuse my eccentricities." He raises his glass and swirls the wine. "This is called Gimli Goose. I acquired quite a taste for it when I went off to school. Just under two dollars a bottle, as I recall. Canadian." He nods to David and says, "To the past…and to the future." They drink.

The courses come and go and much later, when David recalls the events of this evening, their substance will go unremembered. What will remain indelibly etched in his memory, however, is that feeling that, for the first time in months, he was beginning to feel that he could carry on. His happiness would remain forever out of the question but at least he was beginning to feel a glimmer of hope, a reason to get out of bed. Something to occupy his waking hours.

An attendant removes a dish and whisks silently away. There is a slight clink as the bottle kisses the rim of his glass and, for a moment, only the raspy efforts to breathe linger in the quiet between them.

"Tell me, David. You said that you and Christiane were deeply in love. If that's so, then why did you let it slip away?"

Though the question doesn't feel accusatory in the least, more bewildering if anything, David responds defensively. "I didn't *let* it slip away at all. It just did. It's as I told you, I stood there like a frightened child and did nothing." He slides his glass away and repeats defiantly, "Nothing!"

"And you feel that your inaction changed her feelings for you."

"I know it did. It's a moment I wish I could take back. I've relived it a thousand times."

Andrew nods understandingly. *"Le point tournant,"* he offers. *"Voltaire.* The turning point."

David raises his brow. He does not respond.

Andrew continues. "That moment in time when fate intervenes, and the course of our lives is altered irrevocably. And it is a moment over which we have no control. We are merely its pawns."

"I've no interest in philosophy." David tosses back the remaining liquid in his glass and reaches for the decanter.

"She begged you not to intervene."

"It doesn't matter."

Andrew draws deeply from the tank. "Then tell me this. How would things have been altered if you had responded differently? What if you had acted the hero and confronted this man? What if he had killed you right there on the sidewalk? Would you have preferred to have died in that instant... in the arms of your wife?"

David seethes. Of course, bloody not, he thinks to himself. What he wants is for it never to have happened in the first place. Not to have been there at that moment in time. "I just want to go back to the way things were. To have been somewhere else than on that bloody street corner." he offers defeatedly.

His host softens. "I'm sorry, David. I don't mean to be so objectionable. But you see I have had a lifetime to ponder that question." He sips from his glass. "And I will tell you that you are wrong." He regards his guest from over the rim, gauging the reception of his statement. "Voltaire is right about *le point tournant*...and he is not. You and Christiane could not have prevented that moment from occurring. Fate, or as a dear friend of mine might say, *hazard*, brought the three of you together at that place and time. You responded in the same way we all might have done. It was not cowardice...it was common sense. He had a weapon. There was nothing you could have done. He would have killed you and you know it. What's more, you knew it then."

"Come to the point, Andrew."

"Alright then. It's this. We must learn to recognize just when such moments of change actually occur. For example, let us say that a small child strays too near the edge of a balcony and falls to the earth below. Miraculously, he is unscathed. Voltaire's *le point tournant* is not the tragedy of the fall but the triumph of survival."

David says nothing.

"You survived, David. You have misjudged the event's significance. Your moment came much later, when Christiane needed you to be strong. It was your own feelings of inadequacy and failure that you allowed to stand in the way of your love. She did not see those things in you. You saw them in yourself."

David feels the weight of this pronouncement. In such an environment, with the effects of the wine; with his host's affinity for philosophy; with his guilt; it all sounds plausible. He feels that he needs time to digest it, to ponder on its wisdom. To decide that it isn't a load of peat.

"Brandy?" Andrew rises and indicates that David should follow. They wander down a hallway and enter the music room.

"This is my favorite room in this archaic mausoleum. He pours a generous amount of liquor into a snifter and offers it to David. He then takes up his own and they sit across from each other. A grand piano intrudes from the edge of the carpet. David examines the score on the dasher. *Schumann's Symphony No 3*

"Do you play, Andrew?" David nods in its direction.

"Very adroit, my boy. You have hit on the precise reason for our visit this evening."

"I don't understand."

"Well then I shall answer your question directly." He glances toward the Steinman. "Not a lick. I could not locate Middle C with a Geiger counter."

David stares blankly. "Then…"

"You see, most of us are endowed with certain talents. It's true that sometimes we spend a lifetime trying to sort out just what they might be, but, in the end, they generally reveal themselves. Pianist, cellist, painter or mason, each of us is given a gift."

"Speak for yourself, Andrew. It isn't always so."

"On the contrary, David. There are a few rare exceptions, yes, but for the most part, it *is* so. Take yourself, for example."

"I think we have already established my abilities."

"Nonsense." He pauses to allow the moment of levity to pass. "I've read your columns, David. I'm a fan and believe me, you have a talent. These people you interview. They put their faith in you. They open up their hearts…their souls. They trust you, David. That is your gift. They tell you things that they would not dream of discussing with anyone else. Not even a loved one."

David is well aware of this but offers weakly, "they have their reasons."

"Admittedly. But they invariably choose *you* in order to unveil their inner secrets."

"Ok. So, what good is such an inane talent?"

"That is precisely the point. It is very important. To me. And I will tell you why."

The grandfather clock chimes eleven times and the echoes of each peal linger in the air of the room suddenly gone quiet. The guitar, silent witness to a time long past, rests placidly against the ottoman. And its owner begins.

"I have a friend. It pains me to say it but I have not seen him in a very long time. He is in an institution." Andrew draws deeply from the oxygen. "I have recently been informed that, after so many years in what you might call a catatonic state, he is stirring. How this is possible, I can't say, but I am desperate to do whatever I can to help. If he were to be able to communicate…if I would be able to …" He stops abruptly and David cannot help but notice the tears welling up in his eyes. "David, I want you to go to him. *Be* with him. Speak to him and, more importantly, help him to escape that prison which holds him. Use every ounce of your ability. Do whatever you can to bring him back to me…that is…to his family." He coughs, the disease perhaps or cover for his revelation. "He has a sister. She and I have stayed in touch over the years."

Andrew has been spitting out his words rapidly and settles back into his chair, gasping deeply. He manages to say, "Will you do it…please David?"

David is moved by his host's heartfelt plea, his intense emotion. He thinks about his squalid flat. He has no job and no prospects. He knows that, in his present state, he is of no use to himself or anyone else. It is none of these things, however, which impel him to offer his answer. Instead, it is this frail man before him. There is sadness, a desperation which emanates from him, and which cries out for David's help. He simply says, "Of course. I'll do whatever I can."

They sit for a moment in silence. Though nothing else is said, David can feel Andrew's sense of relief as palpably as if it were his own. He moves away from the subject. "Andrew…you say that we all have talents." He silently reminds himself of this man's many accomplishments. His novels, so widely acclaimed, his career as an academic. His infinite charm. "What, would you say, is yours?"

Andrew does not need to think. "I've grown up in a world of privilege, David. Not only was talent not necessary, it was seldom encouraged. In my most cynical moments I even convince myself that growing up as I have, actually inhibited my abilities. But that's a copout isn't it. No, David, you must believe me when I confess to you that I am one of those rare exceptions. I have not a single ability of my own. Not one." He shakes his head to emphasize his certainty. "But look at the time. We will talk again tomorrow. I shall have Fulton drive you home. And thank you, David. I am more grateful than you can know."

David leans against the pillar atop the grand entrance's staircase awaiting the car's arrival. Andrew had bid him goodbye at the door and thanked him effusively one final time. David had the impression that the evening had been an enormous challenge for Andrew and, having secured the acquiescence which he desired, he needed to rest. The car arrives and he ambles toward it, waving away Fulton's efforts to open his door. As his hand settles upon the handle, he turns for one last look at the mansion. It is not the grandeur of this remarkable structure nor is it the scent of the tea roses which line its perimeter that commands his attention. It is, rather, the melody of the piano concerto which drifts effortlessly from the music room window and hovers, like a mourning dove, in the still evening air. David remains, captivated, for a moment and then he is gone.

CHAPTER
Seven

Terri Stafford sits alone in the outside office awaiting the meeting. The interval between visits, though it has been only a week, has seemed an eternity. After meeting with her brother, the previous Thursday, she had been so overwhelmed with emotion that she had left the treatment facility without so much as a goodbye. Today she is hoping to discuss plans for his care with Dr. Belanger and to secure his cooperation in what is, for her, a life changing proposition. And she does not intend to take no for and answer.

Belanger bounds in, speaking as he passes. "This way please, Miss Stafford, this way." She hurries behind and finds him standing behind his desk. "If you would be so kind." He motions toward the chair and waits until she is comfortably seated before sliding into place. "How nice to see you again. Welcome." He smiles engagingly.

Terri manages a thank you and suddenly finds that it falls upon her to begin. She hesitates a moment and then asks, "How is Noah, Dr. Belanger?"

"Ah…right to the point. Excellent." His smile disappears and he is all business. "He is much the same as you witnessed last week but, please, don't let that discourage you." He gazes directly at her, looking for her reaction. "I feel there is hope."

"I am not discouraged in the least, Dr. In fact, quite the opposite."

"Good, good. Then let's begin with a summary of Noah's treatment plan reaching back to his arrival here so many years ago." He hesitates as if cautioning himself for what he is about to say. "I believe that you have a right to know this and, as such, given that I am new to his care, I think that it must fall upon me to discuss it with you. And believe me it isn't my intention to criticize my colleagues."

Terri tilts her head to one side. "I don't follow, Dr. Belanger. What are you getting at?"

He continues. "My review of his care tells me that, aside from a number of electric shock treatments, nothing whatsoever has been done to assist your brother with his recovery in any form. He has simply been left on his own in front of the television set. Of course, his immediate comforts have been accommodated. But treatment…" He takes a moment to temper his rising emotion. "To me, this is unconscionable. Unprofessional. And yet, I suppose that it is not uncommon." He shakes his head. "The receiving psychologist had placed a note in his file to the effect that Noah was probably a chronic drug abuser and that in all likelihood the degenerative brain damage, which he assumed he had, was a result of *continued and habitual use.* He was deemed a low risk for recovery."

"That's preposterous! Noah was an honor student. He never took drugs in his life." She controls her outrage. "Dr. Belanger… are you telling me that he could have been cured years ago. Are you saying…are you telling me… that his life has been wasted unnecessarily…because of some…" she struggles for the words, "fucking idiotic mistake?"

Belanger is shaking his head before she has finished. "Not at all, Miss Stafford. You must understand that your brother has, indeed, suffered a trauma. He has significantly diminished cognitive functioning. Likely caused by the ingestion of chemicals frequently used in the manufacture of narcotics. Possibly Lysergic Acid Diethylamide."

"LSD." She hasn't heard these letters for years.

"But to be clear, I believe that we can make at least some progress. That is to say, I think that Noah might do so. But I caution you not to expect too much. He will never regain full function. You must accept this."

Terri has no use for blame. She may choose to dwell on that at a later time but for now she can only look to the future. It is her turn to be all business. "Fine, Dr. Belanger. Just what are you going to do?"

"Ah, that is the response I had hoped to hear. We have, Miss Stafford, already begun. Please." He rises and indicates that she should follow. "Your timing is perfect."

They retreat through a door in the back of his office and enter a small room. It is equipped with a two-way mirror which allows them to watch, unnoticed, the events occurring in the adjacent area. Noah sits at a table, hands folded in his lap. His expression is blank, his gaze downward. Another man sits opposite.

"He is a psychiatric nurse, Miss Stafford. His assignment is simply to talk to your brother. The nature of the conversation is as wide open as the imagination will allow. It's formally known as Social Communication Therapy, SCT, but let's just say that we are taking the obvious approach. If we want Noah to communicate with us, then we must re-teach the process to him. Model it if you will. It is a technique which has been widely used in the treatment of Autism."

Terri suppresses her skepticism. She looks on as the nurse carries on a one-sided conversation with her brother. For his part, Noah does not look up and certainly does not make eye contact with the nurse. There is, however, something in his body language that Terri finds encouraging. It is subtle but tangible.

"Of course, this is only the beginning. We intend to expand upon it. The treatment room is a sterile environment. We will utilize small groups and also the recreation area. Get him out into the community. I have asked our volunteer services people to prepare a list of individuals who might visit Noah on a regular basis. People with whom he might share similar interests. I understand that he was a graduate student in English."

"He was," she catches herself, "is a writer."

"Excellent. I will pass that on." He taps on the glass. "Now please observe."

The nurse rises and leaves the room. When he returns, he places a lap top computer in front of Noah. Terri looks on in disbelief at what she is witnessing. Noah reaches forward and places his hands on the keyboard. In no time, he is entering something on the screen.

"Sensory Stimulation Treatment, Miss Stafford, in reverse. Rather than filling his head with ideas and images of our choosing, we are encouraging him to do so from within. We began this a few days ago and he took to it almost immediately. We are able to print what he produces."

"Do you mean that he can..."

Belanger anticipates her question. "No, unfortunately not. He can not communicate his thoughts or ideas. Not yet at any rate. At the present he can only repeat words and phrases which have embedded themselves in his long-term memory over the years. Some of these things are likely from his distant past while others are fairly recent."

"I don't understand."

"For example," he reaches into an inside pocket and hands her a piece of paper. "Noah typed this yesterday."

Terri's hand trembles. She is about to read the first words which her brother has produced in over three decades.

You'll wonder where the yellow went when you brush your teeth with Pepsodent. What do you figure we aught to do with him,

Marshall Dillon? Riders on the storm. Riders on the storm. Into this world you're born. Into this life you're thrown. I don't think this is Kansas, Toto. Whatever you drive, wherever you go, trust Texaco. Frankly, my dear, I don't give a damn. Ask not what your country can do for you. Trudeaumania is sweeping the country. He took it out. He what? He took it out. It? It. Out? Out! It's all over folks; the Toronto Blue Jays are the World Series Champs!!

She stares at the page, trying desperately to find meaning amidst the jumble of unfiltered drivel. "It doesn't make any sense."

"I admit that it seems confusing. But it is just the beginning. My hope is that we can help Noah to somehow reach inwardly. Relearn how to process information in a way that is meaningful to him and then to assist him in communicating these thoughts to others. The machine is only a conduit. It will take time."

"I'd like you to save everything he writes, Doctor. I want to read it all. And", she pauses for an instant, "I want to take him home."

Belanger cannot believe his ears. His work has only begun. "You can't possibly mean…" He does not finish.

"For the weekend, Doctor. I will pick him up on Friday." She moves toward the doorway. "Now how do we get into that room, please?"

His court appearance completed, Belinski is headed to Scotia Street. This is a rare day off and he intends to spend it with his son Joey. Although at twelve years of age Joey has outgrown the Children's Museum, father and son still enjoy wandering about The Forks, a collection of shops, restaurants and novelty stores which has risen from the rubble at the confluence of the Red and Assiniboine Rivers. They have history there. Zel and Anne have been taking Joey to this venue since he was able to bounce about in an infant sling. The museum, filled with so many hands-on activities, the ballpark where they had cheered on their local baseball heroes, *The Goldeyes,* and the Pancake House, with its syrupy stacks are familiar stomping grounds. Belinski pulls into the front drive.

"Dad!" Joey is waiting on the front steps. "Mom, dad's here." He bounds down the sidewalk and gives Belinski a bear hug. He's grown taller, thinks his father, and it's only been a week since he last saw him.

"Hiya champ. How's my boy?" He puts him in a headlock, and they wrestle about for a moment. Belinski glances over the boy's shoulder at the two baseball gloves resting on the porch. He smiles. "Wanna through the ball around a little today?"

"For sure. I found your glove in the garage. I thought we could take them with us to the forks. That's where we're going isn't it?"

"If you like. It's your call." Joey spins out of his dad's grasp and bounds up the stairs two by two. He glances up at the doorway. "I was right again, mom. I'll see ya later." He gives him mom a quick kiss and grabs the gloves and ball. "I'll wait in the car, dad."

Belinski stands at the base of the stairs and looks up at his wife. To him, she looks more beautiful than ever before, but then, he feels this way every time he sees her. His feelings, however, rarely translate into language and generally go unexpressed. "How are you?"

"I'm alright, Zel. You look tired."

"Do you need anything?"

She shakes her head. "Notice anything?" She pauses while Belinski silently studies her. "Not me, Zel…look around."

It gradually dawns on him. "The grass. What the…Joey?"

"He worked all morning. He thought it would please you."

It is slow in coming but he finally beams from ear to ear. "It does. It really does. Don't worry, I'll let him know."

She turns and starts back in. "Have him back by five?"

"Why don't you come with us?"

She pauses in the doorway. "I don't think so. You two go and do your guy stuff. I have a lot to get done around here."

"OK. Just thought I'd ask." He turns and starts down the walk.

"Tell you what. Why not stay for dinner. I'll make perogies."

Belinski doesn't even try to suppress the smile. "Great. See you at five." He turns toward the car and shouts, "Hey Green Thumb. Let's get goin'"

Some of the best moments of Belinski's life have come while riding through the streets of Winnipeg. As a boy, he would sit along side his dad and the two would chat amicably for hours on end. That is to say that Belinski Senior, a natural born storyteller, would chatter on endlessly. His son, Zelig, was more of a born listener and was content to laugh at all the right places and add his two cents as necessary. It had been a perfect match. And to his delight, the garrulous gene had only skipped a generation. Joey has taken after his grandfather and, as a result, the tradition has continued.

"How's the week been, dad? Put away any bad guys?" Joey has baseball glove on and punctuates his words with random tosses into it. For his part, Belinski would prefer to avoid too much shop talk with his son and keeps his comments well to the generic.

"Pretty slow week. Guess all the bad guys have left town." He eases the car onto Main Street and picks up speed.

"C'mon dad. This is Winnipeg. It's the murder capital of the country. You're the homicide department's top cop. Even mom says so."

"How's school going? Did you get that Science project in on time?"

"Yep. Got a B. I honestly think that it was worth an A. Dizzy's a tough marker."

"Dizzy?"

"Mr. Dzieziek. No one can pronounce it properly, so we just call him Dizzy. He doesn't mind. I'll bet even he messes it up sometimes."

"You have to try."

"Huh?"

"It's a question of respect, Joey. You have to make the effort. Try and use his name."

His son ponders his reply for a moment and then simply says, "OK dad, I will"

Belinski punches him in the arm. "Thanks." He makes the turn past the ballpark and into the lot. "What else is going on in that world of yours?"

Joey hesitates. He knew this moment would come but he still isn't sure where to begin. He decides that his dad would respect directness and so he simply says, "Mom's signed me up for dance class."

CHAPTER
Eight

The news had come as no surprise. As Belinski hangs up the phone, he offers a silent prayer for Murray and curses the senseless manner in which he had met his end. He had been followed on the standby Darrell the hot dog guy and before he had completed his testimony, Romeo had caved. He had blamed Murray for being disabled. Said it gave him an unfair advantage on the street. He even tried to make it sound as though he was just trying to do everybody else a favor by smashing his head; leveling the playing field so to speak. Who knows, thinks Belinski, maybe he really believes it. He'll likely have seven to ten to convince himself.

He pours from the pot and retreats to familiar surroundings. Darkness has settled in and he leans out from the balcony, searching the far bank for home. An hour ago he had been right there, on the back deck. Right there…where he belongs. He gulps down the black liquid and wonders if Anne is still sitting up. Is she staring out into the darkness thinking about him? "Grow up, Belinski," he mutters to himself.

The evening had gone well. They had talked, reminisced and even laughed. Of course, they had both avoided the invisible elephant which stands between them. Conversations about the job inevitably end in conflict. Belinski knows that if he is to have any hope at reconciliation, things will have to change. His greatest fear, however, will have to be faced if and when he manages to walk away from police work. What if it's *him* and not the job at all? What if the issues between them are, after all, not work related? He knows it is a possibility. He is well aware that he was closed up emotionally long before becoming a peace officer. It is simply his nature.

He settles back into the patio chair and shakes his head. "Dance class." He hadn't raised the subject with Anne, figuring that nothing could be done to change her mind and it might have become contentious. Yet he has a lot of questions. How much time will it take from Joey's hockey? Will the kids at school give Joey a hard time? His mug stops mid air and he holds it absently in front of him. His eyes widen and his jaw opens. What if Joey is…? The phone rings and he spills coffee on his shirt. Anne, maybe?

"Yep."

"It's me."

"Oh."

"You don't have to sound so friggin' disappointed."

"Sorry."

"I don't think so. A guy takes the friggin' time to call up his partner to see if he had a nice afternoon with his kid and this is how he's treated?"

"It was good. Thanks."

"I'm glad. Hear about Romeo?"

"I did. Not too surprised."

"Guess he's Stony's problem now," a reference to the Federal Penitentiary on the outskirts of the city. "Three squares a day and more sittin' around time than even he's accustomed to. And one less panhandler on the street."

"Guess so." There is a lull and then, "Thanks for calling. See you in the morning."

Belinski rings off and collapses onto the couch. He scoops up the newspaper and flips through to the classified section. He reaches for his reading glasses. Someone out there must be willing to hire an ex-cop.

⁓⦵⁓

The *Boston Tea Party* is hardly the place where he would expect to share a cup of Earl Grey with a member of the British aristocracy. It is, however, the venue which Andrew has specified, and David waits patiently at a corner table with a view of Piccadilly Street. Their phone conversation had been, as David has come to expect, a brief one. They are to meet to discuss the details of his trip to Canada, Andrew having already made the arrangements. A server arrives with a menu and a message. The Earl will be along shortly.

David selects a Darjeerling and drifts into thought. A natural inclination toward detail, he is preoccupied with the matters relating to his extended stay abroad. He makes mental checkmarks in his mind's eye as he covers the minutiae of tasks which he has already attended to and creates a new list of those which remain. His overwhelming feeling is one of relief. He has been given the opportunity to leave behind a life in which he finds no meaning. It is a chance to drag himself up from his despair and he knows, intuitively, that he must take it. His tea arrives and he glances up.

"Best table in the place, David. An excellent choice." Andrew slips in beside him and tucks the tank away from view. "Have I kept you long?"

"Just arrived. How are you, Andrew?"

The question goes unanswered as Andrew motions to the server. "The same, if you would be so kind." And then to David.

"Just been with my tailor. Gieves and Hawkes is just around the corner as I'm sure you know. The old man's tailor, really. Never bothered to find one of my own. Shelton was quite perturbed with me. I've lost a bit of weight." He breathes deeply. "Arrangements made, are they?"

"I can leave by the weekend."

"Fine. Fine."

David has the feeling that his answer had been expected and that Andrew's mind was on other things. The tea burns slightly in his throat, and he reaches for the milk. He raises the decanter in Andrew's direction, but his gesture goes unnoticed.

"What memories this place brings back, David. What a time it was." The smile on his face is wistful as he gazes about the space. "Of course, it's greatly changed. Still, I can picture it exactly as it was when I was a lad."

"It's hard to imagine you in a place like this, Andrew."

"The old man would have had a fit if he knew. It was a coffee house then. Swinging Sixties, they called it. I was fifteen or so. Came every Friday night. Folk singers, skiffle groups…even poets and writers. Believe me, David, this place had atmosphere. In the vernacular of my youth, it was happening. Do you know that a lot of those people smoked marijuana here…called it weed, of course, though no one ever offered me any."

"That's probably a good thing."

"Best part about those times is that I actually had the sense that I fit in here. Something I had never felt before…and only occasionally since. Nobody knew who I was…and they didn't care. I wasn't Andrew Sutton, only male heir to the thirteenth bloody earl. I was Andy…the wannabe poet. I even wrote my own songs.'

David finds it impossible to imagine this frail figure as a maverick youth, rebelling against his position of privilege in this hole in the wall haven for drug inspired artists and musicians. Suddenly Andrew begins to sing, although it is barely a whisper.

"They wander through this world and live so freely,
The love they take is never cause for doubt,

I'd give anything if one of them would see me,
As I languish in my prison looking out"
"One, four, five pattern. Everything was a three-chord progression back then." He shakes his head. "Pathetic, I know. But then you must remember I was young. I thought I was deep."

"I'm the wrong person to judge."

"Anyway, this place felt like family. Sometimes, when one of the waitresses missed a shift, Aldo…he was one of the owners…let me serve tables." He sighs at the memory. "Such wonderful times." He takes a sip of his tea, his hand trembling under its weight. "And one night I worked up the courage to ask if I could take the stage… sing one of my songs. I remember it was a Monday and the crowd was pretty thin. Aldo said what the hell, why not."

"The song you just sang?"

"The very one. I walked up to the stage…it was just over there in the corner. I sat on the stool and looked out at the smattering of patrons…familiar faces…encouraging me on. I strummed a chord and took a breath." He takes a pull of oxygen. "And then, without warning, I stood and walked straight off. Surprised myself as much as anyone. I just couldn't go through with it. I chickened out. Headed right out that door." He nods at the same entrance where David had entered. "And I never came back. Until today."

David is moved. He can feel the weight of those memories which Andrew has carried with him for so long. And he knows that, in some way and for some reason, he has been chosen to witness while Andrew laid them to rest. "And now you have finally had your moment."

Andrew fixes his eyes directly on David's. "We are not often given second chances, unfortunately." He reaches into his jacket pocket. "Here is everything you need. I've written out all the travel and accommodation information on this first page. And I have written you a letter. In it, I have given you some background regarding my life in Canada and my friendship with Noah. It isn't complete but it will be enough to help you with your duties. I will send you the rest when I am up to it."

He hands the information to David and offers his thanks. They shake hands and Andrew retreats through that same door he had fashioned his escape so many years before. David sits for a moment, uncertain just what to make of this unusual man who, a few weeks earlier, had been a complete stranger. And now, he has the feeling that he is closer to Andrew than most. He gathers his things and makes his way out onto the pavement just in time to see the Rolls disappear into the fog of Piccadilly Circus.

CHAPTER Nine

The office is Spartan … unwelcoming. It is a reflection of the man himself. Assistant Chief of Police, Homicide Division, Stephen Cuddy has no interest in charming his visitors. In fact, there isn't a single chair other than the one he presently occupies. If you are summoned here, you stand. And Belinski and his partner are no exception.

"It's a courtesy more than anything, detectives. The R.C.M.P. isn't asking for any assistance from us. Not our jurisdiction. They simply want to pick your brains." He shuffles through the papers on his desk. "You both worked the Wentworth case back in '97. Seems they have something similar on their hands."

Lemaire looks at his partner. He knows that Belinski remembers every detail vividly. And so does he. He turns to his supervisor, "Friggin' nightmare, sir. Still lose sleep over that one."

"Here is your contact. Make your own arrangements and let me know if you need anything from this office." Cuddy hands Belinski the information and returns his attention to his desk, a clear indication that the meeting is over. The two detectives are nearly out the door when he calls out. "And Lemaire, keep the language professional, will you. Let's not have the red coats thinking that we're all a bunch of yahoos down here."

Lemaire does not respond. He refuses to make promises he doesn't intend to keep. They are well down the hallway when he turns to his partner. "Wentworth, for Chrissakes." Belinski doesn't acknowledge him. He is lost in thought. He's standing on the sidewalk of a home in the exclusive area of Tuxedo. The Forensics Team and several uniforms are already on scene, but nothing is disturbed. The victim is a woman, her body posed as though she is merely reclining against the steps without a care in the world. There is, however, no mistaking the violence which has been inflicted upon her. Though she is fully clothed, her garments are slashed in a dozen places with a jagged edged blade. Blood oozes out from her wounds and has begun to congeal around the edges of her shredded clothing. The corners of her mouth have been viciously carved upward toward her ears and the assailant has painted a grotesque clown-like smile in what is likely her own blood.

"Zel!" Lemaire growls. "Press the friggin' button for Chrissakes."

They are standing inside the elevator. Belinski returns his thoughts to the task at hand. He taps the number for the underground parking lot with his knuckle and takes out his cell phone. "Do these things work in here?" He enters the phone number of his Mounties contact. "No sense wasting time." He is surprised to hear the thing ringing and arrangements are made.

"Selkirk Steelers. My cousin played his junior hockey for those guys." Lemaire is looking out the window at the many signs which punctuate the roadside as they approach their destination. "I swear he would've made pro if he didn't blow out his knee."

"Cuddy asked you not to."

"Huh?" Lemaire tilts his head at his partner. Then it dawns on him. "Good one," he mocks, "Belinski made a joke. Lemme make a note of that. Funny. First day with the new sense of humor?"

"Just trying to keep up my end. See the McDonald's?"

"Up there on the right. What kind of cheapskates are these friggin' guys, anyway. McDonald's for Chrissakes."

"Maybe they think you're buying."

"Keep it up Belinski…that's almost two jokes in one day."

They pull into the lot of the only McD's in town. Selkirk is a small centre thirty kilometers north of Winnipeg. Poised at the lower bowl of the largest lake in the province, it represents home to those who work both in agriculture and the fishing industry. A number of provincial government offices are also located here including the Selkirk Mental Health Centre. Belinski and Lemaire are soon sitting opposite two uniformed officers already well into their big breakfasts.

Sgts. Weatherdon and Ebby are cut from the same cloth. Square jawed, cropped hair and ramrod backed, they exude strength and efficiency. One of them waves vaguely at the seats opposite.

"So, what do you have?" Belinski is always direct and to the point.

"Female victim. Cut to shreds. Face carved to the ears. She was found on the steps of the mayor's house, of all places."

"Leads?"

"Nothing so far. That's why you're here. You had a similar case, yes?"

"Wentworth. Five years back. Sounds pretty similar." Belinski provides the officers with the specifics. "I've still got my notes. I'll have everything sent out."

The Mountie looks across the table at the shorter of the two officers and surmises that he is the infamous *Grunt* and asks, "Did you have any suspects back then, detective?"

"Not a friggin'one. We questioned everyone close to the victim, canvassed the neighborhood and even did a few spots on Crimestoppers. Everyone checked out. We drew a friggin' blank. It went cold," he glances at his partner, "at least til now."

They discuss both cases at length and, with the promise to keep in touch, Belinski and Lemaire excuse themselves leaving their fellow officers to finish their breakfast. Neither one speaks. Both have been reminded that there is every likelihood that the same bastard they had failed to apprehend is still out there. They begin the trip back to the city in silence. Finally, Lemaire speaks.

"Isn't this where they keep the friggin' nut jobs?"

"If you mean the Selkirk Mental Hospital, then yes I 'spose so."

"That's where Loony Lenny is locked up, right?"

"What's your point?" Belinski is not in the mood. Like most everybody, he has heard the media reports in recent weeks indicating that the man responsible for a savage attack on a stranger a number of years back had been granted day passes into the community. His psychiatrist had argued, successfully, that he no longer represented a danger to the public.

"My friggin' point is that they let that asshole out to wander wherever the hell he likes." He waves his hand menacingly in the air. "He cuts the friggin' head off some poor old bastard sitting on a park bench and the friggin' psychiatrists say he's not a friggin' threat. He's friggin' *Loonie Lenny* for Chrissakes."

"So"

"So, what if he's our guy? What if he's off his friggin' meds again? Hearing those voices he claims tell him to slit people's throats. Who the hell knows if he takes those friggin' pills? Do you think anyone actually checks that shit?"

Belinski just doesn't want to go there. Not now, anyway. "I'll mention it to the boys. Get them to check into it. Good point, detective." He settles in for the drive.

Business class is an unfamiliar luxury for David, and he feels self conscious as the rest of the passengers file past him enroute to their seats in the back. He fumbles with his carry on and tries not to make eye contact. It's an over night flight and will land in Toronto early the next morning. From there it is a short two-hour flight to Winnipeg International. Terri Stafford, an acquaintance of Andrew's is to meet him there. She is also the sister of the man whom David has come to see. He settles into the oversized seat and closes his eyes. He wouldn't turn down a drink.

It isn't long before the craft is airborne, and he gets his wish. Champagne in hand, he removes the letter which Andrew had given him. He thinks back to their meeting and wonders why this is only the first installment. He knows, however, that Andrew will provide the rest in his own time and his own way. A pocket of turbulence buffets the cabin and David glances about, trying to read the expression on the faces of those around him. He detects no signs of concern, and the smiles of the flight attendants remain in place. Reassured, he opens the envelope.

David,

Thank you, once again, for agreeing to help with what you must, most assuredly, regard as a highly unusual request. I reiterate to you that your action is the most important thing in my life, and I would certainly undertake it myself if health would permit. That said, I feel that I could not have enlisted a more suitable emissary.

As for a starting point I am decidedly less certain. Let us adopt the principle that forewarned is forearmed. I will give you as much information about my time in Canada and also my friendship with Noah Stafford as I am able. I entrust you with this in the hope that, in your communication with Noah, some of my distant memories may trigger a response in his own. You will tell him, of course, that you are there at my request; that I am present through you. I recognize that this manner of thinking is not likely to be supported by existing scientific research but then, neither you nor I have a great fondness for modern science, do we.

    I shall begin by confessing to you that I was not much of a student. I loved to write, of course, and I enjoyed discussing works of fiction, particularly my own. But the rigors of academia were too much for me. Of course, at the time I believed that I was a rebel and simply refused to be constricted by the narrow-minded system of education presented by those antiquated dons at Cambridge. I know now that I was just another layabout who lacked the character necessary to put in the work required for success. At any rate it was late in the Michaelmass term that I turned in a research paper containing ideas which my tutor knew to be well beyond my capacity and intellect. He accused me of plagiarism. I didn't appeal and I was sent down.

    The old man was furious. Of course, he made the necessary financial arrangements with the college and a scandal was avoided. Thus, I was banished, for that is what I perceived it to be, to the provinces, and I enrolled at the University of Manitoba. And, yes, I will admit to you right here and now that I failed to graduate from that institution as well. The honorary doctorate which allowed me to take up my duties at that same esteemed college, which only a few years earlier had sent me down in disgrace came later, after I had demonstrated success as an author.

    And so, I took up residence on my own in a strange country, insulated by time and distance from a life which I had come to resent and a father with whom I had little connection. I loved it from the moment I arrived. And I will tell you that I believe that you will like it as well. There is a freedom of being which is hard to articulate but which is so refreshing. People say and act as they please without pretense or constraint. Canadians have a reputation for being polite and retiring but believe me, I did not see it. I learned to swear and curse with the best of them. I made a point of wearing my shirt tail out over my chinos and went wherever and whenever the hell I wanted to. I even had holes in the knees of my pants. To this day it gives me great pleasure to recall that nobody knew me there and nobody cared. And I am grateful to this day to my tutor for turning me in.

I met Noah Stafford, quite by chance, on the campus of the university. We hit it off immediately and the fact that we were both would be writers cemented our relationship. We became roommates in the apartment, (the Canadian term for flat), which my father had rented for me. I found it curious that, although his parents were quite well off, I think they owned a chain of jewelry shops or some such thing, he preferred to pay for his education and living expenses out of his own pocket. He took summer jobs and, of course with his ability, he was awarded numerous scholarships. In that regard, you could say that we were an odd pair. Still, it seemed to work for both of us.

We lived in the 'village', which is Winnipeg's equivalent of our West End though on a much smaller scale, of course. I have compiled a list of many of the places where we spent our time and placed it at the end of this letter. You will want to familiarize yourself with them before you make contact with Noah. There is no telling what may trigger a memory. Two places in particular were favorite haunts of ours. The first was an ice cream parlor called The Dutch Maid. I can't tell you how many meals we skipped so we could gorge ourselves on the most delicious hard ice cream I have ever tasted in my life. We have absolutely nothing to equal it in England. Noah was a huge fan of licorice if you can believe it. Just imagine…black ice cream.

Our other favorite place to spend time was the local watering hole. Officially, it was known by the name of some hotel or other. Its punters, however, knew it as the 'Menagerie'. Believe me, it was a veritable zoo. Individuals from all walks of life socialized there and draft beer was the drink of choice. We would sit for hours on a Friday night reveling in the atmosphere. There were a few other writers whom we got to know, and we never tired of the people or the music. Noah, in particular, developed several characters for his stories based on the individuals that we met there. Canadian beer, by the way, is surprisingly good and they serve it cold.

I am not certain exactly when or how we came to discuss the possibility of experimenting with psychedelics, but one thing led to another, and it was decided that we would try them together. I volunteered to make the purchase and although I had never obtained illegal narcotics before in my life...nor have I since, of course, it was surprisingly easy. Within the hour Noah and I were sitting in our flat staring at a couple of sugar lumps the size of pair of dice.

I remember that he turned to me and asked if I really wanted to go through with it. Now I realize that he was uncertain...maybe even frightened. Then, of course, I was thinking only of myself. I mustered enough bravado to reassure him that, not only was I ready...I couldn't wait for the experience.

We picked up the cubes and he turned to me. He made a toasting motion with his and said, 'to us'. And with that he tossed it down and leaned back into the sofa. I did likewise. But then, without any conscious thought at all, it was more simply an impulsive...I spat it into my hand. I couldn't go through with it. I chickened out.

You will remember our conversation about Voltaire, David. About the 'moment'. And of course, I cannot argue that this wasn't such a time for as you must surmise, the drug that I had purchased was laced with much more than LSD. And Noah has been institutionalized ever since. And as for me, my life ended that night as well. I was...I still am...devastated. And of course, in the same way that you hold the guilt for the loss of your Christiane, I have always felt responsible for what happened to Noah. More importantly I wish that I, too, had eaten that damnable sugar.

But my 'moment', David, came a few seconds earlier. I have always wondered...no it would be more accurate to say that I have always been tortured by those two words which Noah chose prior to ingesting the chemicals. 'To us'. I so wonder what he truly meant. I have always hoped that it was meant to reveal something to me. For you see, David, that, although I never told him...could never bring *myself to do so for fear of his reaction; his rejection, I loved him with all my heart. And I could never tell him. And that is why I am relying on you. You, David, for as you must realize, not only are you Noah's last hope…you are mine as well.*

CHAPTER Ten

The light touch on his shoulder is sufficient to rouse David from his slumber. The sun is glowing brightly in the east and a patchwork of earthy tones rises up to meet the aircraft. Before long he is standing in front of the luggage carrousel searching for the ribbon he had chosen to mark his bag.

"David Whittier?" An attractive woman, late forties or early fifties, stands behind him. Her expression, although not unfriendly, is curt and businesslike. She holds out her hand.

"For my sins." He turns and smiles. "You must be Miss Stafford." They shake. "It's a pleasure to meet you." He spins back just in time to scoop his bag from the roundabout. Back to her he says, "Not the only blue ribbon in the bunch. Thank you for meeting me."

She takes a moment to study him. Deciding that further conversation can wait she says simply, "This way, Mr. Whittier. I'm in the lot."

They make their way across a sea of rental cars to the public parking area and are soon loaded and out of the gate. Andrew's instructions had provided the name of the hotel with a month's stay paid for in advance. Neither initiates conversation and David busies himself looking about the surrounding area. He cannot but feel somewhat disoriented. They are traveling on the wrong side of the road. After an awkward few minutes, he asks.

"Is it a long drive to the city centre, Miss Stafford?"

"This is Winnipeg, Mr. Whittier. Everywhere is within a thirty-minute drive." She turns toward him and continues, "Can we be less formal? My name is Terri. Do you mind if I call you David?"

"That suits me just fine. It's a pleasure to meet you, Terri."

"Nice to meet you too." She smiles for the first time.

"I'm staying at The Hotel Fort Garry. Do you know it?"

"It's a landmark. Maybe some day I'll tell you the history of the CP Hotels. Right now, I want to ask you a direct question and I want an honest answer." They are stopped at a light, and she looks at him intensely. "Why have you come?"

He is taken aback. It is his assumption that she and Andrew are old friends; that she and he had coordinated his role together. He's the newcomer in the scenario. David stumbles over his reply.

"It's my understanding that your brother is institutionalized. He has recently shown signs of emerging from some sort of oblivion…I'm sorry, that's not the word…he has been non-communicative for many years…and I have been asked to spend time with him. Andrew feels that I might be able to help him in his recovery."

It fits with what Andrew has shared with her and although she has a bent toward over protection, especially when it comes to her brother, Terri is reassured that David's motives are as they seem. "I hope, for Noah's sake, that Andrew is right."

They cross a bridge and enter an area along the river where the great mansions of Winnipeg rise arrogantly against the skyline. The winding roadway is divided by a median where ancient oaks hover over the sidewalk like protective wings and where walkers and their pets vie for space among a throng of joggers and cyclists. David is reminded of the many pathways which spread, in spider-like fashion, throughout London's Hyde Park.

The car slows and takes a side road. Terri negotiates a narrow driveway, and the vehicle comes to rest in front of a large three story dwelling. She turns off the ignition and regards her passenger. "We're here."

David looks at the house and then back to Terri. Surely even in Canada they wouldn't situate a hotel in the middle of a residential area. Besides, he had expected something on a much grander scale. He searches for something to say but Terri beats him to it.

"I'm sure the Fort Garry would meet your needs well enough but if you are intending to help my brother then you are going to stay here. This is my where I live. What's more, so did Noah. He grew up here. And this afternoon you and I are going to pick him up." She pauses, as if considering the significance of the situation. "I'm bringing him home."

It doesn't take long for David to settle in. He stands before the third story window and gazes beyond the front drive to an enormous green space filled with walkways and flower gardens. Off in a distant corner a group of men, dressed in whites, are playing, of all things, cricket. In another direction a towered building, in traditional Tudor fashion, holds court over the grounds. The area teems with people and their pets and a steady stream of automobiles roam, bumper to bumper, about the lanes which spread in several directions throughout the park. David recalls Andrew's comment that Noah's family had owned what he had thought might be a chain of jewelry stores. They had done very well David surmises.

He makes his way down to the kitchen and stands awkwardly in the middle of the room. Staying here is an unexpected twist and he doesn't presume to know his place. What the hell are the ground rules, he wonders. He runs his hand over the surface of the fifties style dinette suite whose chrome trim reflects the sunbeams which peek in through the glass panes.

"Make yourself at home," Terri throws over her shoulder as she scurries past and heads toward the sink. She is carrying a small potted plant and water is dripping from the saucer beneath it. "Let me just take care of this and then well have some tea. You *do* drink tea, David?"

He jerks perceptively but recovers quickly. "Only when I'm out of Laphroaig." He smiles. "A cup of tea would be perfect, thanks."

Terri busies herself with the kettle while David rummages about for a start to the conversation. He is in a foreign country, staying in the home of a total stranger at the bidding of a man he has known for a few weeks at most. The request he has agreed to, when he takes the time to articulate it to himself, is highly unusual if not bizarre. And later today, if he has understood his host correctly, he will meet a man who has been in an institution since the time that David had played with his first toy train set.

"You have a lovely home, Terri."

She turns and looks directly at her guest. "This is pretty awkward for both of us isn't it David. I'm sure you're uncomfortable but let's make the best of it, ok? The doctor says that my brother's condition is improving and I'm going to do everything I can to help him. I honestly don't know if your presence here will do any good, but Andrew has insisted, and I have agreed to give it a try." She pauses. "Do you take milk?"

He nods and, in a moment, she joins him at the table. Her direct manner is oddly reassuring, and he settles into a vinyl covered chair. Terri sets his cup gently upon the surface.

"This was one of my parent's favorite pieces. They bought it at auction not long after they were married. Dad always insisted that it once belonged to Elvis though how it got to Canada he never did explain."

"Family histories are often best viewed with a grain or two of salt," offers David. "My parents were convinced that we were direct the descendants of Robert The Bruce." He pauses and sips his tea. "Old Robert must have been very prolific because the vast majority of my classmates in primary school were told the same thing." They share a smile. "Are your parents still living, Terri?"

She shakes her head. "Mom went first. She passed away the first of January two years ago. She insisted on seeing the century roll over and, against all the medical predictions, she succeeded. Dad hung on for a few months, but he was lost without her." The fondness in her voice indicates to David that theirs was a close family.

"It must have been difficult for them when they learned about your brother."

She takes a moment before responding and David wonders if Terri is open to discussing such a private matter with a perfect stranger. He wouldn't blame her if she told him to go to hell. He tries to backtrack. "What I mean is..."

"They were devastated." She doesn't look up. "Who wouldn't be? And yet, they never let anyone see their sadness. They put on a brave face for the rest of us." She hesitates and then continues. "But I also think that they never forgave themselves for leaving him in the hospital."

"What else could they have done, Terri? Especially considering the times. It's the way things were done then, wouldn't you agree?"

"They had no resources to deal with him. They had the business to run. Of course I agree. And they never talked about it. I just know that's how they felt."

"But they visited him?"

"Every weekend." She looks up. "Every Sunday for thirty years."

They fall silent as the magnitude of her words soaks in. David cannot but help visualize the scenario. Years of expectations giving way to resignation, the solemn drives to the institution followed by silent tears on the return. The guilt they must have harbored in those moments when they had temporarily given up hope. The overwhelming grief that they must have felt sitting there with Noah week after week with no way to communicate; with no way to reach him.

"He's never been home in all that time?"

"Once." She smiles sadly. "A few years before mom passed. There was some problem at the institution. Necrotizing Fasciitis. They had to move everyone out for a few days. So, my brother came here."

"Flesh eating disease. I've heard of it. How did your parents cope? They must have been very frail by then."

"The hospital sent staff along to help them out. It actually went very well. Noah ran every morning, did his push ups and chin ups in the basement. In some ways it was as if he had never been gone. But mostly he sat right here at this table…in his bubble, oblivious to everyone around him."

"And today?"

"We'll see."

⧖

The Selkirk Mental Health Centre sits on a large acreage in the west end of the small town. An aging brick structure looms protectively over a collection of smaller and more modern satellites while an array of elms and evergreens softens the space and provides both shade and shelter to the many residents who wander the grounds. David notes that their attendants are close at hand. There is a gentleness to this scene which clashes in stark contrast with his all too vivid memory of St. Bartholomews, where Christiane had spent so much of her time. They enter and are met in the foyer.

Introductions are perfunctory and David senses that Belanger harbors questions about his presence which, for the time being, remain dormant. They sit in the Doctor's office separated by the laptop while Terri outlines the weekend's agenda. For his part, Belanger seems impatient, as if he has something on his mind. Finally, he interjects.

"Yes, yes. That sounds fine, Miss Stafford. There is something I would like you to see. Will you come this way please?" He rises and whisks them out of the room. Down the hallway they come to an entrance to a larger space. Belanger places a finger to his lips, and they slip inside.

They find themselves in what, to David, looks like some sort of classroom. Chairs have been arranged in a circle and a small group of individuals are engaged in conversation. At the centre is the same man whom Terri had seen with Noah on a previous visit. He looks up momentarily and acknowledges their presence but quickly returns his attention to the group.

"Lawrence Blessing," says Belanger for David's benefit. "He's one of our psychiatric nurses. He runs this group every Friday. He is also Noah's primary care giver."

They remain standing in the doorway as the group carries on. David scans the members until his eyes fall upon a thin individual who, by anyone's standard would be described as handsome. His sinewy frame leans guardedly against the chair's back, while his feet are firmly rooted to the floor. Interlaced fingers lay calmly in his lap and his head rests placidly upon his shoulders. Dark hair without a hint of grey, parted down the middle, sweeps back over his ears in the fashion of a rock star. Large eyes stare straight ahead and, although they are not subject to the ebb and flow of conversation, seem to be at peace within the space. He sits motionless as if deep within himself. He looks to be in his early forties although David knows him to be ten years older.

"Noah," he whispers and Terri gestures in the affirmative.

The group continues, oblivious to their audience, and the nurse goes about the business of eliciting opinions and validating responses. He makes every attempt to involve each member and the collective mood is one of acceptance and safety. Noah, however, does not contribute anything and when the discussion concludes and the patients file out, he remains in place.

Belanger motions for them to follow and he moves into the circle. They take up chairs opposite Noah and for a moment all are silent. David is certain that there is a glimmer of recognition in Noah's expression as he regards them each in turn. His focus holds on his sister an instant longer that the other two and then his eyes draw downward toward the floor. Terri is the first to speak.

"Hello Noah. How are you?" There is not a hint of condensation in her tone. She does not talk down to him in the manner adopted by an adult when addressing a child, nor is her voice laden with exaggerated patience that many would address someone with an intellectual disability. It is a question posed between two equals, honestly put, as if the two siblings had spoken together just the other day…as if an answer is expected.

But that answer does not come. Noah's eyes remain fixed and after a moment it is Belanger who speaks.

"Noah, I would like you to meet someone." His voice is soft but clear and it has a calming effect on all of them. "This is Mr. Whittier." He glances in David's direction. "He has come all the way from London to meet you."

A few seconds pass with no obvious reaction. "My name's David. It's a pleasure to meet you, Noah." He rises out of his chair and holds out his hand. An awkward moment comes and goes, and David returns to his seat. Finally, it is Terri who takes charge of the situation.

"Noah, please look at me." Her words hang in the air and Belanger begins to explain why this is an unreasonable request. Movement from the chair opposite, however, halts him in mid sentence. Slowly Noah contracts the muscles in his neck as though he is moving a great weight. He raises his chin and gazes directly into the eyes of his sister. He remains motionless.

"I would like you to come home for the weekend, Noah." She pauses to let her words sink in. "But only if you feel up to it."

Belanger feels the need to come to Noah's rescue. He is certain that his patient is neither capable of a full appreciation of this request nor does he possess the capacity to formulate a response. He is certainly not able to reply. Communication on any level would be impossible; has always been so. Yet he remains silent, deciding that this is something that Terri will soon discover for herself. But he is wrong. Like the visitors sitting beside him, he stares, open mouthed, as Noah takes in a lungful of air, unlaces his fingers and places them on his knees and slowly nods his head. He maintains eye contact with Terri for an instant and then returns his gaze to the carpet in front of him, unaware of the tears which have found their way onto her cheeks.

With the necessary documentation completed, they make their way toward the exit. Belanger provides escort and wishes them well at the door. As they cross the parking lot, a voice cries out from behind.

"Miss Stafford. One moment, please. If you don't mind, I'd like to wish Noah well." Nurse Blessing bounds across the lot and stands for a moment to catch his breath. He turns to Noah, who does not look up and says, "Have a great weekend, partner. You'll want this." In his hand he holds a black case which David assumes contains the lap top computer. Noah absently reaches out and takes possession of it. He smiles and pats Noah on the shoulder. Then to the others he offers, "I didn't think this day would come. Good luck." And with that he heads back inside.

The return journey passes quickly. Noah sits in the passenger seat beside his sister who maintains a steady stream of conversation, much of which is related to family history and shared experiences from their youth. She tosses in a few snippets of local trivia for David's benefit; the local fort constructed by the Hudson's Bay Company, Portage and Main, allegedly Canada's windiest corner, the Via Rail Terminal, but her focus is clearly on her brother. For his part, Noah sits silently, seemingly oblivious to what is passing by his window, his gaze fixed firmly on the dashboard in front of him.

David's thoughts are elsewhere. Now that he has met Noah and has been able to gauge firsthand the nature of his condition, whatever optimism he may have felt previously has quickly evaporated. He feels like an imposter. He has no training in psychotherapy and certainly no practical experience in working with people with mental health issues. He is no Nurse Blessing and definitely no Dr. Belanger. He is merely a journalist to whom celebrities have turned when they had stories to tell; axes to grind. What the hell was he thinking when he agreed to take this on? Where would he even begin? He cannot imagine how his presence here can result in anything but an imposition at best.

Terri guides the car into the drive and, for a moment, the three occupants remain in place. David searches Noah's face for any glimmer of awareness and, to his surprise, he is certain that Noah has recognized the home where he had grown up. Its just a glance, held only for an instant, but sufficient to indicate, to David, that the man sitting in front of him knows this place. They exit the vehicle and, in minutes, are sitting at the same kitchen table where, hours earlier, he and Terri had begun the day. Noah looks around the room. He rubs his hands on his thighs and his breaths come more rapidly. He rocks slightly from side to side. Suddenly he turns and looks fully into the face of his sister.

Terri has anticipated this and begins calmly. "I have some bad news, Noah." She pauses and maintains his stare. "Mom and Dad are not here. They've passed away."

He doesn't look away but rather gazes directly at Terri, as if he is searching desperately for some way in which to communicate. But no words are spoken. No thoughts are formulated. As if he has given up in frustration, he slowly lowers his eyes. As he does so, he reaches out his hand and places it on hers. A tear gathers in the corner of his eye, and he nods his head. David knows that he comprehends.

A moment passes and then Noah turns his gaze toward the stranger in his home. Though his look is impossible to read, David knows that it falls upon him to explain his presence. But where to begin? He has no real sense as to Noah's capacity for understanding. What effect, if any, would the mention of Andrew's name have? A person he has not seen for the better part of thirty years. Taking his cue from Terri, he speaks directly.

"My name's David, Noah." They hold each other's stare. "I've come to meet you on behalf of an old friend of yours. His name is Andrew Sutton."

For an instant Noah does not move. Then, as if a wave has suddenly crashed over him from behind, he pitches forward and steadies himself, hands on his knees. His breath comes in fits and starts and he rocks his shoulders. He looks up bewilderedly at David and then toward his sister. His eyes widen and he looks frantically around the room. They fall upon the laptop resting on the kitchen counter and he pushes back from the table sending the chair tumbling. He reaches the machine and fumbles with the catch. When he has it open and booted up he begins to type wildly. Although both are caught completely off guard by this reaction, Terri and David settle in behind Noah and attempt to read over his shoulder.

I am the egg man. I am the walrus. God rest ye merry gentlemen. There is a town in North Ontario. A hard rains a gonna fall. Love me tender. She was a tall cool woman in a red dress. Your guitar it sounds so sweetly. Down on the Bayou.

Noah stops abruptly. He glances up toward his sister and then back to the keyboard. He begins again, more slowly this time. *Help me.* His fingers linger on the keys, momentarily suspended under the sheer force of will of their owner. Finally, they can be restrained no longer and they resume their maniacal pace. *Ronda, help me get her out of my heart. These boots are made for walking. There is a house in New Orleans. Takin' it to the streets. Down down to the water. Amazing grace how sweet the sound.*

He continues at a feverish pitch. David feels his own pulse quicken. He turns to look at Terri who has rested her hand upon her brother's shoulder. She is held spellbound by what she can only imagine has just occurred. Finally, she turns and meets David's stare. Her look begs the question. Could it be possible?

They remain in place as Noah bangs away at the keyboard producing a seemingly random flight of ideas. Nothing else captures their attention and then, like the sudden cessation of a storm, the typing stops. Exhausted, Noah rises and walks past them into the living room. He flops down on the sofa, kicks off his shoes and, in seconds, falls fast asleep.

The house falls silent. Terri moves absently toward the table and slides onto a chair. Her gaze alternates from the laptop to her brother and back again. David peruses the screen one more time, searching for he knows not what. However, with the exception of those two words...*help me*...nothing seems to hold any meaning. Then again, what else is necessary? There is no question in his mind that Noah has somehow found a way to reach through the void which lies between them as clearly as if he had screamed them out loud. As obscurely as they have been uttered and as desperate in nature as they seem, for all of them, those two words herald the beginnings of hope.

Afternoon has turned to evening. David is doing his level best to chop the peppers and onions which Terri is passing his way, something he has not done in some time, and he struggles to overcome the pangs of emotion which sweep over him. Christiane is never far from his mind and preparing meals together had brought them great pleasure. She joked often that his facility with the cutting knife was not dissimilar to a neurosurgeon forced to use pruning shears. His response was invariably that he was saving his manual dexterity for other things.

"Onions always make me cry too," offers Terri. "I guess it's just one of those tough jobs that somebody has to do, eh?"

"Just trying to earn my keep. I guess I'm a little rusty."

"You'll do. I was just thinking that Noah hasn't had a home cooked meal in a long time. He used to love stir fry when we were kids. He would never dream of eating meat. He was the original Vegan before they invented the expression."

It's been more than three hours since he had collapsed on the sofa and Noah is still deeply asleep. In the interim, Terri and David have dissected the measure of his response to hearing Andrew's name and although neither can speculate as to its exact meaning, both agree that it has touched a nerve deep within Noah's psyche. There is no question that it's had a powerful impact and, although caution will be needed, both also agree that no further discussion about Andrew should take place this evening.

The floorboard creaks and they turn abruptly. Noah is standing behind them, arms hanging at his side. Before Terri can speak, he staggers toward the basement doorway and disappears down the stairs. David moves quickly to follow but Terri is quick to intervene.

"Wait." She raises her hand and listens.

A few moments pass and soon the straining sounds of a workout echo up the stairwell. David glances back inquisitively.

"Chin ups." She offers. "He's done them every day of his life. Even in the institution. Dad put up a bar when he was a kid. Push ups and crunches too."

David shakes his head but says nothing. He glances down briefly at his own midsection, feeling a little self conscious that, in all his forty some years, he has not once heeded the call to exercise.

"How's your wind?" Terri's look is almost playful.

"Pardon?"

"Noah runs every morning at 6 am. Five k."

"But surely…"

"Believe me, he won't make an exception. It's probably not necessary but one of us should go with him. At least for tomorrow. Can you ride a bike?"

"Good lord," David mutters to no one in particular.

David is awake by four. He lies on the bed staring up at the ceiling, vaguely aware of a strange sensation. His head is clear, and his stomach settled. No hangover. Save for the Champagne he had consumed on the plane, the events of the previous day had provided a distraction from his usual routines. He rises and by the time Noah ambles down the stairs, he is waiting at the kitchen table.

"Good morning, Noah. Like some company on your run?"

Noah does not make eye contact. He sits down at the table without a trace of acknowledgement and ties his track shoes. Then he is off. David scrambles to the door in his wake and fumbles with the bike which is leaning near the side of the house. In a heartbeat, Noah has bounded down the drive and out into the street. It is a route embedded in his muscle memory and, although he has only taken it a few times in the last three decades, he navigates it with certainty.

David struggles to keep pace. Peddling desperately, he rounds the corner in time to see Noah disappear under the canopy of trees which lines the median of the broad street. There is virtually no traffic and only a handful of joggers are out and about this early. To his dismay David finds that, although his legs are racing, he is making very little headway. He glances down at the rear wheel, worried that the chain has come loose. "Sprockets," he mutters to himself. "Change gears." Frantically he grasps the lever in front of him and yanks it back and forth. It is a mistake. His attention momentarily distracted, he wobbles and, as the ground rushes up towards him, he covers his head with his arms. When he finally shakes out the cobwebs, he looks up. Noah is nowhere to be seen. A red-faced David takes up the bike and heads back the way he came, hoping against hope that he will be able to recognize the right house.

CHAPTER
Eleven

Belinski flashes his shield and the uniform steps aside. The entire area has been cordoned off for half a block in either direction and the normally light Sunday morning traffic has been diverted. A few Gawkers rubberneck from across the crescent but, for the most part, the majority of the residents of the affluent neighbourhood remain blissfully unaware of the tragic intrusion on their doorsteps. He treads cautiously down the walk which wends its way to the front of an enormous stone mansion. Lemaire is already on the scene and intercepts him mid-stride.

"You're not going to friggin' believe this, Zel."

Glancing past his partner, Belinski is able to discern the cadre of officials, garbed in white coats, which marks the periphery of the crime scene. It isn't his partner's warning but simply his gut that tells him that what awaits will be all too familiar. And though he is sickened, he is not surprised. He proceeds toward the victim.

She has been positioned against the concrete stairway, arms outstretched in either direction, as though she hadn't a worry in the world. Belinski knows otherwise. Her clothing has been shredded and the blood, which oozes out, has begun to congeal upon the fabric. Her throat has been cut deeply and her assailant has slashed the skin from the corners of her mouth upward in a garish attempt to reach her ears. The blood which has filled the ensuing crevasses is still moist, resulting in the grotesque suggestion that she is smiling.

Belinski acknowledges his partner for the first time. "Wentworth."

"Down to the last friggin' detail. Even the same neighbourhood."

The scene is commotive and the detectives retreat to allow the forensic team to complete their tasks. A familiar voice calls out.

"Morning Zel. Hope we're not taking you away from Mass." Johnson steps away from the stairway and removes his mask.

"That guy has no friggin' soul," mutters Lemaire under his breath.

"What can you tell us, Johnnie?"

"It's déjà vu all over again, detective. I know you worked the Wentworth case."

"Victim?" Belinski switches to auto. Years of experience have taught him to bury his emotions from this moment on until such time as the case is resolved. The time for reflection will come later.

"Female. Twenty-five to thirty, maybe. Out for a run by the looks of it."

"Any ID?"

"If she had any, the assailant took it with him. We got a Jane Doe here."

"I'll need a picture." He glances downward. "Cause?"

"Loss of blood. Looks as though the jugular was severed. Not here though. There isn't sufficient volume. It's probable that she was killed nearby and then placed on these steps."

"See if your team can find out where. Time?" Belinski looks at his partner who is making some initial notes of his own.

"Last eight hours at most. After midnight for certain. No rigor yet and the blood's barely cool. I've contacted Dr. Jenkins. He'll do the autopsy this afternoon. I can have a complete report for you by tonight."

"Who found the body?"

"How the hell should I know? Check with your guys inside." Johnson fusses with his mask, the dismissal a clear indication that his work is not finished.

"Ok, Johnnie," Belinski hesitates. He doesn't want to ask. "Message?"

"Yep." He points to the concrete along the side of the front steps. "Same as Wentworth. Printed in red lipstick."

Belinski takes a glance as he and Lemaire step off. The word bangs around against the inside of his skull. One nonsensical word. How many times has he awakened in a sweat with that word on his lips? The truth is that he isn't certain that it is a word. Not English any way. He quickens his pace.

"Have the uniforms gather statements from the neighbors. I'll take the people who live here" He looks back toward the crime scene. "Just want to give Johnson and his team time to wrap up." He looks at his watch. "And Guy…see if you can get hold of the Mounties. I don't recall them saying anything about a message when we met with them."

"On it." Lemaire takes a few steps and then turns. "You know this is gonna be a friggin' nightmare." Receiving no response, Lemaire is in motion.

Belinski waits impatiently near the street. His eye is drawn to a lone figure on the far side of the crescent. An elderly woman, standing on her veranda is gesturing subtly with her hand, trying not to be seen by anyone but Belinski. He waves and makes his way across the street and down the winding sidewalk. She greets him with a question.

"Are you in charge, officer?" Her voice quivers, as if carrying a great weight.

"Detective Belinski, maam." He reveals his badge, but she takes no notice. "And you are?"

"The young lady on the porch, detective…is she…"

"It's a crime scene, maam, that's all I can say at this time." He glances upward toward the second story window where a shade is partially open, a second pair of eyes looking out.

"Oh dear. The poor thing." She cinches the rope on her dressing gown but holds her ground.

Belinski has no time for gawkers, but dismissiveness is not in his nature. "Do you have any information that could be important for the police to know about this crime, Maam?"

She hesitates. Belinski takes that for a no and prepares his exit.

"Well, detective…I don't think I have a choice. Yes…I think there is."

"Alright," he responds, "let's make it official then." He takes out his notebook and records her particulars. Then he asks, "what would you like to tell me, Mrs. Bakerstream?"

"Well, detective…where should I begin?" She looks back over her shoulder through the glass front door.

"I'm not the deepest of sleepers, you see. In fact, most nights I wander around the house aimlessly…pacing to and fro." She looks to Belinski for understanding. "I suppose it comes with age. Sometimes I look out the front window…it helps to pass the time. After all, the nights can be so long." She takes a deep breath. "I use a pair of field glasses. They're Henry's, you see. My husband. He says he likes to look at the birds in the trees along the crescent, but I know he enjoys watching the pretty girls jogging by the house." She gauges Belinski's reaction to this over the top of her glasses. "There's a steady stream, don't you know."

"What did you see through your field glasses, Mrs. Bakerstream?"

"Well, detective, it was getting late…maybe one o'clock. Not many cars were passing, and the streetlight has been out for some time." She glances toward the nearest pole. "Henry has phoned the city several times to let them know about it but, well, things move slowly, don't they?"

"Please continue maam."

"Well…I saw a flash. I looked toward the veranda, and I saw someone lighting a cigarette. It could have been a pipe, I suppose, but not many people smoke a pipe these days, do they. Now, mind you, the field glasses aren't as new as they could be and my eyesight is rather compromised you understand, but I know what I saw." She pauses for effect. "It was Charles Palasades. You know, of the furniture chain. He lives there, of course. But I will swear to it, detective. Charles Palasades was on that very porch," she points dramatically, "early this morning. I'm *certain* of it." Having hit her crescendo, in her finest television courtroom fashion, she sags slightly, rests her hand on Belinski's forearm and repeats, more softly now, "I am certain of it."

Belinski smiles appreciatively. He knows that every street has them. Neighbors who like to take an interest in the comings and goings of those close by. He also knows that he has solved more than a few cases through their observations and, as such, does not disparage their efforts. He thanks her for the information and assures her that, should her testimony be required in any form, someone would be in touch. He retreats and leaves her to relay the details of their interaction to her husband, Henry. The FIU is wrapping up and, tucking his notebook into the pocket of his jacket, he heads back over to meet with the furniture magnate and his spouse.

The vibration in his jacket takes a moment to register but the number on the screen demands his attention. He stifles his surprise. After all, it's early on a Sunday morning.

"Belinski," he answers.

"What can you tell me, detective?" Assistant Chief Inspector Cuddy doesn't waste words.

"Looks a lot like Wentworth, sir. Also similar to the case in Selkirk," he offers, "though I think we need to use some caution. It's pretty early on."

"I'm heading to the office right away. Meet me there as soon as you can. Let's get ahead of this thing."

He rings off, leaving Belinski with little doubt that he means right away. The Palasades will have to wait.

They sit at the kitchen table, Terri fussing with the jam for Noah's toast and David examining the scrape on his forearm. Noah's stare is fixed on a bird perched on a branch outside the window. David had returned before Noah to a perturbed look and had offered his explanation, and apology, clumsily. An hour or so later, Noah had entered the back door unnoticed and gone straight up to shower and change. David had been struck by the absolutely mundane nature of this.

"I hope you had a good run, Noah," offers Terri. "It's a beautiful morning. I'm glad you're here."

Her brother redirects his stare in her direction and taps his fingers absently on the table. It is a gesture which David had noticed during the previous evening. He imagines that it is a form of conditioned response in that the computer has become Noah's only means of communication.

"Did you enjoy your bike ride, David? She renders this so casually that even David has the feeling that they are old friends. Statements to Noah, which require no answers and questions to David. He follows her lead.

"It's been a while since I've cycled." He turns to Noah. "You're not easy to keep up with." A genuine smile and his gaze lingers.

"I suppose, David, that you use the subway to get around in London." Terri's inviting manner would put anyone at their ease, he thinks.

"We call it the tube. And yes, it gets us wherever we need to go." A glance to Noah. "That is, unless you're in the mood for a joke or a good tale. If that's the case, then I would suggest a cab. Someone once said, 'there are two kinds of London cabbies...story tellers or comedians.'" David chuckles at his own anecdote and reaches for the tea. He raises the pot and looks at Noah.

"In that case," Terri begins, "Noah would fit right in. He is a writer, David." She looks at her brother. "Mom used to say that he was born with a story in his head and a pen in his hand." Back at David, "I have some of his work in the office. You have to read some of them." She pauses and then adds, "if that would be okay with you, Noah."

David searches Noah's face for a sign of acknowledgement as Terri continues.

"And David is a writer of sorts as well, Noah. He works for the *London Times*. He's quite well regarded in England, I'm told. That's where he met Andrew."

David does not correct the inaccuracies and although this conversation has not been rehearsed in any fashion, he senses an opportunity. He excuses himself and heads off to retrieve one of the books that he has brought with him. He's back in a moment and fumbles with the bookmark.

"Noah…I wonder if you would like to hear a passage or two from one of Andrew's novels. He's a gifted writer, as I'm sure you know." He opens the book and holds it before him. For a moment, Noah shows little response but then pushes his plate from him and leans forward.

"His aching heart was like a drop of blood on virgin snow. So beautiful and so tragic. It was at this moment that his dream, so gently caressed in slumber, died like the smoldering embers of his love."

Suddenly Noah's hands begin to tremble. He rocks back and forth, and his breath comes in fits and starts. He grasps his forehead as though it will explode at any moment and then looks frantically, first to his sister and then to David. Tears well up in his eyes and then he flings his chair backward and rushes from the room.

Terri jumps up but does not follow. "Noah…," she calls as his chair crashes to the floor. Absently, she lifts it and puts it back in place while she looks helplessly down the hallway. David, book suddenly cast aside, rises but shock renders him speechless. He tries to read the expression on Terri's face. Is it recrimination? Does she hold him responsible for provoking Noah's outburst? He is more than surprised at what he sees.

Her hands fly to her face, and she wheels around to regard him. She smiles through her tears. "Oh my god, David," she whispers, "My dear god." She reaches vacantly behind her for her chair. David darts quickly and slides it behind her just as she falls back into it. "I can't believe it." She buries her head in her hands and, for a moment, falls silent. Then she looks up once again and blesses David with her most radiant smile. "He felt something, David." Her hands begin to tremble. "You saw it. Emotion. He hasn't done that since he went away. Her head sways back and forth as though she has just won the lottery and her thoughts are already on the many ways in which she can help people with her windfall.

"The book." David looks down at the table. "Those lines struck a chord." He picks it up and holds it like a crystal bowl. Andrew's photograph stares out from the jacket's back. "Or was it the picture?"

"The words…the image…I don't think we can know," Terri replies. "And right now, it doesn't matter." She looks down the empty hallway. "What matters is that something is stirring in him. It feels like a new beginning." She rises once more. "I'm going to comfort him." And before David can respond, she is gone.

⁂

"Bring the Detective a chair," Assistant Chief Superintendent Cuddy barks at his assistant. Belinski is surprised at this breech of protocol and stands patiently by. A card table chair is proffered, and the assistant slips away.

"So, let's get to it." He taps the desk between them impatiently. "I don't have to tell you that I'm up to my ears in calls. The mayor...Chief Petroni...the media. Everybody wants an answer." He swats away an imaginary pest. "This thing's got more legs than a centipede." He grimaces. "And the body's not even cold yet."

"That's just it," begins Belinski. "We can only move as fast as the evidence takes us. What I suggest..."

"They all want to know if we have a serial killer out there, detective. Hell, for what it's worth, I want to know it too."

"Of course. But we need time to determine whether we're dealing with the same perpetrator or some sort of copycat. Right now, it's impossible to say."

"Ok, Ok, I hear you. So, let's cut through the muck and make a start. You handle the investigation and I'll take care of the questions. I don't have to tell you that manpower will be an issue." The same pest again. "What do you think you're going to need on this?"

Belinski is no rookie, and he knows that asking for the moon won't get him any cheese.

"Well...the conference room will do for operations. I've got Detective Lemaire. I could use two or three people to do legwork, follow up on any leads...handle some interviews."

"Uh huh. I can give you Ginelli and Templeton. I don't know what the hell to do with them anyway."

"The 'speakergate guys'?"

"Is that what they're calling it?" Cuddy shakes his head. "Shoulda figured." A chuckle. "Look, they're good cops. One just happens to have a big mouth. He's young. Should get on well with your partner."

"Fine. I'll be glad of the help." Belinski looks at the laptop sitting idly on a corner table. "I'm going to need a tech guy. Someone who can do some research, check data bases...that sort of thing."

"See what I can do. That it?"

"Should be for now. We'll get started right away. Protocol for reporting?"

Belinski knows that, like most in administration, Cuddy wants to know what's going on before it happens. He also knows that that can be a pain in the ass. Any time taken away from the case can have a critical impact on results.

"I trust you, Belinski. Do your job and let me know what I need to know when I need to know it." His look is genuine. "But if this is the same guy as Wentworth…I want to hear from you. Clear?"

"Crystal." They both rise and, to Belinski's amazement, Cuddy offers his hand. Another precedent broken.

Belinski is on the phone before he has left the outer office. Multitasking, a necessary talent in his position, has not come easily to him. He is a plodder by nature but, like most things, once he has taken it on, he has become adept at the intricacies of it. A system, he has often reminded himself, is the key. And while he doesn't necessarily see himself as a concrete thinker, he is definitely sequential. Step by step.

Lemaire answers on the first ring. "What took you so friggin' long? How did it go with Cuddy?"

"We're good to go. Operations out of the conference room for now. What have you got so far?"

There is static on the line and after a moment Lemaire's voice returns. "Sorry about that…just pulled into the basement. Not sure if you caught it all…got an update from the Mounties. Also, we have an ID on the victim. I'll be up in ten minutes."

The conference room is a large rectangle with white board along the longest wall. Belinski operates from memory as he begins to fill in a section of the blank space.

Angela Wentworth Age 24 at time of decease. (August 97) Travel agent…lived with parents (real estate agents) Graduate of Red River Community College Volunteered at Winnipeg Humane Society Tennis Running

He drops his hand to his side. He isn't sure whether the information he is recalling springs from the actual investigation or from her obituary. Right now, he decides, it doesn't matter. It will do for the purposes of providing background for the new members of his team.

"A lot of bad memories." Lemaire is standing in the doorway. "I still feel like we let her down." He tosses his keys on the table.

Belinski steps away from the board. "I know how you feel." Then more briskly, "Alright, detective, what have you got?"

"Ok. The friggin' Mounties are getting nowhere. I swear they were happy to hear that we got another case over here. Said they'd send everything they have over to us. I took a few notes to get us started." He shuffles through his book.

"Their victim is Rosamie Pagliani. Nineteen years old. Worked part time in a flower shop in Selkirk. She was a student at the university. Engineering. Valdictorian of her graduating class." He looks up. "What a friggin' waste."

Belinski agrees but says nothing. Sentiment won't help their case. He waits for Lemaire to continue.

"She was also the Provincial cross-country champion twice at Selkirk Regional High School and was a member of the track team at the U of M." He puts away his notebook and, knowing what Belinski is waiting for, adds, "yes…the killer left his calling card."

He moves to the whiteboard and prints 'IISTITIA' in block letters. He steps back to examine his effort. "What the hell can it mean? It's friggin' gibberish."

A flood of random thoughts rush through Belinski's head. With Wentworth, so much effort had gone into deciphering those letters but every attempt had ended with frustration and failure. In the end, no meaning could be assigned to them and their significance, if there had been any, was never discovered. Now, however, with the same letters present in both new cases, there could be no doubt. They provided undisputable proof that the three cases were linked. Moreover, they established without a doubt, the presence of a serial killer.

Before Lemaire can continue, there is a knock at the door. Standing in the entranceway is a young man in jeans and a cardigan sweater. The T shirt that peaks out from under it has a picture of a double decker bus and the logo that says 'The Original Tour Company'. To Belinski's eye, he could be sixteen or thirty-six. His dark hair is longer in the front, ala Elvis, but is shaved close around the ears. His green eyes twinkle from behind stylish dark framed glasses and he stands easily in open toed sandals.

"Excuse me, fellas." He pauses. "I'm looking for Detective Belinski."

Belinski nods but says nothing.

"Ethan Mansbridge." He moves forward and extends his hand. "Assistant Superintendent Cuddy suggested I come by. "Said you could use a hand with some research."

"Yes. Of course." He moves forward. "Zelig Belinski." A much firmer handshake than he anticipates. "This is Detective Lemaire."

The two nod from across the room. Any reservations that the Grunt has about the new guy's abilities are kept silent for the moment and he returns to his work at the board.

"Have a seat." Belinski motions to the closest table. "I'll bring you up to speed. Mind if I ask you a few questions first?"

"Not at all," comes Mansbridge's response as he slides into a chair. "Is this an interview?"

"Let's call it a conversation. If we're going to be working on the same team, I think a little background would be helpful." Belinski smiles his best professional smile.

"Ask away." The same smile reflected back.

"Let's start with your educational background…personal history…that sort of thing."

"Sure. Well, I grew up on the coast. Salt Spring. Advance Placement in high school. You could color me the guy who wasn't the quickest or the slowest, I guess. For example, when my class would enter his room, our Latin teacher, Mr. Pristako, would greet us with "Ah, here comes Ray of sunshine Rathert and the Happy Gang. You could put me in the *and the* category."

"For Chrissakes, he doesn't care about that shit." Lemaire spits from across the room before Belinski can stop him.

"Why don't we move it forward a bit," he suggests.

"Understood. I'm a graduate of the Canadian Military College in Kingston, Ontario. I went into the purple trades, specializing in Logistics. I then moved on to Communications which we called SIGNET. My final posting was at the Communications Intelligence headquarters in Cheltenham, England. I speak three languages, not counting Latin, which is more than a little rusty, and, when I ended my time with the military, I was Section Chief."

His eyes never leave Belinski's. "From there, I joined the Toronto Police Department. I was a research specialist for four years before moving here at the beginning of the month where I am about to serve in the same capacity." He pauses a moment before addressing Lemaire.

"And by the way, Detective, it's *Inspector* Mansbridge."

Lemaire's head hangs lower than his jaw.

A smile tugs at the corner of Belinski's mouth and he's pretty sure he's not the only one enjoying the moment.

"So, what about you, Detective, what can you tell me about yourself? This is, after all a conversation…yes?"

"Well," Belinski begins, "My chief focus was hockey if I'm honest. I was always more interested in the results of my last game than my next test. In spite of myself, I managed to graduate with a Criminology degree from the University."

"He was the captain of the Bisons for three of his four years there." Lemaire has recovered somewhat.

"Two years of Law School and then joined the force. After a stint in vice, I transferred to homicide."

"Law school not for you?" Mansbridge's interest is genuine.

"Let's just say I wasn't for it."

They share a moment of reflection. For Belinski, he knows that Mansbridge will be an excellent addition to the team. That's good enough for him.

"So, you transferred from Toronto *to* Winnipeg?" Lemaire is nonplussed. "Most people are looking to go the other way."

"It was love, Detective." Mansbridge is quick to answer.

"She must be pretty special." Lemaire shakes his head.

"Oh, believe me, detective…he is." Mansbridge's gaze is direct.

Belinski clears his throat. "Ok. So here it is in brief." He pauses awkwardly. "I gotta ask, is it Inspector Mansbridge…or sir…how do you want it?"

"This is your case, Detective. I'm not official yet. Why not just Ethan? I'm good with that."

"Good then." Belinski starts again. "We've got three victims. One is a cold case from five years ago. Two are recent…few weeks apart. Signs are that it's the same perp. The team consists of Lemaire and me, you if you're interested, and a couple of uniforms. I suggest we meet this evening and sort out the priorities. That should give us a chance to get this place set up. Say seven?"

"Seven it is. Anything I can do before then?"

"Yeah…get a good nap in," Lemaire calls from across the room. "Once Zel puts us to work, rest will be out of the friggin' question."

"Understood, detective. See you both at seven bells." And with that Ethan Mansbridge is out the door.

Lemaire saunters over and flops into a chair. One leg finds the chair opposite.

"So, Zel…what do you think?"

"That's a hell of a resume. Bright guy."

Lemaire takes a moment. "Ya know…for once I gotta agree with you. I think he'll work out." Then he looks at his partner. "You went to friggin' Law School?" He shakes his head. "I don't think I can be your friend anymore, for Chrissakes."

Noah has spent the entire day sequestered in his room. His laptop remains on the dining room table where he had left it the previous evening and although his sister has looked in on him periodically, she has decided to maintain her distance. An injured animal, she surmises, often seeks refuge in a solitary place and she is certain that Noah has been wounded emotionally. She has spent much of her day providing David with many of the events and experiences of Noah's early life. So much of what she provides centers on Noah's academic success and, in particular, his many literary accomplishments.

"When Noah was twelve years old, he entered a national short story contest. Now, keep in mind, it wasn't only for children. According to mom, Pierre Berton, a well known historian here in Canada, was one of the entrants." She searches David's face for recognition. "He won first place, David. It was a wonderful story. You'll have to read it."

She smiles at the memory. "He called it *A Day in the life of a Catholic School*. It was based on the elementary we both attended. We called it 'god school' because it was run by the church. Just up the road from here." She looks out the window. "There was one teacher, Sister Agatha. Noah used to call her Attila the Nun. Not certain she was his favorite."

She carries on in this fashion, much like a proud parent, but also, David observes, as a barrister might, pleading a case before the court. It is the outpouring of one whom, for so long has kept her emotions locked up inside, and who now finds that she has someone to share them with. She feels that, in David, she finally has an ally.

"I wonder if…"

David's question is interrupted by a knock at the door. Terri flashes him a puzzled look as she rises. She peaks out the window on her way to the entrance. "It's my next-door neighbor."

"Eileen," she says by way of greeting. "How is everything?"

"Hello, my dear. Right as rain. And you?" She smiles and crooks her neck to get a glimpse into the hallway.

David is uncertain of his place but rises and awkwardly steps in behind his host.

"Hello, young man," comes the greeting from the steps. Though it has been some time since he has been referred to as 'young man', David figures that, given the thick glasses and grey hair observing him, anyone under sixty might appear so.

"This is David Whittier, Eileen. He is visiting from England."

"How nice to meet you, Mr. Whittier." She smiles a knowing smile at Terri and then says, "very nice, indeed."

"Is there something I can help you with, Eileen?" Terry returns the smile minus the innuendo.

"Well, my dear, I'm going to hobble up to the Bulk Barn." She looks at David. "Need some peanuts for the squirrels. Would you like me to pick up anything while I'm there?"

"Thanks for asking, Eileen, but no, I don't think so."

"Ok, luv. Just thought I'd ask." She remains in place. "Have you seen the news, dear? Just terrible, don't you think?" She shakes her head. "Can't feel safe in your own neighborhood anymore."

"Actually, I haven't," Terri replies. "What's happened now?"

"Another murder, dear. Oh my. I thought you would have heard." She turns and looks up the street. "Right around the corner…again. Over on the crescent."

For a moment, Terri is silent. Thoughts from another time compete for her attention but she finds her voice.

"Well, that *is* terrible, Eileen. Thanks for telling me. I'll catch up on the details on CBC at six. Are you sure you should be out and about?"

"I'm eighty three years old, my dear. And while I'm still in my prime, I might not be what they're looking for. You keep safe, now."

She starts to turn and then, "very nice to meet you, Mr. Whittier."

Terri moves way from the door and sighs. Her eyes linger on her neighbor momentarily as she powers her way down the sidewalk. David is distracted by movement on the periphery and, before Terri can speak, they notice that Noah has resumed his seat in front of his laptop.

She calls out to him as she closes the door. "Good to see you up and about, Noah. Hope you're doing ok."

Greeted with silence, she and David move into the dining room and she rests her hand on Noah's shoulder as he types.

His aching heart was like blood on the pure virgin snow. His aching heart was like blood on the pure virgin snow. His aching heart was like blood on the pure virgin snow. Why do birds suddenly appear every time you are near…just like me, they long to be close to you. Why do birds suddenly appear? Why, why, why Delilah? Why, why, why Delilah? Why why why, why why why…And I

As Noah finishes the last word, he flings himself backward, distancing his arms from the laptop and willing his fingers to stop typing. It seems to take everything he has and he slumps in his chair. His gaze spins around the room and settles on David. With pleading eyes, he strains forward, desperately trying to break through the barrier which, like a sealed tomb, binds him in space and time from the world around him. He raises his hands and buries his face into them before lowering his head onto the tabletop.

※

"That about covers what we know about Wentworth and Pagliani." Belinski summarizes. "Detective Lemaire can fill us in on the little we've gleaned from this morning." He motions toward his junior. "Guy…"

The white board has begun to fill in. The three victims' names head columns of information, hastily scribbled in point form, which, though scant, present the sum total of knowledge of each case thus far. Black lines, drawn in tangential directions, connect the details of three shattered lives. And there isn't much to go on.

The team has assembled, and introductions have been made. Ginelli and Templeton sit stiffly, neither knowing why they have drawn this assignment and both wondering how the hell they can contribute. They are street cops. Uniforms, with little or no practical experience in investigative work. Whether punishment or promotion, neither is certain but their money is on the former.

Though he has three years active service on the force, Beto Ginelli has yet to reach his twenty first birthday. Close cropped black hair and compact frame, he has the fit look of a soccer player which, in fact, he is. He sits in stark contrast to his older, and rounder, senior partner. Constable Templeton, mid forties and sagging, is checking off each day as he clings to the notion of early retirement. A career of sitting in a squad car is on full display.

"Jennifer Grant, age 31." Lemaire pushes up from his chair. "Married to an investment broker. No kids. She was a lawyer with Cromwell and Fertado. Member of the Winter Club and active in her church. That's all I could get out of the husband before he threw me out. He was pretty friggin' upset."

"Ok detective. It's a start." Belinski nods in the direction of the empty chair and Lemaire complies. "Alright. Here's how I'd like to proceed." He leans forward and regards the members of his team. "We'll meet in the evening…similar timeframe. This isn't going to be easy, people. The Mounties have turned their investigation over to us so not only do we have three separate cases to run down, we have to look for links between them all." He rises and moves to the whiteboard.

"We don't have a lot to go on, but I suggest that we focus on the commonalities here. Victims are all young women. Each was out running at the time of their deaths. Familiarize yourselves with the cause of death and the sadistic way in which they were killed." A nod to the folder in front of each man." They were all left on a doorstep. Posed. No sexual interference in the first two cases and, though we don't have the report yet, my guess is that that will hold with Ms Grant as well."

Ginelli raises his hand like he's back in school. "Sir, if you don't mind…"

"For Chrissakes, constable, let the man finish." Lemaire shoots him a glare.

"Go ahead, Ginelli," Belinski rescues.

"Well, I don't know how Dave feels…that is, constable Templeton, but I'm not sure why I'm here. Can you…"

"That's on me, Ginelli. I had hoped to find some time to fill you in but it didn't happen. I can provide some details after we're finished but, for now, this will have to suffice. This is an important case…manpower is limited, and I needed some help. You and constable Templeton were available, and I jumped at the chance to get you." He smiles and says, "I know you both will be a big help."

"Sir." Ginelli settles back into his chair.

"Ok." Belinski recommences. "I want to start in this direction. Constable Templeton…do you mind if I call you Dave…by this time tomorrow that phone will be ringing off the hook." A glance at the desk in the corner. "You'll take the calls and log them. Separate list for anything you feel might be helpful. Situations that you deem critical, you pass on to me or Detective Lemaire immediately. Clear?"

"Yes, sir."

"Guy. When we were in Selkirk, you raised the question of Leonard Lee. I'd like you to pay a visit to The Selkirk Medical Facility tomorrow, take Ginelli here with you, and see what you can find out about any day passes he may have been on. Let's determine one way or the other if there's any connection there."

"Got that Ginelli. You and me...and Loonie Lenny." Lemaire pulls his finger across his throat.

Belinski lets it go. "Ethan...why not begin with the phone records of the three victims. See if you can come up with any overlaps. People they all might have known...businesses they all may have frequented. That sort of thing."

"Understood. What about you, boss?"

"I've got to get back to this morning's crime scene. I have to follow up on information about the resident there." He takes visual inventory. "Anything else?" But he gets no response.

"Good then. Let's meet again here tomorrow evening. Same time."

CHAPTER
Twelve

Although she tried several times to encourage him, Noah did not emerge from his room for the rest of the day. Even the prospect of a home cooked meal failed to entice him. David and Terri had spent the rest of the day in reflective conversation regarding the weekend's events. They had taken a few moments to watch the local news and digest somewhat absently, the information about the attack in the neighborhood.

David sits, lost in his own thoughts. It does not register that Terri has turned the television off and has left the room. Something about Noah's writing earlier in the day is not sitting right. On the one hand, he sees it as real progress. Clear indication that Noah has been able to transfer thought to word…at least in his unusual way. David sees this as a genuine indication that Noah's consciousness is expanding. He knows that Andrew would be most interested in that. On another level, he is pleased for Terri. If not happiness, he feels that she at least has hope. But it is none of these things that whisper at the edge of his sub consciousness. The words themselves, maybe?

"Can we talk about tomorrow, David?" Terri calls from the kitchen.

David snaps his head back and settles his nerves before answering. "Of course. Be right there."

"Noah has to be back by 9 o'clock," she carries on. "I can't believe they are such sticklers about these things. He's a grown man, for Pete's sake. They treat him like a prisoner."

He joins her in the kitchen. "I can escort him if you like. I know you're anxious to get back to your business." He adds, "besides…I plan to visit him every day during the week anyway. Happy to begin tomorrow."

"David. It's an hour's drive and you don't have a vehicle. How on earth…"

"I'll take a cab," comes his quick response, "after all, I have a very liberal expense account." He displays his first smile of the day. "Andrew is paying the freight."

"Well…"

"Besides, it will give Noah and me a real chance to get to know each other. Captive audience."

"And you intend to visit him every day?"

"And then bring him back home once again on Friday. Sound good?"

"Sounds very good, David. I like the thought of Noah having someone to spend time with every day. Thank you."

There are few, if any, signs that a brutal crime had been investigated here just yesterday. The blooms on the rose bushes are radiant and the sidewalk has been power washed. Traffic eases by with a routine which belies recent events. Occasionally, a car slows, and a picture is taken, the story behind it to be relayed over a later dinner. All in all, however, the day to day has resumed.

Belinski waits for an answer to his knock. Although he is expected, he finds himself in a holding pattern. Finally, Palasades opens up and steps through the entranceway. His suit jacket is under his arm and a cup is in hand.

"Forgive me, detective. I'm on my own this morning. My wife had an early meeting. Can we talk on the way to my car? The garage is round the back."" He brushes past and makes his way down the steps.

"Just a moment, Mr. Palasades." Belinski hasn't budged. "I'm afraid that won't do. I'd like to ask you a few questions about your movements last night." He pauses. "And I'm sorry if it's inconvenient for you but we can do it here or we can do it at the station."

The two men eye each other for a moment before Palasades responds. "*My* movements?" His surprise is genuine. "What on earth for?"

"Well, to begin with, a dead body was found on your property early yesterday morning. You and your wife both gave statements to the officer on scene. In yours, you said that you were supervising an inventory at your warehouse until midnight."

Palasades shifts his weight. "Do you mind if I smoke?"

Belinski ignores the request. "I did some checking. Seems that your plant manager…"

"Ok detective. I see where this is going." He lights up. "It's true. I wasn't there." He looks around like he's just discovered that he's lost his keys and has no idea where to begin his search. "I made that up." His hand is in the cookie jar, and he knows it.

"Do you have any hobbies, Detective Belinski?" He dispatches his coffee to the garden soil. "Poker? Do you play golf?"

Belinski waits for him to continue.

"Well, I don't. Not really. I've got an enormous billiard table… the whole room if you must know." He shakes his head. "I maybe get to use it once every couple of months. When the in-laws come over. Rest of the time I work."

An SUV has stopped on the Crescent in front of the house. A look from Belinski encourages them to move on.

"I've got a grass guy." He grimaces at his lack of respect. "That's not fair. I have a company that comes and looks after the yard. They do a wonderful job as you can see." A wave of his hand. "Well, the owner is a great guy. I just love talking to him. In fact, I go out of my way to bump into him whenever I see him in the yard. You wouldn't believe his knowledge of music trivia."

Belinski adjusts his position and nods, wondering where this is all going.

"Turns out, Tom, that's his name, plays in a snooker league. They meet every Saturday night at one hotel or another. Maintain standings and everything." He smiles. "Well, we got to talking and then he asks me if I'd be interested in subbing in. Said his partner couldn't make it." He holds his arms outstretched. "You might think me foolish, but I leapt at the chance. Had a fantastic time. We won every game."

"And you got home…when?" Belinski calls Mrs. Bakerstream to mind.

"Around one. Sat on the porch for awhile. Savoring the moment."

Belinski leans forward. "But your statement…"

"Look, Detective. I'm not sure how to put this but my wife… well, it's not snobbery really but…well she has a certain image of the sorts of people we should associate with if that makes any sense.?" He searches Belinski's eyes for understanding. "She's the president of the College of Physicians and Surgeons. "If I had said that I was out playing pool with the grass guy, she would have had an embolism." His look is honest. "So, I lied."

"And the owner of the maintenance companies name…?"

Before he can finish, Palasades has written out the particulars.

Noah has been checked back in and he and David sit in the atrium looking out over a garden. David is reading passages from *A Tale Of Two Cities*. He stops from time to time to gauge Noah's investment but, aside from an occasional shifting of his weight in the chair, he finds none. Eventually he rises and, resting his hand on Noah's shoulder, bids farewell with a promise to return tomorrow. He is tempted to discuss the weekend with Dr. Belanger but accepts that he would be out of line. Whatever information is to be shared with Belanger will have to come from Terri.

David's taxi nears the end of the drive when the cabbie screeches to a halt. Barreling around the corner and into the grounds is another vehicle. Its driver has the window down and waves his fist wildly.

"Watch where you're going for Chrissakes!" he yells as he passes.

It's been a long drive and the air conditioning in Lemaire's unmarked squad car is on the fritz. He is less happy than usual. He's spent the time passing on his vast knowledge of investigation techniques to his totally captive audience. For his part, constable Ginelli has been an enthusiastic listener, asking appropriate questions and prodding his new mentor as necessary. Lemaire does not look for parking, choosing to leave the car near the entrance.

"We're here to see a Dr. McKenzie," he asserts to the receptionist at the first desk he comes to.

"Of course, sir." The young man's tone is flat but not impolite. "Who should I say is here, please?"

Lemaire turns sideways and looks Ginelli up and down from his crisp blue shirt to his pressed blue pants, and finally his badge, before returning his glare to the face behind the desk.

"Who the frig do you think is here, for Chrissakes?"

"Yes, of course, officer. My bad. "Just one moment, please."

Lemaire shoots a sideways glance to his protégé that says, 'you might do it differently, but my way works for me.'

It's not long before they are approached by an older man dressed in a perfectly tailored navy suit. His outstretched hand bids his visitors welcome.

"Dr. McKenzie…you must be Detective Lemaire." He smiles as though he has just eaten something unpleasant, ignoring Ginelli altogether.

"I'm told you're here about Leonard Lee, yes?"

That's Loonie Lenny to me, Lemaire thinks to himself. "Just following up on his whereabouts on a couple of occasions recently. I understand that you let that guy out on his own."

The doctor clears his throat. "That *guy* as you put it, detective, has rights under the law. And as a consequence of those rights, he has been granted periodic day release. It should…"

"I couldn't give a crap about any of that, doc…he chopped the head off a guy in the park and I want to know where he was on these dates." He thrusts a crumpled piece of paper forward.

Ginelli thinks that the doctor's head is about to explode. Instead, he shows restraint and takes the paper, smoothing it out before turning to the receptionist who, up til now has busied his head as low behind the desk as possible.

"Please cross reference these dates with any day passes issued to Mr. Leonard Lee." He turns back to Lemaire. "It may take a moment. Would you like to meet him while you wait?" Dr. McKenzie has fully regained his composure.

Lemaire is surprised by the offer. "Meet who…Loonie Lenny?"

"No, detective. Mr. Leonard Lee. I'm sure you will find it most illuminating."

Before Lemaire can respond, his host turns and starts down the hallway.

"This way, please. You too, constable."

The two officers exchange worried looks and, for the first time, Ginelli notices a potential chink in the grunt's armor.

They find themselves at the entrance to what appears to be an art room. McKenzie disappears momentarily and the returns with a diminutive man in what Lemaire surmises to be his early forties. The doctor makes the introductions.

"Detective Lemaire has some questions for you, Leonard." And with that he heads back the way he came. "I'll meet you at the front desk when you're finished, detective," he tosses over his shoulder.

The three men assess each other. Before Lemaire can open his mouth, however, Leonard Lee speaks.

"I think I know what this is about, officers." His voice is thin and measured. Each word is deliberate and seems to come from a great distance. He taps the paint brush against the outside of his pant leg as if his arm is independent from the rest of him.

"You're here about the murders." He stands defiantly. Then he adds, "They actually let us watch the news in here."

Ginelli absently takes a step backward. His eyes don't move from the business end of the brush.

Lemaire finds his voice. For once, if an altercation breaks out, he will be the larger combatant. "That's right, Lenny." He stares into the face in front of him. "Did you friggin' do them?"

Leonard Lee raises his hand to his forehead. Both Lemaire and Ginelli tense.

"Look officers. I have a medical condition. I know that. And believe me, I wouldn't wish it on anyone. And yes, I am responsible for Mr. Jamieson's death." He slowly lowers his arm. "I was off of my medication at the time. And I am so very sorry for his family."

"But what about…"

"No detective. I didn't have anything to do with any of them. I'm sure that you will find that I was here on every occasion when they occurred. I don't go out as much as you might think."

"And you take your medication regularly?" Ginelli enters the conversation.

"As regularly as clockwork, constable. Those were dark days for me. I don't intend to go back."

The three men stand there in the ensuing silence, two of them uncomfortably so.

Then, out of nowhere, Lemaire's hand appears, and he and Loonie Lenny shake as if they were old friends.

"Well, thanks for clearing that up, Mr. Lee." He glances down at the paint brush. "And good luck with the painting... and everything." He looks him in the eye and then adds, "and you better not be friggin' lying to us." And with that they go their separate ways.

They catch up with McKenzie, more by chance than design, as they near the exit. He is engaged with a staff member and fails to see them coming. He dismisses her and turns his attention to another matter.

"One second there, doc. Just one more request." Lemaire seizes on the opportunity.

McKenzie doesn't make the effort of smiling. "What is it, detective?"

"You can forget about Loonie Lenny. That's not going anywhere. What I want is a list of every patient who had a day pass on those dates I gave you." He nods in the direction of the front desk.

"Oh, for god's sake..." he catches himself, "that would take up valuable time." And then another tact, "Do you have any authority here, Detective Lemaire? You said yourself on the phone that you were from the Winnipeg Police Department."

"I'll tell you what doc." Lemaire raises himself up to his full height. "I'll have the Mounties pay you a visit and you can waste *their* valuable time. See how they friggin' like that. And while I'm at it I'll let them know that you are obstructing a murder investigation. They're gonna be real happy with you for Chrissakes." He thrusts his card forward. "Here's where you can reach me."

And with that, the newly formed partnership turns and head out the front doors.

As they approach their unparked vehicle, a tow truck is idling near the front bumper. Lemaire has no doubt that his ungracious host is responsible for its appearance and waves his shield menacingly at the driver. They are soon off without incident.

Lemaire, as is typical in any setting, initiates the conversation. After all, as he likes to tell people, 'I'm French Canadian, for Chrissakes. If I stop talking, I might have to listen.'

"So, what kind of name is Beto?" he asks as he pulls onto the highway.

Ginelli is somewhat caught off guard with the question. He had more or less figured on a review of the encounter they had just been though.

"Well…it's short for Beethoven, actually," he begins. Both my parents are huge classical music buffs. Growing up, it's all I heard around the house. You wouldn't believe the vinyl collection they have amassed over the years. You might not know this but…"

The return trip has lasted just over an hour. Lemaire eases the squad into its space in the underground parking lot of the Public Safety Building. And Ginelli is still talking.

"Now my Guido on my mother's side…"

The air conditioning is still malfunctional, the afternoon is waning, and, in Beethoven Beto Ginelli, the grunt has finally met his conversational match.

Terri returns home to the aroma of a simmering roast and Yorkshire pudding. She drops her keys and a hand full of letters she has scooped from the mailbox on the hallway table. To her surprise, David greets her garbed in a threadbare apron which, she recognizes, belonged to her mother.

"You're cooking," she says as she takes up the envelopes.

"I've got time," he replies as he adjusts the ties at the back. "How is everything?"

She flashes a sliver of a smile and parries the question. "Well, isn't this a fine example of domestic bliss. Makes me wonder why I never married. What's on the menu?"

"Just a little something to show my gratitude. A reminder of home, really. I've also been thinking about how odd this must be for you. I mean…taking in a total stranger. Sharing your home not to mention your hopes." A pause. "I suppose that it's just so very unusual. I'm just grateful…and I'm sure Andrew is as well."

Terri doesn't respond directly. Instead, she holds out a letter. "Speaking of Andrew."

Andrew examines the offering. "Doesn't he know about email? Eccentrics and their ways." He stashes is in the pocket of his apron and says, "I'll set the table."

Throughout dinner, David can sense that Terri has something on her mind. He wonders if he has overstepped his bounds by presuming that she would be amenable to his meal making. He chastises himself for not being sensitive to the situation and he starts to make amends.

"Terri I…"

"David, I've been thinking." She beats him to it. "It's just that I'm not certain if we should continue what we've set out to do. With Noah, I mean." She casts him an uncertain look. "I mean, what if we are pushing too hard? What if he is happy the way things are?

"I'm not certain I follow?" This certainly is not about food, he muses, and a distant voice in his head chastises himself for being so shallow.

"Well, you saw him yesterday. The way he reacted to Andrew's book. He was so upset…so angry." She tosses her napkin on the table. "I just don't want to hurt him anymore. Hasn't he been through enough?"

David feels disoriented. He can't help wonder what has transpired over the course of a workday. This morning Terri had asked him to pass on her love to Noah and now she wants to disengage.

"Has something happened to change your mind," he prods gently.

He interprets her facial response as defensive…cautious. She doesn't answer immediately and when she does her demeanor softens.

"Well, maybe I'm overreacting. But I feel so overwhelmed. I just don't want to do the wrong thing." She doesn't allow for David's reply, opting instead to end the conversation. "Let's carry on for now. But I'm going to do my best to feel how all this is affecting Noah. I'm not going to allow anything to hurt my big brother."

The evening has passed with little conversation between the two. Terri had said something about inventory and had busied herself in her office. For his part, David spends the time planning for the next day's visit with Noah. He vacillates between another reading from Andrew's book and something less provocative. He keeps coming back, however, to the phrase that Noah had perseaverated on.

'like a drop of blood on the pure virgin snow'

He studies it intently. Finally, he rises and rummages through his bag, returning with Andrew's book. He fumbles through the pages, removing the various bookmarks and checking the many dog ears he has creased until he finds what he is looking for. He skims silently at first and then reads in full voice. Then he whispers the line once more.

But what can it mean? Or for that matter, how can it be? He sits on the edge of his bed, astounded. He tucks Noah's printout into the pages and places the book back into his suitcase. And he doesn't know what to do about it.

David wrestles himself from his thoughts. Then he remembers the letter. Absently ripping it open, he begins to read.

Dear David,

I do hope that this letter finds you well. I can only imagine how things are going for you over there, but I have faith that you are finding your way. I know its early days. I thought that it might prove useful were I to provide you with a contact or two with whom you could speak. Someone who knew both Noah and I back in our school days and whom, if you should deem it appropriate, might pay a visit to Noah.

There was a young solicitor who lived in the same complex as we. Bryce Taylor I believe. The three of us spent more than a few aimless hours listening to music and discussing plans for our collective futures. I'm afraid I don't have much more for you to go on but, after all, you are resourceful in your own way and I'm sure that you can track him down.

The second individual may present somewhat more of a challenge. He was our professor. Dr. Emmett Jacobs, faculty of English Literature at the University of Manitoba. I say challenge because we found him to be an old coot even back in the day, so lord knows if he is still alive. I did hear from him once upon my return to England. Sent me a congratulatory note on my first book. I have to say it was grudging and somewhat sarcastic. He never did have any confidence in my abilities. Noah, on the other hand, found his great favor.

If you are able to uncover either of their whereabouts and, should you deem it helpful for them to visit Noah, then by all means, my boy, make it happen. I firmly believe that such triggers from the past hold the key to Noah's future.

I eagerly await your communication if or when you have something which you feel will interest me. God speed, David. You must know that time is of the essence.

Yours sincerely,

David rests the letter in his lap. A wave of emotion sweeps over him. He looks down at the letter and then to Andrew's book and he retreats, once more, into the reaches of his imagination. Of his suspicions, he has one question. What does he tell Terri?

CHAPTER Thirteen

"Couple of housekeeping items before we get started." Belinski stands against the backdrop of an ever-growing spider web of information on the whiteboard. "I met with Assistant Superintendent Cuddy this afternoon and I'm pretty sure I don't have to tell you that he's breathing fire." He pauses. "He wants results."

"Don't we all, for Chrissakes. Did he offer more help?"

"So that's just it, Guy. For now, we're it." He pulls at a nearby chair and slides it up to the table. "But he's put a timeline on things. We're on the clock."

"It's understandable." Mansbridge pipes in. "Case like this really places him in the spotlight. Until it's resolved, he's likely to be pretty uncomfortable."

"Exactly, Ethan. But we can't let that be our focus, can we. We have to take our time and follow procedure. Step by step, gentlemen." Then he adds, "oh, and one other thing. Templeton...Ginelli, you can dispense with the uniforms if you like. Your option."

Ginelli absently fingers the sleeve of his shirt while he surreptitiously glances around at the attire of the other members of the team. He remains silent.

"I'm good with this," offers Templeton. "Government issue is fine with me."

Belinski rubs his forehead and takes in a breath. "Alright, let's get to it. Guy, how did you make out in Selkirk"?

Lemaire rises and picks up a marker. As he approaches the board, he makes a dramatic letter x through the name of Leonard Lee. "Loonie Lenny is out," he pronounces. "He was locked up safe and sound inside the friggin' nut house for every one of the murders."

"Alright," confirms Belinski, "Leonard Lee is not a suspect. Anything else, detective?"

Lemaire is surprisingly succinct. "Not a friggin' thing. What about you, Ginelli?"

"No, detective. I think you've covered it."

As Lemaire returns to his seat, Belinski redirects to Templeton. "Anything of interest on the tip line, constable?"

"Couple of points, sir," he begins. "First, you were right. My right ear is swollen. Phone's been ringing nonstop. Mostly bupkis. One lady was convinced that her second cousin on her mother's first husband's side…or something like that, was our man." He glances up from his notepad. "I checked it out. Turns out he's been dead for twenty years."

Some snickers…Templeton is finally starting to feel like he's part of the team. And then more seriously, "One tip…or should I say several tips about the same thing, stood out as something we might follow up on." He shuffles through the pile. "A number of women have reported an incident where they had been out for a walk or a run and had found a wallet. Apparently, it was lying right in the middle of the pathway. Out of nowhere, some guy approached them and said that he was looking for …any guesses… his wallet. When they returned it to him, he tried to strike up a conversation. They all said that they felt creeped out about the whole thing."

"Good work, constable. Anything else?"

"Well, yes there is sir. If you don't mind my paraphrasing my fellow co-worker here," a glance at Lemaire, "every incidence happened right in the friggin' middle of our crime scene. Wellington Crescent."

Every set of eyes widens. Belinski makes a few notes and then says, "that sounds promising. Definitely need to move on it." He turns his attention to Mansbridge. What about you, Ethan?"

"Sure. I started with the phone records. Not too terribly much there. The credit card information should be more promising but I'm still waiting on that." He opens his laptop as he speaks.

"I first looked at each victim's incoming calls hoping to find commonalities of any kind. If, for example, a single caller showed up on all three of the victim's numbers...well you can see the ramifications of that." He glances up. "Unfortunately...nothing there."

"Outgoing," Belinski prods.

"Sure. Conversely, if all of the victims had made a call to a single individual, well that would be interesting as well. Results here were slightly more promising. Three numbers came up. First one was a pizza restaurant. This is likely pretty common, but it might bear further investigation." He provides the name to Belinski.

"The second was a dry cleaner. Again, over a five-year period, the odds are pretty high that any of us might use such a company. Then again, step by step...right boss?"

A nod.

"The third was to the box office of the Winnipeg Jets. Sports fans we can presume. This may have no significance at all, but it would be a more likely option, if looking for tickets, to use a generic source...Ticketmaster, for example. Could be something, could be nothing. I will follow up on these matters tomorrow."

"Thanks, Ethan. Is that it?"

"If you can bear with me." Back to the laptop. "Well, we spoke last night about the similarities across the three crime scenes so I got to thinking about what the differences might tell us. It might not be much but, taken together, it may add to our overall picture." He steps to a free section of the whiteboard and begins.

"The first item is the most obvious. Location. Two of the crimes were committed on the same street, less than a mile apart. The third, however, is sixty kilometers away in Selkirk. Our killer is mobile. But it may be important to follow up on what connects these two seemingly dissonant locations." He scribbles a few notes.

"The second is the time of day. Again, Wentworth and Grant were both murdered in the early hours. Pagliani some time around noon. Not clear what this tells us but it is noteworthy." He taps the marker against the side of his head.

"I also took a closer look at the reports. Another thing that separates the Pagliani case from the two on Wellington Crescent… she had dramatically fewer slash wounds." He motions towards his own legs and torso. "It may suggest that the killer had less time available. Could be that, as it was later in the day, there was a greater risk of being discovered."

"So, what makes us so sure that these murders are even connected at all?" Ginelli stirs. "Maybe we have two killers out there?"

"There's a friggin' secret code word or somesuch," Lemaire spits out. "The nutjob prints it on the stairs…in lipstick." Lemaire points at the nonsense phrase at the top of the first panel. "One killer, period."

Belinski steps in. "That's the premise we are going on, Beto, but you make a good point." Then back to Mansbridge. "Ethan?"

"So again, back to the dissimilarities. Hair color and style of all three victims…completely different. Age…bit of a range as well. Even ethnicity varies."

"So then why…"

"By themselves, they don't tell us anything. Collectively, however, they have a high probability of significance."

Lemaire opens his mouth but thinks better of it. Why not just let him make his point, he thinks. Why appear thicker than necessary.

"It tells us something about motivation. Or at least it rules something out."

Ginelli doesn't try to conceal the fact that he's lost. "I don't get it."

"He's...I'm assuming our killer is male...isn't after a particular personality type...or a look-alike." He looks at Ginelli. "He's not trying to kill his mamma."

Beto cringes.

"Or the woman who rejected him."

Lemaire chimes in. "That's right. Some of these guys are trying to off the ones who have screwed them over. Like the girlfriend who took up with the best friend or the teacher who never called on them when they knew the answer."

"Precisely, detective. So, while it doesn't tell us why he *is* killing, it does give us an idea of what rabbit hole we can avoid looking down."

"That's good work, Ethan. You raise the issue of motivation. We can rule out a few things but let's look at it from another angle. Are these crimes simply opportunistic or are they premeditated?" Belinski looks around the room.

"Or both." Mansbridge again.

"Both, for Chrissakes?"

"Sure. Let's say a criminal commits a crime...on impulse or by design...doesn't matter. Gets caught and does five to ten. He's got a lot of time on his hands...scheming, fantasizing. Then he gets out. Bides his time until the right situation presents itself and ..."

"Preparation meets opportunity." Templeton's thoughts manifest aloud. "Bobby Knight." He looks around to blank stares. "Indiana basketball coach."

"Bingo." Mansbridge puts down the marker.

The whiteboard is filling up with every report. Belinski allows a moment for the new information to sink in and then says, "Let's see if we can get some head shots of our victims. I want visual reminders of just who we're doing this for." He looks at Templeton. "Can you see to that, constable? And not from the file. Something appropriate."

"Consider it done."

"Good." He steps to the board once again. "For my part, we can eliminate our Mr. Palasades as either suspect or witness. His alibi checks out." He draws a diagonal line through another dead end.

He pushes ahead. "Alright. Guy, I'd like you and Beto to get on this wallet thing. Maybe you could follow up with the complainants while Ginelli covers the scene itself." He looks for a nod. "Maybe our man is searching for his victims in plain sight."

He scans the list generated by Mansbridge. "Ethan lets get on the credit card information. I want to know if the victims have any links to specific individuals, businesses, vacations… whatever else you can find."

"What about you, Zel?" asks Lemaire as he struggles to unwrap a muffin.

"I'm going to meet with the Mounties who investigated the Pagliani case. I want to find out if there's anything else we should know about." He scans his team. "Ok. That it?"

With no response, he adds, "Alright then. Let's get our reports in. Everyone up the chain wants to know what we're doing and how we're doing it."

⁓∞⁓

The sun has already set by the time Belinski opens the patio door and falls into the deck chair. The moon is low in the western sky, and he's already thrown a frozen dinner into the microwave. Of all the competing thoughts scrambling around his head for his attention, he settles on the image of Palasades and his pool buddies. What kind of life, he muses, is it when you have to sneak off to do the things you enjoy? The sacrifices we make for scratching out a living. It isn't long before a tangential nudge takes him to his own situation. The bell on the counter comes to his rescue and he wills himself out of the chair.

He peels back the cellophane, shaking his hand at the bite of the steam and reaches absently for his phone machine. Having always been insistent that he keep his private and work life at a distance, his land line often goes unchecked for days. He presses the play button and vaguely takes in the myriad of detail about his upcoming physical, the cable install and his boat mechanic advising that it's going to cost more than he thought for the new prop. Then a familiar voice begins to speak and he snaps to attention.

'Hi Dad. Want to let you know that summer league is going great. I've got a game tomorrow night at Dutton Arena. Seven o'clock. We play the Riverview Ravens. Remember them…from last year's playoffs. That goal I scored in overtime? Well, anyway, I know you don't like me to brag so…but I know what you're thinking…better keep my head up…never know who might try to get me back, right. Don't worry, Dad. I got it. Hope to see you there.'

"Shit!" Belinski racks his brain. Did he check his messages yesterday? If he missed the game…

He grabs up the phone and hits the speed dial. Anne answers on the second ring.

"It's me," he blurts. He bangs his elbow on the edge of the counter at the sound of her voice. Tell me I didn't miss it."

"Zel," she says. "It's nice to hear from you. How is everything?" He can't read her tone. It's calm but that, he knows, doesn't mean anything.

"Joey's game," he stammers, "is it…"

"Relax, Zel. He just called you half an hour ago. It's tomorrow night."

Belinski eases himself into a chair and exhales. "Thank god," he mutters. Then he rallies. "That's great. Is there anything I need to know?"

"I think you know pretty much everything there is to know about hockey games. Starts at seven. Just show up."

Belinski is about to offer to pick them both up when it hits him. His team meets at seven. He'll have to make some arrangements.

"Ok. Seven's good. How have you been?"

"I'm getting on alright. Work is hectic but you know how that goes." She tacks. "I've been worried about you. Are you on this case I've seen in the news?"

"It's mine. Not much I can say right now, though." Then he adds. "Listen…are you still running along Scotia…you know, along the riverbank?"

"Same as always," she replies, "girl's got to keep her figure."

"You don't need to worry on that count. I want you to do something." He waits for her to ask but she remains silent. "Use the treadmill for the next while. A week or two."

"But it's the middle of…"

"Please, Anne. It's important."

"Ok."

"Thanks. That's good. Alright, then. See you tomorrow at seven."

"Goodnight."

Belinski lets out a sigh and leans forward. He rests his head in his arms on the tabletop and he allows his eyes to shut. And he wonders how the hell his team is going to react when he changes the meeting time to ten o'clock.

CHAPTER
Fourteen

David sits across the desk from a concerned looking Dr. Belanger. He had been advised that the doctor wished to see him before proceeding to meet with Noah. Belanger is fussing with his laptop and making vague excuses for his lack of technological prowess. David mutters something about occupying the same vessel but his comment goes unacknowledged. Finally, Belanger looks up.

"So, Mr. Whittier," he begins. "As Miss Stafford has given me the authority to discuss matters of her brother's well being with you, and given the fact that she, herself, is not present," he pauses briefly, "then that is precisely what I will do."

"Alright, doctor. What's happened?"

"Well…there has been a development. Whether we view it as progress or, contrarily, as a set back, is open for debate."

"That sounds ominous, doctor. Would you please elaborate?"

"Of course. From my own observations with the work I've begun with Noah and a review of his file going back several years, I can not find a single incident of violent behavior. Not an outburst, not even an angry look." He studies David's face for understanding. "This morning, however, that has all changed. Please."

He swivels the laptop around so that David can better view the screen. "This happened earlier." The video is paused with Noah and his Psychiatric nurse sitting face to face across a small table.

"Noah has known nurse Blessing for many years," says Belanger. "They have spent countless hours together. Lately his nurse has even escorted Noah on various trips into the community. He reads to Noah, and he has been instrumental in our communication therapy program." He initiates the video. "If anyone could be considered to be close to Noah, it would be his nurse."

The video is shot through a one-way mirror and there is no sound. It opens with Blessing reading from what looks to be a book of poetry. Noah sits placidly and seems to be attending to whatever is being read to him. He shows no affect. Then the nurse puts down the book and speaks directly at Noah. His manner is calm, and he smiles as he talks. After a few minutes, Noah's entire demeanor begins to alter. He rocks forward and back and his head jerks from side to side as if he is reluctant to look straight ahead. David is reminded of an interrogation scene where a prisoner has been bound and beaten. Suddenly Noah raises his arms and, with surprising vigor, smashes them down upon the table. This he repeats several times before pushing back from the table and lashing out at his startled nurse. He slaps him about the neck and head and then turns and rushes from the room. The video ends with a shaken Blessing kneeling on the floor.

David's stomach turns over. Shock, disappointment…even guilt surge through him. He finds it difficult to look away from the screen. And words are not forthcoming. It is Belanger who breaks the silence.

"I agree, it's hard to watch." He closes the cover. "And I'll be the first to admit that I felt like a failure when I saw it earlier." He removes his glasses and rubs his eyes. "Naturally, I felt responsible." He stands and takes a few steps away from the table, as if his movements represent a new frame of thinking.

"But as I said a moment ago, it is debatable as to how we might view this change of behavior."

"Blessing or curse sort of thing," David offers.

"In a nutshell, yes," Belanger continues. "After all, we are hoping for progress with Noah. The status quo has gotten us nowhere, yes?" He doesn't wait for a reply. "Well, this is definitely a change. And change can also be seen as progress."

This is music to David's ears. He now sees Belanger as more ally than adversary and he ventures to get some answers to the many questions that have been plaguing him over Noah's treatment.

"Will there be any consequences for Noah's outburst, doctor?"

"No, no. Of course not. These things happen quite often. Nurse Blessing is fully aware of the dangers inherent in working with some of our patients. I have spoken with him, and he has no interest in pursuing it further. Nor has he requested to be reassigned."

"That's good to know." David extends his hand in the direction of the chair just vacated by Belanger and, surprisingly, the doctor resumes his position. "I have a few ideas of my own about how to reach Noah, but I don't presume to understand his condition. And…I don't want to interfere in any way with what you are doing here."

"Fair enough." Belanger is intuitive. "So, you want to know my honest opinion about his state of mental health." He hesitates. "And his prior treatment to date."

"As far as your professionalism allows, of course."

"Very well. Then let me be perfectly blunt." Belanger leans forward. "As far as I'm concerned, Noah has been treated… and I should really say mistreated…as an animal who has been abandoned to live in a cage, with little or no interaction and absolutely no attempt to treat or advance his condition in any way. I view it as shameful and in every sense of the word, criminal."

His words hang in the air like cordite. Their ramifications are staggering and, as David well knows from a previous life, unusually candid. On one level, he is outraged but, at the same time, he feels a sense of hope.

"I know it isn't easy for you to vocalize that, Dr. Belanger. And I assure you that it won't be repeated. His look is sincere but garners no response, so he carries on.

"I'm wondering how you view Noah's potential, both to communicate and also to process what is spoken to him. You see, I have the strong sense that he is much more alert than it seems. Call it a gut feeling…intuition, whatever you like. When I sit with him, I feel his presence."

"What do you know about Autism Spectrum Disorder, Mr. Whittier?"

"Little to nothing, I'm afraid," comes David's reply.

"Now, mind you I'm not saying that Noah is autistic. Merely that he exhibits many of the symptoms of the syndrome. I am, therefore, treating him in much the same manner as I might with someone with that condition."

"So…"

"For example, we know that many autistic patients are nonverbal. Some studies say as high as forty percent. That doesn't mean that they are not aware of their surroundings or, for that matter, capable of thought. They have what's called 'apraxia of speech', which means that they cannot find words to express what their brain wishes them to communicate." He looks up. "You can imagine just how exasperating that might be. So, over time they essentially give up trying to do so."

In his mind, David sees a frustrated Noah, sitting in a room by himself, day after day, year after year, with no one to interact with, his ability to communicate ebbing along with his hope. He asks, "So the drug that he ingested so long ago caused this condition?"

"Well, we can't say with certainty, and we don't fully understand the underlying causes of ASD but we know that it derives from a chemical change in the structure of the brain so, yes, it is possible."

"So, doctor, if Noah can't retrieve the words he needs to articulate his thoughts, then what would you say is the significance of the phrases and slogans he generates on his laptop?"

Belanger considers for a moment. "A good question. At first, I dismissed them as meaningless." A sigh. "Now I'm not so sure. He does seem to have a photographic memory…again that's commonly linked to Autism…but I think there's more to it than just random recall. In addition, he seems to have a rare form of eidetic imagery."

"Eidetic imagery?" David is unfamiliar with the term.

"Forgive me. It's the auditory equivalent of a photographic memory…or close to it. Suffice it to say that, in Noah's case, he seems to have total recall, not only what he has seen or read, but also what he's heard."

"So…the question is whether or not he is able to use this stored information as a substitute for his own words."

"That is precisely the question."

David finds Noah sitting alone in the corner of a large gathering area. Although several patients and staff members are scattered in small groups throughout the space, he has retreated, much as an animal does when injured and feeling vulnerable, as far away as possible. There is a large picture window and Noah, sitting with his back to the room, watches the chickadees at their feeding station.

"Noah?" David says softly. "It's me, David. Would you mind if I joined you?"

To his surprise and delight, Noah makes eye contact. David takes this as acquiescence and, moving slowly, sits in the neighboring chair. He notes that the laptop is resting on the floor between them.

"Birds are fascinating, aren't they? Though I can't say I know that particular species." He smiles and expecting no reply, carries on. "My flat in London overlooks a park. I have spent more than a few hours watching them."

They share the moment, side by side, gazing out the window. David, for his part, wonders whether his hasty research of Colonial culture will fail him when he needs it. Nevertheless, he initiates the attempt.

"Noah, I wonder if you would do something for me. I would like to use your laptop for a moment." He waits for Noah's response. A movement, a shift of position…anything that David might take for understanding. And he gets what he is hoping for. Noah turns and glances downward…at the laptop. And David scoops it up.

When it is responsive, David takes a breath and types.

Old MacDonald has a farm

He then passes it to Noah. The look he receives is, at first, neither blank nor expressive. That, however, soon changes and Noah glances sideways as if David had just spoken in tongues. He returns his gaze to the unfinished phrase staring up at him. And he writes.

EIEIO

David feels a shiver down his back but reaches out for the laptop and keys in

Amazing grace how sweet the sound

This time it is Noah who reaches for the machine.

That saved a wretch like me

Both men look up from the screen and into each others faces. And both men notice a tear gathering in the corner of the eye of the other.

And then David writes the phrase that he wasn't sure he wanted to risk but, if his suspicions are to be validated, has to be written.

His aching heart was like a drop of blood on the pure virgin snow. So beautiful and so tragic. It was at this moment that his dream, so gently caressed in slumber, died like the smoldering embers of his love.

Noah takes the laptop. The tear is larger now. Laden with memory. It trickles down his cheek as he writes

He picked up the pistol which had, til this moment, rested on the stone before him, and he placed it gently in his mouth. He whispered her name, tasting her essence on his lips. And he pulled the trigger.

Noah's breath oozes out of him. His shoulders sag as he slumps forward. He remains still for a moment and then, with one final resurgence, returns to the laptop and writes

Help me Rhonda

Freedom Mission is a stone's throw from the Public Safety Building and the walk gives Belinski a chance to clear his head. The night cleaning staff had yet to finish with his office when he had disturbed them earlier this morning. He had not been surprised when the crime scene report could not uncover any DNA evidence. This was consistent with the other reports. A predictable setback. Still, it was disappointing.

As he walks up the concrete steps to the entrance, he is surprised at what he doesn't find. As a rule, the immediate surroundings of the Mission…steps, sidewalk and alleyway…play host to a collection of street people. Particularly near mealtime. The Freedom Project, he knows, fills an important void for the have-nots of the city and without the tireless efforts of its staff and volunteers, far to many of the less fortunate would have no where to turn. This morning, the area is vacant. Moreover, a collection of media vehicles is parked along the curb at the building's frontage. He steps through the door guardedly.

"Detective Belinski...how nice." Klaus Sigfisson strides toward him. His energy, which is most often boundless, seems supercharged today. "Always glad to see the local constabulary."

"Mr. Sigfisson." Belinski extends his hand.

From over his host's shoulder, the sounds of laughter resonate from the main hall and Belinski can discern that a gathering has assembled.

"So, what brings you here today, detective? Did you hear that we are in need of an extra chef in the kitchen?" His twinkling eyes belie his seventy some years.

"Unless breakfast comes frozen," Belinski replies, "I'm afraid I can't be of any help." He reaches for the envelope in his jacket pocket.

"I just came by to thank you for everything you did for Murray. And to give you this." He hands him the offering.

"And what would *this* be?"

"Just a small donation to the cause. I wish it were more."

"Well, well. This is turning out to be quite a day." He rests his hand on Belinski's shoulder and offers a sincere, "thank you. Thank you very much."

As Belinski turns to leave, a roar of laughter erupts from the meeting room.

"Why don't you stick around for a moment, Detective Belinski? This is quite a day for us. There are some people I would like you to meet." Hand on his shoulder again. "Like you, they are making a donation as well. This way."

They stand in the doorway that leads to the large gathering room. The chairs are full of staff, volunteers, and several of the patrons of the Freedom Mission. There are even a couple of individuals in wheelchairs and Belinski can't help recalling the tragic images he has of Murray. Members of the media have set up along the far wall and the cameras are rolling from the back. The event must be newsworthy. Behind the podium stands an elegant woman, mid sixties maybe, with an infectious smile and a cheerful disposition.

"Bonnie Biekler," Sigfisson informs. "She and her husband, John, have made a substantial donation to the Mission. Millions actually. It's a great day for us and it couldn't come at a better time."

Anyone who has lived in Winnipeg for any length of time has heard of the Beiklers. Their generous donations have blessed countless community groups from hospitals to research organizations to grass roots rehabilitation centres. The list is endless and several buildings around the city proudly display their name.

"They are two of the best people I know. Let's listen in."

Mrs. Biekler is rounding into form. "It really is such an honor to be with you today and to be able to make this contribution to the Mission. And I have to tell you that Johnnie is thrilled as well. In fact, he said to me just this morning...Bonnie, in your wildest dreams, did you ever think that I would be able to make a contribution to such a worthwhile cause?' I smiled at him...and then I asked him...Johnnie, what ever gave you the idea that you were in my wildest dreams?" She winks and the audience roars.

Sigfisson and Belinski exchange smiles. Mrs. Biekler finishes to great applause and her husband, John, steps forward. His look says that he won't be outdone.

"Well...as Bonnie has already mentioned, I am thrilled to be here and to be able to make this donation. You know, I too am a dreamer. Since I was a kid, I have dreamt of building tractors. And I set a goal to one day have a hundred employees. And I'm proud to say, I reached that goal." The audience shows their appreciation. "But what I really want to say today is this. "I'd like to thank our children." He peers out over the rim of his glasses. "I'd like to thank our children for allowing us to give away their inheritance."

Belinski feels an elbow in his ribs as his host chuckles audibly. The ceremony raps up and tea and an assortment of pastries appears. The Bieklers are surrounded but Sigfisson is persistent. "I'd like you to meet them before you go. Just give me a second." Before Belinski can argue or make his escape, Sigfisson returns with the two guests of honor. "Bonnie and John Biekler...I'd like you to meet Detective Belinski. A cop with a heart." Small talk ensues and as often happens in such social situations, the conversation ends abruptly as others join in. Eventually Belinski slips, unnoticed, from under the throng and out the door.

⁓∞⁓

Wet grass cushions the worn soles of his jogging shoes as Ginelli slows to a crawl. By his calculations, he has already logged around ten kilometers but, to his disappointment, he has nothing to show for it. Still, he enjoys the thought of drawing pay for something he would readily engage in anyway. He is patrolling the crescent, hoping to blend in with the many others who seek their daily fix of endorphins in the form of running, jogging or walking. From behind dark glasses, his eyes scan relentlessly for what he and Lemaire have taken to referring as wallet guy.

He finds a bench and slumps down, pretending to tie a lace. From the many tips that had been reported, he knows that the majority of incidents have occurred within a tight radius and his current location is at the epicenter. It is also midway between two of the crime scenes and the team agrees that this may be no coincidence. He leans into the bench and flashes a smile at a young lady as she passes. Old habits die hard. He watches her as she disappears past a cedar and then resumes his task. After a few strides, however, he pulls up.

On the path, not thirty yards from where he is standing, he sees the same young lady. She is kneeling down and examining something on the ground in front of her. Ginelli edges closer to the shrub and observes, his senses tingling. The young lady, he reasons, has found a wallet. She rises and looks about, ostensibly in hopes of finding its owner. She looks perturbed. Ginelli knows that look. Runners don't like interruptions.

Ginelli suddenly tenses. A man approaches and a conversation ensues. The young lady hands over the wallet and then turns. Before she can move away, however, the man reaches out and takes hold of her shoulder. Ginelli springs to action. He charges forward, screaming, "police, get out of the way," and plows, elbow first, into the man's side. After a tussle, Ginelli pins his adversary, face down on the pathway, and places him in a hammerlock. The man tries to speak but Ginelli only applies more upward pressure, rendering him immobile. He clamps on a pair of handcuffs and reads him his rights. Then he yanks him to his feet and whirls him around.

He is older than Ginelli had anticipated. Wisps of grey hair escape from under a Jets baseball cap and he is breathing heavily. A wet stain is spreading down the front of his cargo pants and one of his shoes has come off.

The woman stands by in shock. She splutters out a thank you and steps cautiously away from both of them. Ginelli hands her a card and says, "I'll need a statement. Call me at this number." Then as roughly as his conscience will allow, he pushes his quarry forward. "Cars this way…lets go."

Belinski and Lemaire examine the septuagenarian through the one-way mirror of the interrogation cell and the lead detective is not pleased with what he sees. On the one hand, he realizes that it could be possible. On the other, however, common sense tells him that there is no way in hell that this aged specimen would have the strength, let alone the desire, to carry out three brutal murders.

The suspect has been processed and even fingerprinted and his particulars have revealed a couple of interesting facts. The first is his residence which, according to his ID is close to the two Winnipeg crime scenes. The second is his name.

"What were you thinking, Guy?" spits Belinski. "Leaving the rookie on his own like that." His head tilts sideways. "Why weren't you there to back him up?"

"I had a commitment." Lemaire studies his shoes.

"A commitment? What does that mean?"

Lemaire stares his partner straight in the eye. "My front cap fell out." He absently runs his tongue over his teeth. "I was at the dentist."

"Your cap? You left the kid on assignment with no backup because of a tooth?"

"I looked like an idiot. Besides, I figured he could handle it."

"Well, you figured wrong." Belinski seldom criticizes his co-workers, and he silently reprimands himself. He recognizes nothing good can come from it and tries to ease the tension. "Got any other dental concerns that I should know about?"

"You're not the only one who played hockey, you know. This is friggin' Canada for Chrissakes."

"Alright, partner. You've made your point. Now let's get in there and talk to this guy."

The room is a twelve-by-twelve shell with a single chair tucked into one corner.

The clang of the door causes the room's occupant to jump but he quickly regains some of his composure. He rises and takes what he feels is a defiant stance. Belinski and Lemaire enter, each with their own stool which they set down just a little too close for comfort.

"Have a seat," Belinski takes the lead. "We have a few questions we'd like cleared up."

"Well, I have a few questions of my own," the man splutters. "I was a lawyer for forty-seven years and I know my rights. I've been assaulted by a police officer and confined against my will. I'm telling you that there is going to be hell to pay and someone's head is going to roll. When I..."

"How about a friggin' charge of unwanted touching?" Lemaire jumps in with both feet. "Who's head do you thinks gonna roll for that, for Chrissakes? And that doesn't include the murder charge we're thinking of slappin' on you."

Their suspect stiffens and takes in a heavy breath. He looks about the room like a trapped animal but finds no reply save for a few unintelligible sounds. Then some of the color drains from his cheeks. He retreats into the chair and stares blankly at the detectives.

"Ask your questions, officer," he utters.

"Ok, Mr. Bakerstream," Belinski begins, "do you mind if I call you Henry?"

The suspect nods.

"Ok, Henry. Please tell us about the wallet."

Belinski reads his face. Although he expects to see remorse... shame even, he observers neither. Rather, he sees smugness. Bakerstream has the look of a man who is pleased by his own cleverness.

"It started as something to pass the time." He looks up. "Retirement isn't anything I had even contemplated. I thought I would work until I dropped. Would have too but, well, a lawyer needs clients, doesn't he?"

Belinski senses that his partner is about to come to life and puts a hand on his forearm.

"I have these binoculars. Who knows where they came from? I started watching the girls as they passed by. And lord knows, they go by in droves. Right past my window."

"But that wasn't enough after a while?" Belinski prods.

"Well, I though...wouldn't it be better if I could talk to them. You know...get right up close. So, I came up with the wallet idea. Oh, I didn't put any money in it. Nothing of that sort. Just a few old company cards...the kind a plumber might hand out." The look he gives the detectives confirms Belinski's earlier notion.

"I'd walk a ways down the path and then, oops, drop the wallet and step off. Before long someone would inevitably pick it up and there I was. Of course, it wasn't always a pretty girl but I got quite good at my timing. And I had some wonderful conversations you know. I made quite an impression on some of them."

"And what does your wife think of all of this?"

"It was practically her idea. She once said, 'why don't you just go out and talk to them, Henry'. I don't think she was being sarcastic, detective."

Belinski is satisfied that, although a mystery has been solved, its perpetrator has nothing to do with his investigation. For the record, however, he has to ask.

"Henry Bakerstream, did you have anything to do with the murders of Angela Wentworth of Jennifer Grant?"

"Oh, dear god, detective, absolutely not. I give you my word as an officer of the court."

Belinski looks at his partner.

"I'm satisfied. What about you, detective?"

Lemaire looks his suspect up and down and nods. "Let's get a uniform to drive this guy home." He sniffs the air. "And they better find some friggin' clean clothes for him. He stinks like hell."

"And Henry," Belinski adds as they leave the room, "no more wallets."

The two detectives suppress a smile as they climb the stairs. Theirs is not the sort of job where humor finds its way into the normal course of a day's work. Today, however, provides a momentary relief from the pressures they are under.

"How did it go with the Mounties, Zel?"

"Not much we can use," Belinski responds, "well, maybe I shouldn't be so quick to judge. They're sending over a profiler. He'll join us for the meeting tonight." He turns and looks at his partner. "At ten. Pass the word along to the others."

"Yes, I think that covers it nicely." The wheezing which has punctuated the telephone call continues long after each phrase has been uttered. "You have my full permission," he inhales deeply, "to publish the entire story. And I will sign…any documentation… that your paper might require."

Although Andrew finds communication increasingly difficult, he is determined to see this conversation through. His words, like the passing of a kidney stone, come hard fought. Yet he knows that this story, unlike any that he has ever written, must be told.

"Send me a copy…before you publish." One last draw from the tank. "That will be all for today."

He hands the phone to his attendant and says, "Westbrooke… send in my solicitor."

David has been stewing for the better part of the afternoon. Since returning from his visit with Noah, he has run the gamut of emotions from incredulity to outrage and his anger has been building exponentially. His first instinct had been to call Andrew immediately and confront him, but he had ultimately decided to wait. A discussion with Terri was, he felt, the more measured approach. After all, she was Noah's sister and had a vested interest in the matter.

She enters the house via the back entrance and drops her bag on the kitchen table. To Terri, David is all but invisible and, filling the kettle, she places it on the stove. She moves in ghostlike fashion, her body going through the motions while her head is miles away. She takes up a position in front of the window and gazes vacantly out at the trees.

"Is anything wrong?" David is standing in the doorway.

She turns slowly, as though her essence is returning to her body in installments. Her look, however, is anything but vacant. Determined, maybe. As if, having reached a momentous turning point, she has accepted that there is no turning back. She glances at the chair nearest David.

"There's something I need to tell you." She waits til he settles into place. "I've been thinking about it since Sunday."

David feels his chest tighten. He says nothing.

"I have to trust you, David. I have to be certain that, no matter what I'm about to say, you will stand by me…by Noah."

"Of course, I will," he replies, "why wouldn't I?"

"Because if I'm right…that is, if what I suspect is true…then I will have to do everything in my power to protect my brother. Everything." She looks him straight in the eye. "And I will expect you to do the same."

David has no idea what Terri could possibly mean but he senses that, what ever it is, it's monumental. Before he can respond, she continues.

"Promise me, David. Tell me that you will never repeat what I'm about to tell you. And tell me that you will help me to protect my brother…whatever the cost."

David is transported back to another time. A time he would desperately return to. And he would choose another course. He would do precisely that. Whatever the cost. And he knows there is but one answer and he provides it.

"I promise.

The kettle whistles and Terri pushes it off of the burner. She returns her gaze to David.

"Thank you." She pulls out a chair. "It hit me when we were watching the news the other evening. The murder on the crescent."

She studies his face for recall. "Well according to the report, it occurred in the early morning. When you were out there, David."

A strange wave of emotion hits him…as if he has just been accused of something…and he opens his mouth. Before he can react, however, she continues.

"And so was Noah." She stares vacantly past him, at the stairwell leading down to the basement. "And you lost sight of him."

David recovers his ground. "But you don't think that Noah had anything to do with that? It's a bloody coincidence, for heavens sakes."

"That's not all, David. I told you that Noah had come home for a visit a few years ago. That my parents looked after him for a time." She stares directly at him and David can see tears forming in the wells of her eyes. "There was another murder." She wipes her eyes with the back of her sleeve. "I wasn't living here at the time but I remember my parents telling me all about it. It was the talk of the neighborhood. Do you really think it's a coincidence that he was home at the time of both of them? And he has only been home twice in all that time."

"But surely that's exactly what it is. A coincidence. You don't really think…"

"That my brother could do such a thing? Of course, I don't." She fumbles through her purse. "I haven't smoked in ages," she says as she grapples with the cellophane.

"But that poor soul has been virtually imprisoned for years. God knows what they've done to him in there…or not done. How can we possibly understand what he's been through?"

David feels like he's standing on ground during an earthquake. If true, then what the blazes are the options? Noah is already under psychiatric care. Surely it would serve no purpose to involve the police.

"But he's making progress. Even Dr. Belanger would agree with that. Do we just throw all that away?"

"David, that's exactly the point. I don't care what has happened in the past. It's Noah's future that concerns me. If we can continue to help him to regain his true self, to whatever extent that can happen, then I know we will have done the right thing. Noah is not a murderer. He is the gentlest person I've ever known."

"So, you want to continue to bring him home…to keep doing what we've been doing? But how can we be sure…"

"We watch over him, David. Every moment he is here. It's the only way."

⁂

The sounds of the arena are as familiar to Belinski as his own name. He and Anne stand, side by side on the top tier of the bleachers. Joey's team is finishing their pregame skate as parents and relatives crown in around them. Belinski wanders back to his youth, where his parents, if they could find the time, would stand, hand in hand, on the snowbank surrounding the outdoor rink, stamping their feet to ward off the chill.

"This is nice," says Anne as she sips a Tim's coffee. "I'm always surprised how cool it can be in here. It's the middle of summer, after all."

"Summer…winter. Ice is ice. It's cold and it's slippery. Do you remember when we went skating at St. Vital Park?"

She smiles. "How could I forget? Even if I wanted to, you would never let me."

"One minute you were standing beside me, and the next, you were flat on your back. I've never seen anyone go down so suddenly. It was like the earth slid out from under you." He smiles the smile that this remembrance always elicits.

"And on the way home, you asked me how my 'clb' was. It took me a while to figure out what you meant."

"Well, it was cute then and it's cute now."

She nudges him and her coffee dribbles over the rim.

The game begins and the proud parents share in the enjoyment of watching their kid play Canada's national pastime. It isn't until the end of the period that Belinski opens up.

"I'm getting out," he says, and he waits a moment to let it sink in. "This is my last case."

The look coming his way is hard to read, especially when hope clouds objectivity. It could be skepticism, maybe guarded optimism. But it is direct and there is no doubting that she has heard him clearly.

"Are you sure? The force is your life."

"It's my job. Nothing more. What an idiot, I've been. You and Joey are my life." He turns to face her. "I've never been more certain of anything."

"But what will you…how will we manage. I'm not making all that much and…"

"I'll have a pension. Plus, I'll find work."

The buzzer sounds and the teams return to the ice. So much is left unsaid, but Belinski feels a sense of hope that, for so long, has seemed unattainable. And right now, that is more than enough.

∽∞∽

"So, the devil says, 'what did you think, Chomsky…that you were the only one trying to get outta here?'" Templeton slaps his thigh. The resultant laughter suggests that Belinski will not suffer any repercussions for the reschedule. He shuffles some papers while he awaits the appearance of their guest and, in short order, an unfamiliar face peeks into the room.

"Detective Belinski?" He extends a hand. "Morley Osborne. I believe you're expecting me."

Introductions are brief and Belinski kicks things off. He is grateful for any assistance he can get, and he is aware that the profiler's time is in demand.

"Alright then. It's late and we have a lot to cover. Morley, if you don't mind, we'll start with you. What can you tell us about the kind of suspect we're looking for here?"

"Thank you, detective. Let me just say, this must be a diligent group. I don't remember the last RCMP meeting I've attended that started so late at night. I'm impressed."

"You better friggin' believe it, mister."

"So, I've been through the files. You've got your work cut out for you. I can give you some impressions…call them educated guesses, try to paint a picture of the individual behind these crimes." He scans the group. "Feel free to stop me at any time…questions…what have you."

He rises and takes in the white board before beginning.

"Although we have three crime scenes, we have one basic motis operandi. And one personality type. We call these people slashers. Our killer likes to inflict pain. Case in point. He doesn't kill quickly. He takes his time…cuts and watches. Taking pleasure in each wound."

"Excuse me, Morley," interrupts Belinski, "I notice that you say 'he'. Can you confirm that we're looking for a man?"

"Most definitely. I'd say male, thirties or forties…you might stretch that out a little on either side…history of poor relationships…unfulfilled in his professional life, if he has one. And I cannot stress this enough…he has a hatred of women."

"Don't we all, for Chrissakes."

Belinski's glare stifles any laughter that Lemaire was hoping for.

"Forgive the poor taste, Morley. Please continue."

"Let's look at the placement of the victim's body for example," he says, returning to his theme. "She is reclining…almost leisurely. Satisfied, if you will. And a grotesque grin has been carved onto her face. The killer is indicating that she has been pleased sexually... and that he is responsible."

"I prefer the old-fashioned method," laughs Templeton, 'but hey, that's me."

Belinski makes a mental note to avoid another late-night meeting. This bunch is far too giddy for their own good.

"So, we're looking for a male with poor social skills who can't get it on with women and enjoys stickin' it to them with a knife." Lemaire provides a surprisingly competent summary.

"Well...not the words I would use...and I didn't...but, yes, essentially."

"One more question, Morley," asks Belinski. "What do you make of the time frame? One murder five years before the others?"

"Two possibilities there, detective. One, our killer may have been out of commission for a time. Incarcerated, perhaps. Or two...he is exceptionally patient. He's got time on his hands, and he is in no rush.

"Will he kill again, Morley?" Mansbridge has been listening intently.

"What would stop him?" Morley Osborne's reply resonates with each member of the team.

"Alright. Morley, thank you for your help. It's appreciated. Of course, you're welcome to hang around for the rest of the meeting, but I understand if you have somewhere else to be."

They take a break while Osborne gathers his things and makes his exit. Templeton takes the time to add this new information to a corner of the white board and Lemaire corners Belinski.

"Did we learn anything new, for Chrissakes?" He shakes his head in disgust. "Any one of the old geezers in your mom's apartment block could have told us the same thing. Where the hell do they find these guys?"

"It's information, Guy. Maybe it'll help us...maybe it won't."

"Well, my friggin' money is on won't." He wanders back to his seat, still shaking his head.

"Alright. Let's get at it. You all know that constable Ginelli made an arrest today." He glances at the junior member of the team. "After interrogation, I can tell you that he isn't our man."

"You mean wallet guy?" Templeton throws out.

"That's right, constable. Wallet guy is off the list. But I should point out that, because of constable Ginelli's diligence, that particular threat has been resolved." He looks at a red faced Beto. "One question for you, constable. When you realized that you were wrestling with a seventy-year-old man, why didn't you let go of him?"

"Sir," he begins, "Well, I thought it might be a disguise, sir."

"That was very cautious of you, constable Ginelli. Good work."

"Ok Templeton. You're up. Anything we need to know?"

"Sir, I can honestly say that not a single call, in my estimation, gives us anything remotely resembling a line of inquiry. Total bust today, cap."

"Good enough. Ethan?"

"Couple of things. I started in on the credit card records of all three victims. Looking for any consistencies or crossovers…places they all may have frequented, individuals they might each have made payments to. That sort of thing." He reaches for a marker. "These are pretty low probability of significance…one-time sorts of things…likely coincidence." He lists a number of places of business…convenience stores, service stations and clothing outlets. "In a city like this, people are bound to overlap somewhat."

"I'm sensing a 'but' here, Ethan."

"That's right. There's a restaurant. All three of our victims have eaten there…more than once. Though I have to add …never on the same day." He prints in block letters.

"Zorbas. On St. Mark's Road."

"That scumbag, for Chrissakes," Lemaire spits, "I remember this guy, Zel?"

Belinski raises his brow

"I was still with vice. It was before you and I teamed up…when I was with Doncaster." He searches his memory. "Smaller place… converted gas station or some such…yeah, that's it."

"Why the pejorative, Guy?"

His partner shoots him a look, "do you mean, why is he a scumbag? We busted him for having a camera in the chick's washroom. Taking movies of the customers takin' a…you know. Is that scumbag enough for you?"

Belinski turns the attention back to Mansbridge. "What do we know, Ethan?"

"Owner is a forty-seven-year-old male. Vasilios Bouras. Single…lives in the village. Two prior complaints for domestic but neither went anywhere. Different women…live in girlfriends… both ultimately refused to cooperate." A nod across the table. "And we have no reason to question Detective Lemaire's memory. He was initially charged in the camera incident but, again, nothing concrete came of it. Crown decided not to pursue it. Tough to prove that he was the one who installed the camera."

"Friggin' slime ball."

"One thing more thing that may be of interest. He owns guns. Checked with registry. He's some kind of hunter, if the calibres are any indication."

Belinski raises a finger. "So, if he has guns, then we can assume he has a collection of knives as well. Anything else, Ethan?"

"That's pretty much it." He glances at the whiteboard. "Except to state the obvious. He checks a lot of Osborne's boxes."

His pronouncement lingers for a moment as a new section of the board is filled in. Lemaire catches his partner's eye and leaves no doubt that he wants to be included in the follow up on this one.

"Alright." Belinski pushes forward. "Guy, what have you got?"

"Received the list of names of patients who where out of the friggin' bin at the time of the crimes. I haven't had time to get into it yet but I gotta say, it really makes you wonder. These nut jobs are out and about like squirrels in the trees. Might take a while to follow 'em all up."

"Alright. Anything else, anyone?" It's late, the mood in the room has darkened and the reports have yet to be written. No response is forthcoming.

"Good. Guy…you and I will tackle Mr. Bouras. Ethan, keep on those credit card records and see if you can dig up anything more on our restaurateur." He looks at Ginelli. "Beto, get on this list of detective Lemaire's. We're looking for anyone who may have been in Winnipeg on the days of the crimes. Selkirk as well. If you need a hand, maybe Constable Templeton can assist." He glances over. "If the phone ever stops ringing."

The team filters out of the conference room. Mansbridge hangs back and as Belinski nears the door, he calls him back.

"Just a minute, Zel. I think I have something that will interest you."

Belinski turns to see Mansbridge at the whiteboard where he has begun to print.

"What have you got, Ethan?"

"I've been thinking about the notes that our killer leaves. Or letters…whatever they are." He prints 'I I S T I T I A' on the board in capital letters and taps the ledge with the end of the pen.

"Tried creating acronyms out of the letters. Moving them around etc. Came up with a few phrases but nothing, really, that would make any sense." He looks up, "so I think we can eliminate that as a possibility. If the killer is trying to communicate with us, I don't think he would be quite so vague."

"Ok. So, what does that leave us with?"

"Well…the next thing I considered was language. It's obviously not English so I played around with as many other tongues as I could think of. Some common, some more obscure."

"And you found?"

"Well...that's just it. I didn't exactly." He looks at Belinski and tilts his head. "But...there's a chance it could be Latin." A smile. "That is, if our killer is a poor speller. Here...take a look."

Mansbridge takes the eraser brush and rubs out the second 'I' so that it appears,

I S T I T I A

"Now if the 'I' could be a 'U' instead. Like this." 'I U S T I T I A'. He substitutes the letter and turns to Belinski.

"Then we have, in Latin, the word, *JUSTICE*"

Belinski stares, transfixed. Mansbridge's discovery barrels over him like a tsunami. His gaze shifts to Ethan and then, like a magnet, back to the white board.

"Justice," he mutters. His eyes remain on the word. He allows a moment to pass...to let the word settle in.

"Justice." He looks up at Mansbridge. "So, what is the bastard trying to tell us, Ethan?"

◦∞◦

It's almost 2 am when Belinski finally gets to his machine. The message from Anne is encouraging and it brings a smile to a tired face. He plays it twice. The next voice he hears is only vaguely familiar.

Detective Belinski. I hope you don't mind my calling you at home. It's John Biekler here. We met earlier. I got your number from Mr. Sigfisson. If I'm out of line, please forgive me but Klaus said that you might be able to advise me on something. I'm looking for someone to head up our security division. I'm hoping that you might know someone who might be interested. If you can call me tomorrow at our home office, I would appreciate it. Good night then.

He doesn't even attempt the packaging on the frozen macaroni. Instead, he slides it back into the freezer drawer and puts a battered kettle on the burner. Tea and a piece of dry bread will suffice. Dinner, if that's what you can call it at this hour, is inconsequential. Since leaving his office a half hour earlier, a single thought, or word, his been on his mind. Justice. And he knows that sleep, tonight, is out of the question.

CHAPTER
Fifteen

David stares up at the slanted ceilings above his bed. Although the sun has yet to rise, the birds in the trees outside his window herald the coming of an unpredictable, and he is certain, contentious day. His thoughts vacillate between two people whom, only a few weeks prior, were complete strangers to him. This morning, however, they occupy his world like intimate family members.

His host, on the one hand, with her single-mindedness of purpose, as genuine a person as he has ever met, is devoted to her brother as only the most loving sister could be. David has absolutely no doubt that she would go to any length to protect Noah. And if he has done things that, under normal circumstances, would elicit repulsion and certainly incarceration, she is willing to sacrifice her beliefs for a greater truth. For in her mind, it is her brother who is the victim.

And Andrew. A study in contrast. The very man who, having openly professed his love for Noah, has shown a level of betrayal that elicits David's most profound disgust. And today, whatever the cost, David silently promises himself that he will bring that betrayal to light.

But the question he has been avoiding the most, remains on the periphery of his consciousness. And so does the promise that he has made. When the time comes, and he is certain that it will, for him to honor that promise, will his principles allow him to do so? If Noah has, in fact, committed the crimes that Terri suspects him of, then will he stand by quietly? After all, innocent people have had their lives taken from them. Brutally. And if the demon that is responsible lives somewhere deep within Noah's subconscious, can he be party to the cover up?

He throws his legs over the side of the bed, wrenches himself upright, and is grateful for the immediacy of more practical matters. He washes, dresses and selects some reading material to take with him for his visit with Noah, leaving the future to unfold in its own good time.

The unmarked squad eases into the lot and Belinski makes note of the time. The place is much as Lemaire had described it. Back in the early seventies, so many of the independent service stations that had dotted the landscape of prairie cities like Winnipeg, had suddenly found themselves unviable. Many went under and their shells found new life in the form of restaurants, convenience stores and pizza take outs. Zorba's has been a fixture on this thoroughfare for as long as Belinski can remember. Its one of those places that you pass by so often that it becomes invisible.

As he throws the shift into park his phone rings, causing his partner to jump.

"Zel...Ethan. Looking over some bank records. Something pretty interesting." He pauses but Belinski remains quiet. "Jennifer Grant worked there...at Zorba's. Direct deposits for about a year. By my calculations, it was likely during her first year of Law School. Thought you should know before you got going."

"So that would make it around five years ago?"

"About right. I'll keep digging."

Belinski mutters a thanks and turns to his partner. "Let's make sure we do everything by the book, Guy. No mistakes."

The entrance is small and cramped. Competing lines of patrons waiting to pay and those having newly arrived, jostle for position in the narrow foyer while a cashier struggles to keep pace. There can't be more than twenty tables and booths, but business is booming and not one, it seems, is empty.

Belinski steps in front of a waitress with an armful of empty dishes and holds up his shield. "I'm looking for the owner," he shouts over the din.

He doesn't have to wait long. Stepping forward, as if he had been watching their arrival, is a heavyset man in an open collar shirt and dress pants. He moves in the manner of a wrestler, slowly; guardedly, as if he is assessing his next attack. Belinski senses that, although past his physical prime, he is not one to be taken lightly. He peers defiantly outward through angry eyes at the two detectives and then says.

"Oh shit. Not you."

He is looking past Belinski at his partner.

"That's right, numnuts…me." Lemaire hoists himself to his full height.

Belinski steps between them. "Are you Vasilios Bouras?"

"Depends," he spits, "who's asking? And it better be important. We're right in the middle of the breakfast rush."

"Belinski. Homicide. And I gather you've met Detective Lemaire."

"What the hell does homicide want with me, Detective Belinski?" He exaggerates each syllable of the last name.

"Is there somewhere we can talk?"

Bouras exhales dramatically and mutters something. Then he summons someone from behind a counter and snaps at him in Greek. He returns his gaze to Belinski and says, "Not exactly a goddamned wine lounge we're running here…this way."

The back hallway is cluttered and only somewhat less noisy. The three men stand facing each other. Bouras' positioning is openly hostile, as if he is ready to spring forward at any time. He initiates.

"Look, detective. What the hell is this all about? I've got a…"

Belinski is quick to interrupt. His tone is measured and direct. "Mr. Bouras, I'm going to be honest with you. I don't like your tone and I don't like your attitude. We're investigation a crime and I'm about ten seconds away from ending this conversation and taking you downtown. Understood? So, I'm asking you for your cooperation."

Bouras reels himself in, demonstrating that his mood, as well as his demeanor are a function of circumstance. "Alright detective…what do you want to know? If this is about that bullshit camera thing," he glares at Lemaire, "I never had a damn thing to do with it. That was…"

"It's something entirely different so let's move on."

Years on the job have taught Belinski that guys like Bouras use bluster in order to divert and deflect. He's also learned to attend to the little things. Tells or tics, whatever his fellow detectives like to call them, are invaluable assessment tools. A blush in the cheek or a tinge on an ear might indicate a change of blood pressure. A look, particularly to the right, he has discovered, might show deception. A change of subject, much like Bouras' just now, tells him that his suspect is uncomfortable. But in this case, it's the glance that gives him away. Belinski noticed it the instant they had entered the hallway. Something about the walk-in freezer at the end of the hall has Bouras worried. And he's deliberately trying not to look that way.

"Let's start with your whereabouts from this past Saturday around midnight til Sunday morning."

Bouras looks puzzled. "You're asking me where I was Saturday night?"

"Up until Sunday morning, numnuts. And don't tell us you went to church, for Chrissakes."

Bouras stiffens and then thinks the better of it. "You saw what it's like out there, detective," he says to Belinski, "business has never been better. We close at ten...we prep til midnight...I'm back here at six." He pauses. "Well, Sunday I was a little late getting here. Had a few mouse traps to set."

"For the record, what time did you arrive?"

Bouras hedges. "Eight for sure. You can check with my cook if you need to. He'll confirm."

Belinski looks at Lemaire and he steps out. "Can anyone verify your whereabouts from the time you left the restaurant til the time you returned?"

"Look. I live alone," he can't stop himself from bragging, "in a big house. This place is a goldmine."

Belinski ignores the braggadocio. "Tell me about Jennifer Grant."

Bouras handles the curve ball easily. "Jennifer who? Never heard of her."

In any interrogation, there are moments which present forks in the road. Belinski chooses not to pursue this line and, instead, he keeps the information in his back pocket. The fact that Bouras is lying is sufficient for the time being.

"Alright, Mr. Bouras. Thank you for your time. I'll find my way out."

Belinski wends his way through the crowd and nods at his partner through the commotion. As the exit, Lemaire confirms that the cook backs up Bouras' claim and they head for the car.

"That guy's a bigger scumbag that I thought," Lemaire spits, "he's also a lying bastard."

"I agree. He's hiding something," his partner replies, "lets dig a little deeper into our Mr. Bouras. I'll contact Cuddy...see if he can arrange a search warrant. We can start with his 'big' house in the village."

As they nudge the squad into the senior's rush hour traffic, Belinski reaches for his phone. His gut tells him that the walk-in freezer is on his suspect's mind and he doesn't want it disturbed.

"Ginelli, Belinski. Put aside what you're doing. I have another assignment for you."

Lemaire listens as his partner passes on his instructions and then disconnects.

"Stake out?"

"There's something in that freezer that our man doesn't want us to know about. I don't want to give him a chance to do anything about it."

"Let's just hope that the kid doesn't friggin' screw it up."

"Whittier. Your visits are becoming a daily feature of my rounds." Belanger extends a hand. "Actually, I'm glad I bumped into you." He indicates that David should walk with him as they talk. "Today hasn't started out well for Noah. In fact, he hasn't emerged from his room."

"What about his morning run?" David asks, knowing that it is religiously embedded in Noah's routine.

"First time in memory that he has skipped it."

David feels as though he has just returned home to find his door ajar. He sweeps aside any further conversation and blurts, "I need to see him."

"Of course. You'll find him in his room. If you don't mind, would you check in with me before you leave? I will be interested how things go."

David beelines down the hallway, muttering something or other in his wake, and knocks on the door. He waits a minute, knowing that he will receive no reply, and then enters. He finds

Noah sitting on the edge of his bed, looking up at him as if he had been waiting for David's arrival.

They look directly into each other's eyes. There is an intensity about Noah's gaze, a desperation, and he has his laptop at the ready. David pulls up the only chair in the room and sits down opposite. And this time, it is Noah who initiates.

Help…I need somebody

He spins the computer around for David to respond.

Help…not just anybody

And then Noah.

Help…you know I need someone

David takes a chance and changes the lyric.

I will help you, Noah.

Noah sways from side to side, the frustration at his inability to communicate, manifesting itself in sheer physical distress. He stares at the door, as if willing David's attention from the room. To the world outside his walls. He pulls at his hair and then returns his hands to the keyboard. And he types.

At break of day when that man drove away, I was waiting
I crossed the street to her house, and she opened the door
She stood there laughing
I felt the knife in my hand, and she laughed no more.

David pulls back. He feels his stomach turn and he looks vacantly for somewhere to throw up. Noah, however, thrusts the laptop at him, his hands shaking, and insists on a response.

David doesn't react. Noah's confession has struck him like lightning, and he is incapable of a reply. He regards the man opposite, and he is struck, not by what he sees, by what he does not. No remorse, no outward demonstration of feeling for his victims. Just a determined gaze. But is it defiance? Self justification? David is uncertain.

Noah, sensing that David has no intention of responding, takes up the laptop and keys another message.

Blessed are those that mourn for they shall be comforted

David recognizes the line from the Beatitudes of Mathew, but he cannot reconcile the change of tone with the insistent face that stares across from him. And he feels that gap ever widening. A flood of random thoughts washes over him. What trauma has occurred within these walls that could possibly have transformed this mild, gentle man into what he imagines in his mind to be a cold, calculating monster? Who is responsible? And what does his future hold? He takes the laptop, and he writes.

Blessed are the merciful for they shall be shown mercy

The search warrant had come through mid afternoon and Ethan Mansbridge is on scene to supervise. Belinski had been called to a meeting with Assistant Superintendent Cuddy and is just wrapping up his report. Lemaire has returned to the command centre. For his part, Ginelli remains in place in the lane behind the restaurant, thankful to his father's generosity for the use of his Beemer.

Belinski's phone rings and he looks at his boss. Cuddy waves his hand in dismissal, as if to say, 'we're done here' and he answers on the way out.

"Zel, Ethan here. Quick update for you. So far, a lot of weapons. I'll check them against the ones he's got registered. Several knives…and not your kitchen variety. I'll have forensics see if they can match them to any of our crime scenes. And…" he hesitates, "we've got a big box of DVD's."

"Home movies?"

"Looks like. Do you suppose…"

"From the restaurant bathroom. It wouldn't surprise me. Let's get a unit from vice to go through them."

"Already on it."

"And Ethan…Make sure they have pictures of our victims. I want to know if any of them show up in this guy's collection."

"Got it."

Belinski heads down the two floors to the conference room. The phone is ringing and he catches the beleaguered eye of constable Templeton. Lemaire is intent on studying the list in front of him and doesn't see him come in.

"You'll be pleased to hear this, Guy," he says as he walks by. He pulls off his jacket and throws it across the back of a chair. A startled Lemaire jerks sideways.

"Looks like you may get your collar after all. Bouras has kept mementos. A video library for his own personal pleasure. If you can call it that."

"The search warrant?"

"And weapons. Forensics is on it now. Let's hope we catch a break."

Lemaire's curiosity is interrupted by another ring.

"Belinski."

"Sir, it's me. Ginelli. Something weird is going on. I'm watching the back door of the restaurant like you said. There's a van. It's backed in tight. There's two guys…I think they're loading something into it." He hesitates, "It's hard to tell sir, but…I think it might a body."

"Block that van. Don't let anyone leave. I'll call for backup and we'll be there in fifteen minutes."

And with that, Belinski is out the door, Lemaire in tow, and hurtling down the hallway.

When they arrive, an agitated Ginelli is shouting instructions. He's positioned his father's car to block the van from leaving and has backed the two men up against the side of the building. Something, covered by a tarp, lies on the ground by the doorway. Belinski has no trouble recognizing one of the individuals. Vasilios Bouras glowers with rage.

"Sir, I tried…"

"Did you identify yourself as a peace officer, Ginelli? Belinski barks.

"I did, sir. And I…"

"Belinski, homicide," he shouts as he waves his shield. "Let's just stay put until we see what we have here." He motions at Lemaire to remove the tarp. Ginelli prepares for the worst.

"What the frig?" Lemaire tosses the tarp aside and stares down at the ground in front of him.

A carcass, like the side of beef you might see in a butcher shop, lies in the threshold of the entranceway. Belinski turns to the stranger standing against the wall and asks, "Venison?"

"That one, yep," he replies. "Some of the others are elk."

"For Chrissakes." Lemaire's surprise quickly turns to anger.

"And you are?" Belinski continues.

"Don't say a fucking thing," Bouras spits.

"Rupert St. Croix. I know my rights." He glares at Bouras. "I live on Pontiac First Nation. Got a license to hunt year-round."

"That may well be, numnuts, but you can't sell what you kill to a friggin' restaurant, for Chrissakes."

By now, a couple of squad cars have arrived and the uniforms crowd around the perimeter. If Belinski is surprised, disappointed even, he doesn't show it. He issues his instructions in his usual step by step manner.

"Alright. Let's get some pictures. The van, the meat…get an inventory of that freezer." He looks at Ginelli. "Check every corner. Don't miss anything."

He looks at Rupert St. Croix. "Detective Lemaire will take your particulars. You are a person of interest in a crime, and you may be called upon to give evidence in court. For now, once your van is emptied, you are free to go."

Before he can continue, however, his phone activates. He nods as he listens and then turns to the simmering restaurant owner.

"Vasilios Bouras. I am placing you under arrest…"

"This is bullshit," he shouts, "you can't arrest me for buying a fucking side of venison. How the hell can you prove that it isn't for my own personal use? I'm going…"

"on suspicion of the murder of Jennifer Grant," he finishes. "Detective Lemaire read him his rights. Then let's get him downtown."

Lemaire is more than happy to oblige. He spins his old nemesis around and handcuffs his hands behind his back, reads his Miranda, and then, with an extra upward tug on his arm, adds, "let's see you wiggle outta this one, scumbag."

The scene is secured, with Ginelli left behind to supervise, and Belinski and Lemaire are enroute to the station.

"So, I take it, Zel, that vice got something from the DVDs?"

"You're right. Jennifer Grant turns up more than once. Seems she was a personal favorite."

"What kind of friggin' freak is this guy?" Lemaire shakes his head. "I mean who wants to see…"

"It takes all kinds, Guy. I'm just glad we got him. No telling how long he's been at it."

"So, you figure maybe sittin' in his basement, watching his friggin' perverted videos, stopped doing it for him? Lemaire tilts his head. "Wanted more?"

"Let's follow the evidence, Guy. Step by step. See where it takes us."

Lemaire can't count how many times he has heard that line and he knows that it signifies the closing of the door on the conversation. He changes tack.

"Just imagine. That friggin' asshole is buying dead friggin' animals from some guy off a reserve. Then he turns around and serves 'em up to his unsuspecting customers." He waves a finger. "I always wondered what the hell they put into that friggin' souvlaki." He grimaces. "Mutton? What the hell is that, anyway? It's friggin' dead elk, for Chrissakes."

Four walls and a table are all that surrounds Vasilios Bouras. Flanked by his lawyer, he fumes at having been made to wait. A study in contrasts, the larger man, collar wide open, revealing a gold chain as thick as a shoelace, flexes his hands into fists and glowers at the door, willing it to open. His diminutive mouthpiece, meanwhile, replete in a three-piece suit, fidgets continuously through his briefcase. Neither acknowledges the other.

Belinski and Lemaire enter and advise the two that the interview is being taped. They take their seats opposite and the junior officer returns a glare with one of his own. Before Belinski can pose his first question, Bouras smashes his hand down on the table.

"This is all bullshit and you know it," he shouts. "You got no right to harass me like this." He turns to his lawyer. "Finkleman, here, is going to make you wish you'd never heard of me."

Belinski ignores the brute behind the outburst, choosing instead to search the face of the smaller man. "Counselor, we can continue, or we can terminate. And I'd like you to advise your client that it's our choice, not his."

The lawyer turns and opens his mouth to speak but he is rudely prevented from doing so.

"Fuck off, Harvey. I'm not deaf. Let's get this over with."

"Alright." Belinski removes a sheet of paper from a buff-colored file. "The results of the search warrant produced a number of weapons. In particular, officers found five long guns and an assortment of handguns. I want to know…"

"I have them right here," comes the high-pitched response from Bouras' lawyer as he quickly retrieves affidavits from his case. "Each weapon has been registered and I have all the paperwork, in duplicate, for your records, detective."

Lemaire reaches across the table and accepts the documents without taking his eyes off Bouras, whose face, cemented in smug, holds his look, in defiance.

"Like to kill things, eh tough guy," he spits.

"Detective Belinski, I must object to the tone used against my client. I feel…"

"We're not in court, counselor. Consider it a legitimate question."

Finkleman looks to his client, but Bouras ignores him and maintains his gaze on Lemaire.

"Tell us about Jennifer Grant," says Belinski, changing direction.

"I've already told you once. I never heard of her." He places both hands on the table and leans forward. "Quit beating a dead horse."

"We have bank records that indicate that's not true." Belinski waves another sheet from the folder and tosses it on the table in front of the lawyer. "She worked for you for a considerable period of time."

Finkleman studies the document but, before he can comment, his client erupts.

"For god's sake. You've seen my place. It's a fucking goldmine. I go through dozens of waitresses a year. More. I don't know their names. They come and go. I got people to handle that sort of thing."

"But you know she was a waitress." Belinski leaves the comment in the air.

If Bouras is caught off guard, he doesn't show it and he quickly sets the record straight. "What the hell else would she be? Look I'm not saying she didn't work for me. I'm saying I don't know who the hell she is."

"But you like watching her take a friggin' whiz, eh big boy?" Lemaire spits.

"Fuck you, ya dwarf."

Belinski doesn't mind a little tension in an interview. He knows from experience that anger can elicit responses that may never be revealed in a more sedate environment. He allows a moment for both men to escalate but when they pull back, he continues.

"So that everyone is clear on what Detective Lemaire is referring to, the search of your client's premises produced a number of DVD's, taken from a camera in the woman's washroom of Mr. Bouras' restaurant. The camera recorded images of both staff and customers using the facilities."

Finkleman glances sideways at his client but his look goes unacknowledged. Undaunted, he offers up his argument.

"I must remind you, Detective Belinski, that, as you have already indicated, my client is here as the result of a homicide investigation. The DVD's in question are only relevant to a previous case and, as such, cannot be considered evidence in this instance."

"Save it for the trial, counselor. I want to know the connection between a dead girl and the images found in your client's possession."

"And we happen to know that your client's friggin' fingerprints are all over his little homemade movies." Lemaire leans forward and resumes his glare. "And who knows what else forensics will find. Sperm Matta Zoa, maybe."

A shared look between client and lawyer and Finkleman responds. "My client does not have to answer that line of inquiry, detective, and at this time he does not wish to do so."

"Alright. Let's get this on the record. Concerning your client's whereabouts between the hours of twelve o'clock midnight on Saturday night, July 18th of this year and Sunday morning, the nineteenth, at eight am…Vasilios Bouras, where were you and who, if anyone, can attest to it?"

A smile tugs at one corner of Bouras' mouth. He maintains his eyes on Lemaire while his lawyer withdraws an official looking document from the briefcase in front of him.

"Detective Belinski, I have a sworn document, signed by an employee of an escort service and cosigned by her employer, that she was in the employ, as well as the company, of my client, Vasilios Bouras, from the precise hours on the days you have asked about. It speaks for itself, detective."

Belinski and Lemaire exchange glances as the lawyer proffers the document across the table. Bouras rises, pushing his chair away with his legs.

"Shove it, shrimp," he growls as he turns to leave.

"Hold on," Belinski is quick to respond. "Sit down, Mr. Bouras. We're not done, here." He turns to Finkleman.

"Counselor, we're releasing your client on a promise to appear. I've turned the results of the search of his home over to the vice squad. You can be assured that further charges will be pending."

Bouras settles back into his seat. His look is less assured than previously and, for the first time, looks to his lawyer for guidance.

"And you can bet that those friggin' charges will stick, big boy." Lemaire stands and stretches to his full height. He leans forward on the table. "And I'm pretty sure that they won't have any videos for you to watch up at Stoney. At least the kind that turn you on. But, hey, maybe you can get Bruno and Lumpy to take a leak on your face while somebody else is shovin' his friggin' elk meat up your…"

"That's enough, detective," Belinski bellows. "Vasilios Bouras, you're free to go."

Finkleman gathers up his papers and places them fastidiously into his briefcase. His shaken client is already out of the door and is searching for a way out. When they are gone, Lemaire looks at his partner and begins his apology.

"I'm sorry, Zel, I…"

"Not to worry," his partner stops him, "believe me, this time you were speaking for the both of us." He smiles. "Now let's log the tape."

David's emotions bounce back and forth from revulsion to compassion and the result is added fuel for his anger. Since his departure from the hospital, he has been feeling as if he is on the deck of a ship in the middle of a storm. The notion that he, alone, is privy to the most gut-wrenching information, is overwhelming. And even if Terri may suspect, she is able to retreat into her uncertainty. Failing that, she can find her own justification for the defense of her brother. But David has none of that. And what's more, he alone, bears the responsibility for any further travesties that may be committed. Noah is slated to return home for the weekend and who, if not David, will stand guard.

He has, of course, considered contacting the police. It feels, however, like such a betrayal. Of Andrew and of Terri, but most of all, of Noah himself. David cannot begin to imagine what Noah has been through. The abandonment…the neglect. The abject frustration of being alert within his own mind, yet completely unable to communicate to the world around him. Like being imprisoned inside his own head, year on end, moved about like some old piece of furniture. Dusted and forgotten. How, David wonders, can anyone put description to such a situation?

His train of thought turns to Andrew, the fourteenth Earl of Derbyshire. And to his own so-called mission of mercy. How foolish he feels to have been swept away with someone else's delusions. Was it his ego? Maybe it was simply desperation. A down and out excuse for a man, wallowing in his own self pity. Yet he is grateful for one thing. In spite of the bizarre nature of his visit to Canada, he's found a renewed sense of purpose. And he has met two remarkable people in Terri and Noah. Most of all, he believes strongly that he is making a difference. Somehow, he has the feeling that his presence has been instrumental in retrieving a lost soul. Takes one to know one, he figures.

His eyes fall upon his phone. The phone provided by Andrew upon his departure and the irony is not lost on him as he hits the contacts icon. Andrew's number is the only one listed and is that very number that David uses now. He has no idea what time it might be in London, and he doesn't care.

The voice that answers is deep and raspy and no less self assured than David has remembered. Even so, it has its measured effect and David finds his edge softened.

"David, my boy. How lovely to hear from you." He takes a few pulls of oxygen.

"How could you do it?" David blurts the question that has plagued him for days.

"Very well, my boy. And how are you?"

"Let's cut the bollocks, Andrew. How could you do such a thing?"

"My faith in you has certainly been justified, David, though I have to say I didn't expect this."

"But you do know what I'm talking about."

"Of course. And I'll tell you everything. But first, I want to hear whatever you can tell me about Noah. He is progressing, yes?"

David is not to be put off but, with the Andrew's assurance that he will come clean and the relief that he wasn't wrong allows him to exercise patience. He brings Andrew up to date on Noah's condition, the gains made and the struggles which lie ahead. In particular, he discusses the unusual manner in which he and Noah are able to communicate via the laptop and he highlights Noah's trips home on weekends. Naturally, he avoids divulging any information about the secret which only he and Noah share. The sounds which emanate from the other end of the connection are an amalgam of deep pulls from the tank and ahs of great interest and approval.

"That sounds very promising, my boy. You're doing well."

"Don't you think its time you confessed, Andrew?" David's tone is assured

"After all…you're entire success is based on a fraud. You stole Noah's stories and passed them off as your own. How can you look yourself in the mirror?"

There is a long pause on the other end. It isn't, however, the pause of someone trying to drag up a lie to cover a wrongdoing. Nor is it the pause of someone who has been caught off guard. It is the pause of someone searching for a starting point for a story which, although it has long been anxiously keep hidden, the teller is now more than pleased to reveal.

"Let me ask you, David, how did you know?"

The air from David's lungs slips slowly from him and he slumps gently forward. All his suspicions have been validated with Andrew's question. The notion, which seemed absurd initially, but which had grown in spite of his disbelief, has come to light. And, like the feeling one gets having been on the winning end of a long cricket match, he feels the tension drain from his body.

"Well, it was a few things. But in the end, it boiled down to two words, Andrew. Two simple words that have revealed your treachery if I can use that expression."

"Of course, you can, my boy. I certainly have."

"Well, two words within a phrase, that is. The line in the book that you published was, '*his aching heart was like a drop of blood on virgin snow*.'" He pauses to let Andrew recall the line.

"But Noah wrote that same line, unprompted by me, slightly differently. And keep in mind, he has never read your book. He phrased it, '*his aching heart was like a drop of blood on the pure virgin snow*'. THE PURE, Andrew. Because that's how he wrote it in the original manuscript. Your editor removed those two words in the final copy."

"My my, David. You would make a wonderful detective. And you're right, of course. And I have to tell you that I'm thrilled that Noah can recall that beautiful line. He truly has a great gift."

"But don't you feel any shame, Andrew?" David splutters. "You've stolen another person's work and passed it off as your own. Surely you…"

"Of course, I do, my boy. But if you will recall, I told you I was a rare exception. I am one of the few who have no talent of my own. And I let you glimpse into my true character." He takes a long pull of oxygen. "Remember this, David. When someone has everything is provided, when they don't have to work…to struggle for anything, they fail to develop what you might call inner strength. And, as a consequence, they invariably take the easy path." He coughs. "But it isn't quite as simple as that."

For a moment, David is transported back to the evening in the mansion where he sat, spellbound, as Andrew had spun his stories and had ultimately offered David a lifeline from his own abyss. And he finds himself, once more, in thrall of that maleficent voice.

It was a few weeks after our ill-fated evening. The night when Noah, honest and pure of heart, had taken the LSD and I, as I have confessed to you, failed to demonstrate anything but cowardice, and did not. Noah had been hospitalized, although not at the Institute where he resides today, and I sat alone in the apartment. I had no thought of school. I simply moped about the place waiting for word of Noah's condition. Well as you may have surmised, that word finally came, and I was devastated. It was as though my world had collapsed around me. It was so sudden and final. They told me that Noah, the only person I had ever loved, was brain dead. I was shattered. As you can imagine, I went into denial...his condition was temporary, the doctors are wrong, he is going to recover.

But he didn't. And as the days turned to weeks, any hope that I may have had deserted me. I contacted my father and advised him that I was returning. And as I packed up my belongings, it occurred to me that all of Noah's entire collection of work was still there. What was I to do with it? I worried, of course, that it may be displaced, lost even, when his family came for his things. So, yes David, I took it all home with me.

He was very prolific. There were several manuscripts which were, essentially, complete works. Poems, short stories novels in various stages of readiness. They just poured out of him. I took them all...in hopes of preserving them in the event that...well, we both know that that never happened.

It was a couple of years later. I had submitted many of my own pieces for publication and, to no one's surprise, certainly not my father's, I received an equal number of rejection letters. Then I thought, why not. And I submitted on of Noah's manuscripts. The very one which you have used to find me out. And, of course, you know the result. I, or should I say more honestly, it, was a sensation. Well, you can fill in the blanks, now, can't you?

Even my father was pleased. And although he never vocalized it to me directly, I heard from others that he was proud of my accomplishments. So, I kept my dirty little secret to myself. And put out more of his work. And I rode dear Noah's coattails and carved out a career.

"But to profit from someone you cared about..."

Andrew is quick to interrupt. "Oh, gracious me, no. Well, not in the sense that you infer. Every penny that Noah's writing has generated has been put aside. It's all in a trust account, with his sister as executress, waiting for him. Noah is a very wealthy man. Now you can certainly make the argument that I absolutely did profit from his efforts on a different level. And I would not disagree. I have achieved a measure of celebrity that, were it not for Noah, I most certainly never have done. That is one of his gifts to me which, of course, I can never repay. And that is also my great shame."

"But why, Andrew? Why couldn't you have simply preserved them…or found a way to publish them under the name of their rightful author?"

"A most perceptive question, my boy. And I'm afraid that the answer is a simpler one than you are hoping for. I did it for love, David. Specifically, I was hoping that having achieved a measure of success in life, my father would finally say the words that I have craved to hear my entire existence. You think it childlike, I'm sure. But I tell you, David, that to live your whole life and never hear those words…never have the feeling that comes from knowing that someone close to you actually values your being…loves you unconditionally…"

He pauses leaving David uncertain if it is the wheezing of the oxygen tank or something else that he hears in the background.

"Why would anyone want to live at all if they have never been loved, David? And I have lived my entire time on this earth in that state."

David's tone is softer now. "But your father never…he couldn't find it in himself to…"

"That's what I have finally come to realize, David. It isn't that he didn't *find* it in himself…it's that he didn't *have* it in himself…to give to me or anyone else."

"But in a twist of fate, you also see that you are not him. That is, you are not like him."

"I'm glad you understand that, David. And that…is Noah's greatest gift to me. He has shown me that, whether or not I have known love, I am absolutely certain that I have the capacity to give love. And, therefore, I, in turn, am loveable."

David lets those words...the emotion of the moment, linger on the line like gossamer. Yet he does not let his empathy for Andrew sway him from his purpose.

"Andrew, what will you do now. How will you make this right?"

"It's already done, my dear boy. In fact, you will be able to read all about it in the *Times* on Sunday morning. I have told the entire story to a reporter...I don't know if you will appreciate the irony... your replacement, no less. The world will soon know that I am a total charlatan. And Noah will, after all these years, be hailed as one of the great novelists of our time. And rightly so."

David is stunned...and pleased. From the moment he had decided that Andrew must be outed, he had run a dozen scenarios over in his head and none of them had ended in a pleasant outcome. He cannot have imagined that the matter would culminate in such a fashion. He can't wait to discuss it with Terri, Noah's devoted champion and, most of all, he can't wait to inform Noah, himself. How he will do that is another question, altogether, but he is anxious to have the chance to try.

"There's one more thing, David." Andrew breaks into his thoughts.

"Yes, Andrew."

"I want to talk to Noah."

"But I've tried to describe..."

"And, believe me, David, I've heard you. So, make it happen. Create an email account for Noah and set up a link between us. I can't tell you just how important this is to me."

"He will be home for the weekend, Andrew. I'll make the arrangements."

David waits for a reply. None comes. The connection has been lost. He puts his phone down absently and sags into the chair. Thoughts come at him in waves but, for now, his eyelids close and he breathes deeply. He visualizes the scene...Andrew and Noah, each at their keyboards, like their early days in the apartment, creating one final memory together. A smile tugs at the corner of his mouth and a tear finds its way to his cheek. And, were he religious, he would pray for a miracle. That each of these men, whose lives have been irreparably torn apart by one random decision, can reunite, however briefly, in friendship and in forgiveness.

CHAPTER
Sixteen

A Subway wrapper peeks out from a trash bin and the smell of onions lingers. Belinski is early for the evening meeting, and he sits, staring at the board. Competing thoughts vie for his attention and he is only vaguely aware of the voice in his head that repeats Mansbridge's words, *if the I could be a U.* His primary focus at the moment, however, is reserved for his son, Joey, and he reaches for his phone.

"It's me," he offers to Anne's hello. "How is everything there?"

"Zel. I was just thinking of you. How is the case going?"

"You know, you're just like your brother…good old Gordie Good n'you. You never answer my question. Case is going ok. Two steps forward…you know."

"Well, I'm fine if you must know."

"Glad to hear." He pauses. "I was just thinking about Joey. I was wondering how the dance classes are going. He hasn't said anything and, well…"

"Why don't you ask him?" He's right here."

Some small talk between father and son leads to a momentary break in the conversation and Belinski finally asks, "So how is that dance class you signed up for working out?"

There is a bit of a delay as Joey collects his thoughts. "It's ok, I guess. It actually hasn't worked out quite the way I thought it would."

"I don't follow."

"Well, you see, dad, I really only signed up because Jessie Grosvenor told me about it. She's been in dance for a long time. I guess I figured if I joined up, then I could get to know her better." Silence. "But the truth is, she doesn't even know I'm on the same planet. So, I still go but I kinda lost interest."

Never fails. This day has been a long slog but a few words from his family and Belinski is rejuvenated. He smiles and says, "I'm sorry it didn't work out," and then adds, "but I'm glad you didn't quit."

"Mom would never allow it…you know that dad. Neither would you. But it's only for a while. Oh, and by the way, there's a recital at the end. You'll come, right?"

"Wouldn't miss it son. Love you."

"You too, dad."

Belinski slides his phone onto the table and closes his eyes but, no matter how hard he tries, he cannot visualize his son in tights doing a twirl. He's rescued from trying by a tap on the drywall.

"You look like you're on a tropical beach somewhere. Like a maitai?" Mansbridge eases into the room and onto a chair. "Guess we're both a little early, eh?"

"Long days. Nice work on the search. You pulled some good evidence."

"Thanks. No doubt Bouras is a creep. Question is, is he a killer?"

Belinski pulls in some air. "You know, I'm not so sure. I know his alibi is probably bought and paid for, but it really doesn't add up. He's a consumer. Takes what he wants…but, in the end, it works for him. Meets his needs."

"I agree. Plus, we can't really tie him to the other two scenes. It doesn't fit." Mansbridge turns his chair around and leans on the back. "And there's the Latin component. I don't see him as scholarly, do you?"

Belinski utters a sarcastic laugh and rises, ambling to the board. He draws a circle around the letters, 'I S TITIA' that Mansbridge had printed in bold caps.

"I keep coming back to what you said. If the *I* could be a *U*." He taps the marker to punctuate each word. "If the I could be a U." It takes him a moment but then his eyes widen, and his pulse quickens. "What if that's the message?"

Mansbridge is on the same page and pops from his chair. He takes up a marker and speaks aloud as he prints, "*I could be you!*" underlining it with three emphatic strokes.

"I could be you," Belinski repeats. Then louder, "I could be you!"

Mansbridge takes a moment and returns to his seat. He studies the marker, still in his hand and he flips it onto the table.

"He's talking to us, Zel. There's no doubt. But what's he saying? I mean, what, exactly, is his message?"

"Good question. I find it hard to wrap my head around it." He pulls up the adjacent chair. "Is he using the victim as his messenger?"

Mansbridge tilts his head. "I see where you're going. Maybe it isn't the killer talking at all. Maybe he's using his victim to say it for him. '*I* could be *you*.' In other words, take a close look…because what happened to me can happen to you. Like some coded threat."

"Right. So then, the next question is, is he talking to us? Or is he talking to someone else?" Belinski mulls over his thoughts before saying, "Maybe we've been looking at this from the wrong perspective. Our focus has always been on the victims. What they may have in common…why they were chosen. Who might have wanted to harm them?"

"So if," Mansbridge cuts in, "they have been selected at random…wrong place, wrong time, then our killer may simply have been using them to send a message to someone else."

"We need to look more closely at the occupants of the homes where the bodies have been placed. The Palasades, for example. There's a connection there." Belinski looks directly at Mansbridge. "We just have to figure out what it is."

Muffled words find their way from the hallway and the other members of their team tumble in. Something in the expressions worn by their bosses catches their attention and the conversation peters out. There are no racy jokes, lewd remarks or needling of each other as they take up their places and wait patiently to be brought up to speed.

"Alright. Let's get going." Belinski reluctantly transitions from detective to facilitator. "Constable Templeton…let's start with you. Anything on the tip line that you feel is actionable?"

"Well, you may not believe this, cap, but we only logged a few calls today. And of those, nothing of interest at all, really."

"Ok. Thanks constable. We might be able to use your time in other ways then. You're probably itching to get back in action." Templeton nods and Belinski moves on.

"Guy, would you bring us all up to date on Vasilios Bouras?"

Lemaire provides a colorful update on the day's events, up to and including the interview, three piece and all, while shining the spotlight on the part played by Ginelli. He spares the members of the team his parting comments to Bouras as he knows that his partner would likely stop him in mid sentence anyway. He turns to Belinski and asks.

"Anything you'd like to add, Zel?"

"Just this. As Guy has pointed out in his inimitable style, Bouras is a lowlife. No doubt. The bigger question is, is *he* our man?" He looks around the group. "I don't think he is. So, while we will continue to keep him on our radar, I think we need to explore other avenues. And we'll get to that in a minute. Ethan, did you get a chance to look over the list of residents that we got from the Doc at Selkirk?"

Mansbridge nods. "Lots of one offs. People who might fit one day or another. But only a few names came up who were away from the Hospital on all three dates. And, of those remaining, only one is mobile. The others are confined to wheelchairs. It's a long shot at best but the one remaining person who fits our dates is a long-term resident by the name of Noah Stafford. I'll dig up what I can, but someone should really put boots on the ground and check it out in person."

"Alright. Thanks Ethan." Belinski takes up his position at the white board. He outlines the information regarding the message hidden within the Latin word for justice, including the entire conversation he and Mansbridge had had with respect to the new direction they are considering. Then he opens the floor.

"So let me have your thoughts. Let's examine this thing from every angle."

A few moments pass as the team digests the information and collects their thoughts. Lemaire is the first to speak.

"Five friggin' years, Zel. We been trying to figure that gibberish out since Wentworth." He shakes his head absently. "How the hell did you do it, for Chrissakes?"

"It was a team effort." Belinski tosses a glance at Mansbridge. "So, what do you make of it?"

"Well, my first thought is, who the hell talks Latin?"

"Isn't that the language of love?" Templeton throws out.

"That's Italian," replies Ginelli indignantly.

"Alright. So, let's look at the people who live where the victims were placed. What do we know about them?"

"They're wealthy," Templeton says hesitantly, "and they all live on the river. Don't know if that matters."

"Guy, can you remind me? The Templeton murder…I don't think I even spoke to the owners of the house. At the time, it didn't seem relevant. What do we know about them?"

Lemaire pinches his nose. "Yeah. I think he was in construction. You know, commercial buildings like. One of those behind-the-scenes guys that you only hear about when there's some kind of scandal. McCracken somesuch. Don't recall the wife...if there was one."

"So, we're looking at people in positions of power." Mansbridge chimes in. "Starting with those we know, we have the Palasades... the big box furniture store owner. And we have his wife...the president of the College of Physicians and Surgeons, right Zel? Then we have a construction magnate. And, finally, we have a politician, the mayor of Selkirk."

"So, we might be looking for someone who has a grudge, maybe," Belinski synthesizes, "against these particular individuals, or possibly what they may represent."

"Yeah, but Latin, for Chrissakes. Who the hell threatens people in friggin' Latin? I mean, if you're going to try and scare someone...you want to make sure they get the message, right."

Mansbridge turns to Lemaire. "That's a friggin' good point, detective." And he glances at Belinski.

"Alright. For tomorrow. Ethan, start looking at the homeowners from the crime scenes. See what you can come up with and do that thing you do. Look for what they might have in common. Cross reference the hell out of them and when you find any connections, drill down hard. There's something there. We just have to find it."

"Guy, find out what you can about the resident at the hospital. What's his name... Stafford? See if he has any family and if he does, get them to confirm his whereabouts on the dates of the murders. You can take Beto with you. I'm going to have a word with the mayor and while I'm out there, I'll drop by the hospital."

He looks somewhat sheepishly at Templeton. "Sorry constable, one more day on the phones, I'm afraid."

His usual closing remarks regarding reports draws a few groans and then the group begins to disperse. For the first time since the team assembled, there is a real sense of optimism. Belinski and Mansbridge share a look on the way out, each in their own way sensing that the case has taken a turn in the right direction. In Belinski's parlance, they've transitioned from defense to offense.

∞

The jewelry store is located in a trendy area along Corydon Avenue. Specialty shops, restaurants and open-air patios dominate the landscape and, although Ginelli is at home here, it is completely foreign territory for the driver of the squad car.

"Where the hell are we supposed to park, for Chrissakes? This street is like a friggin' phone booth."

Lemaire had spoken to Terri earlier and had made arrangements to meet just prior to day's opening at ten. If she had been surprised to hear from the police, she hadn't shown it, but Lemaire had written that off to the number of robberies in that particular area. Break-ins are a fact of life, and a police presence is commonplace. She buzzes them in through the double glass doors.

"Mrs. Stafford, I'm Detective Lemaire, Homicide, and this is constable Ginelli." He shows her his shield. "Thank you for making time to see us."

Terri's skin tingles. She ignores the error of title and blurts instead, "homicide...is that what you said, detective?"

"That's right, maam. We'd like to ask you some questions about your brother."

"Noah? She puts down the cloth that she had been using to dust the glass counter. "What on earth for?"

"Just routine, maam. According to our information, your brother was visiting you last weekend. Would that be true?"

"Well, yes but...what is this all about, detective?"

"So, you can confirm that our information is accurate, Mrs. Stafford?"

"It's Miss. And yes, Noah was on leave from the hospital in Selkirk. He's a resident there. But…"

"And he was in your home from Friday to Sunday, is that right?"

Terri takes a moment and then says, "That's exactly right, detective. He was in my home. He didn't step outside the door."

"And you were with him the whole time?" Lemaire continues.

"The entire time, detective. And I have a house guest. His name is David Whittier. He can confirm that…if it's important."

Lemaire jots the information into his notebook and thanks Terri for her cooperation. Then he adds.

"If you don't mind, Miss Stafford, and I know this may be a stretch…according to the hospital, your brother was home for a visit a few years ago. You wouldn't know anything about that would you?"

Terri pretends to search her memory. "Of course, I can remember it. It was the first time in many years that my brother was able to come home. I remember ever detail. We, that is, my parents and I, picked him up at the front door of the hospital and went straight to our cottage at Sandy Hook. We had a wonderful weekend together and then returned him safe and sound on Sunday evening." She pauses appropriately. "Why would you want to know that, Detective Lemaire?"

"Again, Miss, just routine. And thank you for your assistance." Lemaire and Ginelli turn to leave, and Terri resumes her dusting when a thought comes to him.

"By the way, Miss Stafford. Do you wear lipstick?"

"Do I wear what? What kind of a question is that?"

"Please maam," Lemaire spits, "just answer the question."

"Well, detective, as a matter of fact, no I don't. Never have."

The door closes and Terri leans forward against the counter to steady her legs. She gulps air in a desperate attempt to quell the waves of nausea building inside and she fights back her tears. How can this be, she wonders? How could the police possibly share her suspicions? And her thoughts turn to David.

It isn't long before the 'closed' sign hangs in the window and she is out the glass door and headed for home, bewildered at the magnitude of his betrayal.

∞

The civic offices of many small centres are often housed in magnificent old historic buildings, proudly located in the centre of the business district. The town of Selkirk's, however, is an exception to this rule. It is a modern, single-story brick building that Belinski finds himself regarding through the side window of his vehicle. As he sips the dregs of his Tim's, he ponders the many incongruencies between the two Winnipeg cases and this one. And he wonders what someone might have against a public official in a small town like this. He exits the car, tosses his cup into the recycle bin and heads in for his meeting with Bently Seaverson.

"Detective Belinski...so nice to meet you." Seaverson glad hands him like an undecided voter. Please...this way."

Belinski is swept through the plant filled rotunda to a modest office with a smallish oak desk. Entirely devoid of pictures, save for one of Seaverson himself alongside Bobby Hull, the famous hockey player who once played for the Jets, the walls are painted in a drab beige. The mayor waves at a leather chair. "Please."

"Now, how can I help? I understand that you are interested in the situation which occurred on my front steps. I'm sure I don't have to tell you just how disconcerting that event was for me. I mean, just imagine my shock to wake up and discover that a tragedy like that had taken place on my very property while I was inside the house asleep. It was..."

"Mr. Mayor." Belinski finally interjects. "I'm sure it was difficult for you. I just have a few questions for you if you don't mind."

"Of course, detective. It's not my place to tell you how to do your job, and I fully understand that you have many other things to do. I have spoken to the RCMP already and I've provided them with…"

"Have you received threats of any kind lately, sir?"

Seaverson chews on the question. He is…has always been, the subject of threats, unkind remarks and bullying. School had been a nightmare and, even though he had reached a vaunted position of authority, it had never really ended.

"That would depend on what you mean by threats, Detective Belinski. Complaints, well that goes without saying in this job, but threats…I shouldn't think so" He slows down, as if recalculating. "There was one, shall I say, disgruntled constituent. And he did vent his frustration on me, as mayor, but…"

"What was that about please sir?"

"Well, he was upset that council voted to scale back refuse pick up to every second week. It was a cost saving strategy, you see. And frankly I agree with the constituent, but I have to abide with the decision of…"

"And he said or did what, Mr. Mayor?"

"He dumped two weeks worth of garbage on my front lawn."

If Belinski is amused, he doesn't show it. And he knows that he needs a couple more answers to confirm his suspicions that the mayor has not been the target of his suspect.

"For the record, Mr. Mayor, you are aware of no other threats to you or your family?"

"Detective, I am quite certain that neither Barney nor I are, or have been, in any danger."

"Barney?"

"My dachshund. The third wife, Doris, left last January. Since then, it's been just us two. You see, having a job like mine…"

"Thank you, Mr. Mayor for being so succinct. You managed to answer both of my questions in a single stroke. I won't bother you any further. I know how valuable your time is. And please, don't get up…I can see myself out."

Belinski slides back behind the wheel, more confused than ever by the logical inconsistencies of the case. If their working theory is that some excessively clever psychopath is targeting individuals whom he feels holds power over him, or maybe for sins already committed against him, and who employs elaborately vicious measures, including threats in a long dead language to do so…then how on earth does this small-town civil servant fit into his scheme? He shakes his head as he drives away, searching for the road to the Selkirk Mental Health Centre, while, at the same time, scanning the route for the nearest Tim's.

"Absolutely not!" David is defending himself against claims which seem to have come out of left field. "Why would I betray the two people that I care most about in this entire country? No… emphatically, no!" He glares at Terri with a look of shock and sadness in equal measure. He had just called for the cab to take him to the hospital for his visit with Noah when she had burst in through the back door.

"Well, if you didn't say anything," she throws back, matching his intensity, "then what the hell's going on?"

David softens. "Look, Terri. I'm not sure," he says sincerely, "but you have to believe me…I haven't said a word to anyone. And I don't intend to."

Terri has been working herself into a lather since the police had walked out her door and her pent-up fury has been released.

She tries for the first time to gather her thoughts coherently. And she knows that David is being straight with her.

"I'm sorry, David. Of course, I believe you. I'm just a little freaked out. I shouldn't have taken it out on you." She forces a smile. "But how could this have happened?"

"Well, let's think for a moment." He motions to a chair and waits until she is settled before sliding in at the kitchen table. "You said yourself that Noah was home the last time there was a murder around here, yes? Wouldn't it be safe to say that the records of his visits would be known to the hospital staff?"

Terri ponders this for a moment and replies, "And I suppose that the police could have accessed that information."

"It's very possible."

"And," Terri says completing her thought, "they were following up as a matter of course. Yes…the officer said that it was routine. Routine, David. Oh, I'm such an idiot. I've completely overacted."

David nods his head supportively. "So, what were they asking specifically?"

"They seemed to know that David had been here on the weekend. But they also knew of his last visit. When mom and dad were here." She hesitates. "But they can't *know* anything, can they David. I mean…if he…there isn't any evidence to…"

"I don't think they can." He looks at her directly. "What did you tell them?"

"I lied. And I'll keep on lying. And I told them that you could verify what I was saying." She holds his stare. "And you will, David. Won't you?"

David knows it isn't a question. It is a demand. Not the demand of an angry child or of a superior, but, rather, one made of desperation. Of fear of what might happen if he failed to support her. And although she is unaware of his promise to Noah, he renews that promise to the sister as well.

"Absolutely yes. I'll back you up on that or anything else that may come up. You have my word."

Terri finally let's go of some of the tension that has built up in her body over the past few hours. She thanks David for his reassurance and then excuses herself. Entering her room, she rummages through her vanity until she finds her cosmetic bag. Removing every tube of lipstick, she jambs them into her pocket and replaces the bag before heading outside to the trash bin. Then she returns to the kitchen where she pours herself some scotch from the bottle in the cupboard. Finally, she slumps down at the table and weeps.

⋘⋙

The phone call to Ethan had been a last moment decision and, as Belinski enters the hospital, the phrase remains fixed in his thoughts. Although Mansbridge has coached him well, he is glad that he had never been selected for the advance placement stream in high school. One language has worked well enough for him even though he lives in a bilingual country. A third would have been too much. Thank god for hockey. He is met in the front foyer by Dr. Belanger.

"Detective Belinski. Welcome. I appreciate your promptness. Bit of a lost contrivance these days, don't you find?"

"Dr. Belanger. Pleasure to meet you. Thanks for seeing me on such short notice."

"This way please." Belanger leads the way through the maze of hallways, each emblazoned with an assortment of colored lines and pictures of bears, kangaroos and eagles, until they arrive at his office. An offer of refreshment is graciously declined, and small talk is dispensed with.

"You mentioned on the phone that you had some questions about Noah Stafford, Detective. Forgive my surprise but...why on earth would that be?"

"I'm interested in his whereabouts on a few occasions. I understand that he is allowed visitations with his sister who lives in Winnipeg."

"Forgive me, detective, if I am a bit reactive but, this isn't a prison...it's a hospital. As a rule, our residents are free to come and go as they please. With adequate support if they require it, of course."

"Alright. Point taken. I wonder if you could tell me a little about Mr. Stafford. Why he's here, for instance. What is his condition...his nature? Is he predisposed to violence? Whatever you can say."

"Detective Belinski, I'm sure I don't have to remind you that patient information is protected by the Personal Health Information Act. We're on thin ice here, I'm afraid."

"I understand that completely, Doctor. So, I'll be direct. Your patient is a person of interest in at least one homicide, possibly more. And it's my job to see that it doesn't happen again. And, that the person responsible is held to account. Now let's work together on this as best we can, alright?"

If Belanger's first instinct is to laugh, he does not. Recent changes in Noah's behavior prevent him from doing so and he acquiesces. "Ok, detective. Let's do just that. Ask your questions. But let's keep it hypothetical, yes?"

"Alright." Belinski takes a moment to frame his thoughts. "Given what you know about patient behavior in general, in your opinion...might someone like the patient in question be capable of violence?"

"In my opinion, and that's all it is, up until a few days ago, I would have answered unequivocally, no. Absolutely not. But..."

"Something's happened to change your opinion, Doctor."

"Look, Detective Belinski. Noah's been an extremely docile patient for many years. Never a hint of emotion." He pauses, uncertain of his ground. "But a few days ago, he attacked his primary nurse. He was completely unprovoked…and he inflicted a serious beating on him. I have no explanation for it, whatsoever."

"And you say that this is only recent behavior?"

"I am relatively new here, detective. I can only speak for what I have directly observed. Naturally I have studied his file, but to give you any real perspective of his propensity to…well, it's impossible for me to comment about his past." He pauses.

"Other to say that there are no recorded incidences of violent behavior that I can cite."

"Alright, Doctor. I'd like to meet him if I might. And also, that nurse if it could be arranged."

"Of course. But I wouldn't expect too much. For the last few days, Noah has chosen to sequester in his room. Refuses to attend group and won't engage with his nurse or any of the other people that we have scheduled to visit with him. Well, with the exception of Whittier, that is."

"Whittier?"

"A friend of his sister. From England. Comes every day and reads to Noah. They also communicate with a laptop. I won't get into it but I do think it is effective. And therapeutic."

Belanger picks up the phone. "Have Blessing come to my office, please."

Then turning back to Belinski. "You realize that Noah Stafford is non communicative. He doesn't speak. So, I'm not sure what you might accomplish by talking to him. But if you insist."

"Let's call it a request, doctor. As long as it doesn't interfere with his treatment in any way."

Belanger waves away the comment. "No, no. Of course not. I merely want to point out that he doesn't have the capacity to answer any questions you have. It will be completely one sided."

There is a knock at the door. "You asked for me, Dr. Belanger?"

"Yes. Lawrence, this is Detective Belinski. From the Winnipeg Police Department. He'd like a word."

"With me?" he splutters, "why on earth for?"

Belinski hurries to put him at ease. "Just need a minute of your time, please. Would you like to take a seat?"

The nurse cautiously slides into a chair. He sits erect with his hands folded in front of him.

"I understand you are Noah Stafford's …how did you put it, Dr. Belanger, his primary?"

"Yes sir. That's correct."

"So, you have a great deal of contact with him…on a daily basis?"

"Yes sir. I meet with him three times a day. I read with him at least one of those times, I also walk with him on the grounds, and I conduct a group session where he is encouraged to participate in social skills activities with some of the other patients. Oh, and once a week, I escort him into the community. He likes to sit in the park and watch the boats on the river."

"And the other day, he attacked you, is that right?" Belinski can't help but notice that a bruise on the side of the nurse's neck has been covered by some sort of skin toned make up.

"Well sir, that is true, but it was just one of those things. It happens in this place."

"And you aren't afraid…concerned, that it could happen again?"

"Detective Belinski, I'd just like to say that Noah is a gentle soul. He doesn't have a mean bone in his body. I don't think he was trying to hurt *me* when he had his…well, when he exploded. I think that it was something else. I was just in the wrong place at the wrong time."

Belinski turns to Dr. Belanger and nods.

"Thank you, Lawrence. That'll be all for now."

The nurse, clearly relieved that his presence is no longer required, rises and slips silently from the room. The doctor gives Belinski a look which he interprets as 'told you so' and then, he too slides his leather chair back from under him. Belinski follows suit but, for his part, he is less than satisfied. His instincts tell him that there is more to the nurse's story than he's revealed, and he makes a mental note to follow up before he leaves.

"This way, detective. I'll introduce you to Stafford."

⁓∞⁓

The man sitting on the edge of his bed, looking out of his window, appears agitated. Belanger has warned that he may be responsive, and he may not. He explains that some progress in this area has been made but Belinski should not have any preconceived notions. When he turns towards them as they enter, however, Belinski is startled and, just for an instant, he is transported back in time. It was another summer, better times for he and Anne, when they had gone to see Sir Paul McCartney in concert in Toronto. A birthday present. He recovers and collects his thoughts as Belanger makes the introductions.

"Noah, this is Detective Belinski. He would like a minute of your time."

Belinski steps awkwardly forward. Looking around, he realizes that there is nowhere to sit and so he steps around to the window wall gingerly.

"Noah," he begins, "it's nice to meet you." He holds his hand out, but the gesture is not reciprocated. "I'm told that you visit your sister from time to time, is that so?"

To Belanger's surprise, Noah makes direct eye contact. In fact, he notices that Noah is more engaged with Belinski than with most visitors. Then he begins to sway from side to side and his breathing becomes strained. He looks about wildly, from Belanger to Belinski to the doorway and back and begins to slap his thighs with clenched fists

The doctor, sensing Noah's physical distress, motions Belinski from the room. A minute or two passes before calm is restored and, as Belanger speaks to him in soothing tones, Noah returns to his position on the bed, where he resumes his outward gaze.

Belanger joins Belinski outside of the room and the two exchange worrisome looks. They start down the hallway when Belinski suddenly stops. He returns to Noah's doorway where he remains silently for a moment. Then he speaks.

"Audaces Fortuna Iuvat." And he studies Noah for a reaction. Then he rejoins his host.

'Fortune favors the bold?', detective?" queries the doctor.

"Just testing a theory," Belinski replies, "taking things step by step."

And the instant he completes his sentence, he feels the skin on the back of his neck begin to tingle.

⁂

The doctor sees him off at the door, but Belinski lingers. He is hoping to catch Noah's primary nurse and he is not disappointed. A group of health care workers are in conversation near the front desk. He takes his chance and approaches.

"Excuse me," he begins, "Lawrence, isn't it? Do you have a moment?"

"Oh, hello, detective," he says haltingly, "well…yes of course. What is it?"

The group disperses, leaving the officer and care giver alone. Belinski speaks plainly. "I have a feeling that you weren't being completely candid, Lawrence. Is there anything else that I should know?"

Belinski can see that the nurse is visibly uncomfortable. He glances back and forth and then turns and says, "detective, I was just about to go on break. Can we talk on the grounds?"

He takes a minute to retrieve his backpack and then leads Belinski out a side door and onto the grassed area surrounding the hospital. They arrive at a picnic table, clearly well used by the staff, and they sit facing each other. Belinski begins gently.

"Nice spot for lunch. Reminds me of Assiniboine Park. By the duck pond."

"Detective Belinski. I have to be honest, I'm really nervous." He looks him in the eye. "So, I'm just going to admit it…I wasn't completely honest."

"That's fine, Lawrence. Why don't you set the record straight, then?"

"Well, it's like this. I take Noah on outings. That part is true. We usually go for an ice cream. At Salty's." He notices Belinski's look. "I know…somebody's idea of clever, I guess. Anyway, we go there a lot. Then we sit by the river and watch the boats. Well, Noah always sits on the bench. Never moves. Just watches the river and relaxes."

"But something changed, Lawrence?"

"Ok. I'm just going to say it. But you have to realize, I love my job. And if you tell anyone…well, that'll be it for me." He searches Belinski's eyes. "I like to smoke a little. You know, when we're away from the hospital. Marijuana. The job's pretty stressful, detective. Well, I usually take a few puffs when we sit on the bench. I even offered it to Noah once, but I didn't get any response. So, one day, a few weeks back I lit up and…well, I sorta dozed off. Not for long…maybe fifteen minutes. I'm not really sure. Anyway, when I woke up, Noah was gone."

"And he'd never done that before?"

"Never. So, I ran up and down the street. Checking all the yards. I was frantic. I'm sure I looked like a lunatic. And then, when I got back to the bench…there he was. Just sitting there, staring out at the river. Like nothing happened."

"Is there anything else, Lawrence?" Belinski asks, maintaining his cool in spite of his elevated blood pressure and racing brain.

"That's all, detective. Except…do you have to say anything to Dr. Belanger? I mean…can we keep this between us?"

Belinski isn't sure whether to harangue this nurse or hug him. On the one hand, he is offended by the irresponsibility demonstrated by a public health official. On the other, the information that he has provided, at risk to his own position with the hospital, may impact greatly on the case.

"Let's leave it this way, Lawrence. I won't say anything for now. But I have to be honest. If you are required to testify in court, it's likely to come out. You might just want to come clean with Dr. Belanger, yourself. Honesty isn't a bad option, you know."

"I'll have to think that one over, detective. But thanks for being straight with me."

Belinski leaves Lawrence to stew in the juices of his own making and finds his way back to his vehicle. He's glad to have the long drive ahead to ponder the information gleaned in the last hour. A pretty successful trip, he figures, and certainly another piece of the puzzle has fallen into place. And he has another thread for Mansbridge to add to his ever-growing list of assignments. Before he starts the engine, he reaches for his phone.

"Ethan. I can be back there in an hour. Can you assemble the team? I think I have some new information which might help us."

"Zel. Glad you called. Did some checking into the wife of the construction guy. You remember, from the Wentworth case. Well…it turns out, she's a doctor. Works in the morgue at the Health Science Centre."

"Ok. That fits, doesn't it? Listen. I'm just not satisfied that the Mayor is the target in the Pagliani murder. See if you can find out who lives next door…the whole block if you have to. We've already determined that our suspect was in a hurry, right? Maybe he got the wrong address."

"On it. See you in a bit."

There is a definite buzz of excitement as the team settles into their places. It's late afternoon and the change of routine indicates a ramping up of the circumstances surrounding the case. Belinski and Mansbridge are huddled around a printout and the name of one neighbor leaps from the page. They look at each other, silently confirming the discovery. Belinski moves to the white board.

"Alright. Let's begin. I want to bring everyone up to speed on a few developments. First, I met with Mayor Seaverson of Selkirk today…you recall that victim number two, Pagliani, was found on his steps. I'll cut right to the chase. I think we can rule out any notions that he was targeted by our suspect. Aside from the fact that the body was found on his property, he simply doesn't fit the profile." He circles the mayor's name in red marker.

"That said, we've checked other residents who live on the same street, and we've come up with what seems the more likely scenario. Ethan?"

"Doctor Sharia Mehta," Mansbridge begins, "lives two doors down from the mayor. Currently, departmental head of Cardiac Medicine at the Health Sciences Centre here in Winnipeg. And a more likely target for our killer. Looks like our man screwed up. He got the address wrong."

Belinski steps to one of the few blank patches the board has to offer and begins his outline. There is a murmur of anticipation, much like that of a university class awaiting their professor's final exam prep reveal. And the clarity is startling.

Dr. J. Palasades	President of the Col. of Physicians and Surgeons		Grant
Dr. L. McCracken	Morgue	Health Sciences Centre	Wentworth
Dr. S. Mehta	Cardiac	Health Sciences Centre	Pagliani

"So, here's the bottom line. The location of the bodies is definitely not random. Our killer has been sending his coded threats to specific individuals. And each of them, as you can see, is a doctor of medicine." He underscores each with the marker. "We need to know what they all have in common. What binds them together."

A moment passes as the revelation sinks in. Pieces seem to be falling into place, and yet, the overwhelming question remains in everyone's mind. Why?

"Zel. I'm curious," Lemaire breaks the silence, "what made you rule out the mayor?" He points at Seaverson's name on the board. "I mean, you seemed to know just who you were looking for."

"Not who, exactly, Guy," Belinski responds, "more like what. I was pretty well convinced that we were looking for a hospital worker. It was a combination of what you said last night." Lemaire searches his memory. "And Beto as well. And then today the doc in Selkirk more or less confirmed it."

Ginelli perks up. "Me?"

"That's right, Beto. You reminded us that *Italian* is the language of love. And Guy, you raised the question regarding who speaks Latin."

"Ok. So..."

"So today, I spoke to Stafford. In Latin." He quickly answers the surprised look from his partner. "Coached by Ethan, here." A glance to Mansbridge. "I wanted to see if I could provoke some kind of response." He rubs his chin. "He didn't blink. But the doctor knew exactly what I had said. In fact, he translated." He turns to his partner, "Latin isn't the language of love, Guy. It's the language of the medical profession."

Lemaire is quick to pick up the train of thought. "So, our guy knows that those friggin' guys…ladies…doctors…whatever…will be able to decipher his message. Because they know Latin, and they're not stupid."

"So why didn't they come forward?" asks Ginelli.

"Great question, Beto," Mansbridge answers, "I think we have to assume that the reason isn't nefarious in any way. Maybe they didn't get the meaning at all. It is pretty obscure. Maybe our killer has given them too much credit."

"That makes the most sense," adds Belinski. Whoever has come up with this crazy threat has had a lot of time to think about it. To him, it's as simple as ABC. But for all we know, the doctors might not have even seen the message."

"Overthink," Templeton tosses out. "Like when the allies stormed the beaches at Normandy. The generals had all these wild plans to take out gun positions that didn't even exist."

"Good point, constable," adds Mansbridge. "Maybe our guy is so far into his own head, that he thinks everybody else is in there too. And it's very possible that he doesn't even want them to decipher his message at all."

"I think he's just a friggin' show off. Trying to prove how clever he is. Look at me. I'm better than the doctors. He's like the kid in school who always thinks he's smarter than the friggin' teacher."

Another murmur, this time of agreement and then Belinski refocuses everyone's attention to the names on the board. "So where does that leave us?"

"To state the obvious, it's a big step forward, Zel." Mansbridge taps a pencil against his knee. "For the first time, we know the exact targets of our killer. His so-called grudge, if I can use that term, is against three specific individuals. It narrows our search exponentially. And it answers a lot of questions." He tosses the pencil on the table. "But it raises another one."

"Which is? Lemaire asks.

"Is he finished?"

Belinski lets the question linger. It's a question he has been asking himself for the better part of the day. The majority of the cases he has been involved in over his career have consisted of a single crime. The question of who might be next had never come up. It just wasn't necessary. But this situation is different, and there are too many unknowns. And he feels the pressure to come through. To sift through the sludge and put an end to the carnage.

"It's our job to make sure that he is," he answers.

There is a collective nod from the team, a metaphorical rolling up of the sleeves, and Belinski continues.

"Alright. Ethan, I want you to cross reference these doctors with the Selkirk Mental Health Centre. See what they all have in common. In particular, I want to know the relationship between any of them may have with Noah Stafford." He studies the picture on the white board. "I think he may be our guy."

"Got it, Zel."

"Good. Now, our suspect is going home to visit his sister. Tonight." He looks at Lemaire and Ginelli. "I don't want him out of our sight for a second. Guy…Beto, you two gotta watch him from the minute he gets home til the time he returns to the hospital. One of you watches the front, and the other the back. If he leaves the house, you follow him. Clear?"

"Like friggin' pit bulls on a poodle. We're on it." Lemaire shoots a look to Ginelli.

Belinski now looks at Templeton. "Constable, I want you to sign out an unmarked squad. We'll set you up a couple of blocks from the Stafford home. And requisition whatever communication devices you need. Stay in constant contact with Ginelli and Guy and be ready to move in to assist at a moment's notice."

"Right you are, Cap." He looks across the table. "Got your backs, boys. Let's get this bastard."

"Alright. We have a few hours. Get some rest and some food on board. It's going to be a long night."

Rush hour traffic through the downtown area of the city has always been an unacceptable yet accepted way of life in Winnipeg and Terri navigates it with the patience of a saint. David takes in none of the landmarks that mark the early days of settlement of the region, however. He is biding his time, waiting for the opportunity to explain Andrew's treachery, uncertain as to what kind of reaction it will elicit.

A lull in the conversation forces his hand and he seizes his chance.

"There's something you need to know." His words linger like lead in the confined space of Terri's vehicle, and she grips down more tightly on the wheel.

"You were absolutely right," David continues, "when you said that Noah was a wonderful writer."

Terri accelerates to make it through the intersection ahead of the light. Then she looks sideways at her passenger. But she says nothing.

"Andrew recognized that early on in their relationship as well." He is floundering, trying to navigate the line between tact and truth. In the end, he decides he cannot and just blurts it out.

"Terri, there's no easy way to say this. Andrew stole Noah's stories and passed them off as his own. The books he published were works that your brother had written before he was…before he went into care."

There are moments in everyone's life when they are hit with information so full of cognitive dissonance, that they are rendered speechless. Like the patient who, having gone through treatment for a serious illness is told that, in fact, the original diagnosis was inaccurate. That resultant feeling of relief, which, all too quickly, becomes overshadowed by fury. Terri is caught between the two. And her thoughts are scrambled.

"Noah's stories? But…how? Why would he …?" She tries to settle herself to one train of thought. "That fucking bastard! How dare he steal my brother's books?"

David does his best to relay his conversation with Andrew. Inclusive in his summary are the clues which had led him to his suspicions initially and his laptop conversation with Noah which had confirmed them. Finally, he comes to the more immediate crux of the matter.

"Andrew has asked if we will set up a link between himself and Noah. He wants to interact with him. I told him that I would do it."

"But you can't just do that." She glares at him across the seat. "You have no right."

"I know. And I won't. Without your permission, I mean. But it's something I'd like you to consider."

"Absolutely not. It's out of the question."

David is silent. He vaguely registers a sign on his periphery. Welcome to Selkirk Home of the…

"How would we do it?"

Terri eases down on the breaks to adjust for the change of speed limit as they enter the city's perimeter and David pounces on his opportunity. He explains that he has already created the email for Noah on his own laptop and so all that remains is to teach Noah how to use it.

"We just need to show Noah how to send and receive mail. He'll pick it up instantly." He takes a moment. "I am convinced that Noah is far more aware of his surroundings than any of us give him credit for. It doesn't take a psychiatrist to see that. When we speak to him, I'm certain he can process it. From what I gather from Dr. Belanger, his biggest impediment is formulating words in his mind and then expressing them coherently. But, because of his superior intellect, he's found a way around that. He's able to use other people's words. That's why he uses lyrics and poems."

Terri shakes her head. "If only they'd found that out earlier. Years ago."

"It would have been life altering," David agrees, "but it isn't too late for Noah to have a life. Now that we do know, that is."

Neither vocalizes it but both are keenly aware of the enormous elephant riding in the back seat. While they are both talking about Noah's future, how can they ignore his past? And although they are both committed to his protection, how can they be certain that other people's safety can be ensured?

"Let's just get Noah home safely and see where this goes," Terri says as she eases into the lot and searches for a space to park.

"Ok boys. Can you hear me?" Templeton's voice crackles into the ears of his partners. He is set up just off the crescent, a block away from the Stafford home. It's just before ten pm and the sun has finally slipped below the trees on the western horizon. The only movement on the street comes from a family a few doors down who seem to be setting up for a garage sale the following morning.

"I hear you just fine, partner," whispers Ginelli into the mic. He has wedged himself into the space between the neighbor's fence and the Stafford's, which affords him a clear line of vision to the back door.

"What about you, detective? Can you hear my enchanting voice?"

Lemaire has the luxury of his own front seat. And he's thankful that on such a pleasant evening, he is in no need of air conditioning. He is slumped down so that only his head is above the dash, and he worries that someone might see him like that and call the cops.

"I hear your friggin' voice, Templeton. But for Chrissakes, turn down the volume. It sounds like you're screaming in my ears."

"HUA detective. By the way, boys, the wife made a giant thermos of coffee so, if you want any, just say the word and I'll bring some to you. Over and out."

"Over and out, for Chrissakes? What are we…flying F16's."?

"Just following procedure, detective. Ok, let's keep our eyes open."

❦

They sit together at the kitchen table. David has explained what is about to take place and shown Noah how to send and receive emails. For Terri's part, she has placed aside any recriminations which she has for Andrew and anxiously anticipates the reunion. The animosity she holds for him will have to wait. She wonders, however, just how Noah will respond when Andrew reveals his treachery. Will he be able to comprehend the magnitude of the act? Will he refuse to engage? She worries that all their preparations will be for not.

When all is ready, David places a call to Andrew and sets the stage. They have agreed to keep the connection open and that, should David notice any signs that Noah is in distress, they should take appropriate measures.

David turns to Noah and says, "Andrew is on the line, Noah, and he is about to send a message to your computer. It may be a few minutes before it arrives."

Noah makes direct eye contact and David has little doubt that he if fully cognizant of what is about to happen. A few minutes pass and then there is a ding on the laptop. Without prompting, Noah opens his mail.

Noah. Oh, how I have waited to say your name. It's me, Andrew. Whittier has explained to me the manner in which we might communicate and, as you well might imagine, I have thought about nothing else since. It seems a most creative way in which to do so but, knowing you as I do, why would I expect otherwise. I will say this, however. I fully believe that you can understand me when I write and, consequently, I have a number of confessions to make to you.

The first, I am ashamed to say, is in regard to my complete cowardice. On the night we were to take the LSD together…and you so innocently did so because you wanted to do it together…with me, I didn't take mine. And my dear Noah, I have regretted that moment my entire adult life. And I am so deeply sorry that you were so badly hurt. I will never forgive myself for as long as I live.

And if that weren't the worst thing I could have done to you, there is something else. This, however, is a little more complicated, as I shall try to explain. It's about your stories, Noah. Your manuscripts. When I left for England…when I knew that you were not going to recover from the trauma you had suffered…I took all of your work with me. I know how selfish that must seem. But the truth was they were comforting to me. Somehow, I felt that you were with me. Your words were all I had left of you. And I read them every night until I fell asleep.

And then I got the idea that they should be published. But, once again, I failed you. Instead of honoring you as the rightful author, I put them out under my own name. God only knows why…many reasons, really, but none of them noble. And whatever you must think of me, I more than deserve it.

But I have finally made it right, Noah. I have given a full confession to the London Times. In a day or two the world will know that you are the true genius behind those wonderful stories. You are on the precipice of fame and fortune, Noah. And although I know that was never important to you, at least you will have the satisfaction of knowing that your work has been well received. Lauded. So please allow me to be the first to congratulate you.

My final confession is this. And what seemed so impossible to have said all those years ago, comes now so easily to me that I would shout it from the roof tops of London or Winnipeg or Timbuktu. Noah Stafford...I love you! I have loved you from the moment I met you and I have loved you every moment since.

It feels so wonderful to be able to tell you that after so so long. And I say it honestly and openly, without any expectation of reciprocation. I cannot presume to know how you feel about me, nor can I have any assurances that, after my previous declarations, that you will respond at all. But I have had the chance to say it to you. And I am overwhelmingly grateful.

Do you remember Taylor, the solicitor who lived in the apartment next door from us? How we used to gauge his trial results by the music he played? I remember it was always Beatles with him. How did it go?

There are places I remember

Andrew sits back and breathes deeply from his oxygen tank. A plethora of emotions sweep over him, but he will reflect on them at a later time. Right now, he takes a deep pull and hits 'send'.

A few seconds pass and then he sees the incoming mail.

All my life, though some have changed

His heart skips and his hands tremble. He quickly composes the next line.

Some forever not for better
Some are gone, and some remain

They find a rhythm with their words.

But of all these friends and lovers
There is no on compared with you

And back and forth they write. Renewing their familiarity with each other, the old feeling of comfort and each is transported back in time to the room overlooking the parliament buildings. They are lost in a world of their own. Space and time are realities which have no bearing on the moment. But Andrew has come to his Rubicon and, although it terrifies him, he crosses it without hesitation. And he writes

In my life

And he presses send. The agonizing moments which pass feel every bit the eternity he has endured for over thirty years. He is waiting for an answer for which he has dreamt, yet never expected to hear. And if it does not come, it will symbolize the end of a journey which, by his standards, will have had no meaning whatsoever. Then he hears the ding.

I've loved you more

David and Terri, who have been sitting by watching, cannot help to have heard a noticeable gasp on the other end of the phone line and David quickly disconnects. Whatever might transpire between Noah and Andrew will unfold on their own terms. He nods to Terri, and they make their way into the living room. David senses that Terri is a little embarrassed. As though she has been witness to two lovers embracing on a park bench.

"I think it's going well," he says. "I wasn't able to see much about what Andrew was saying but it's pretty clear that it had a positive effect on Noah. Would you agree?"

"I'll be honest with you David. I didn't think this was a good idea but now, I'm so happy we did it. My god, just think. Noah has a friend. He has someone to talk with. It's just so…unbelievable. It's like a miracle."

"So how do you want to handle tomorrow?" David says, changing to a less appealing subject. "If Noah goes for his run, I mean."

"You have to go with him, David." She looks at him pleadingly. "Stick with him at all times. And don't let him out of your sight." She punctuates her thoughts. "I have a feeling that if we can just get through this weekend, things will be alright."

Back at the kitchen table, the typing continues.
Love, love me do
You know I love you
I'll always be true
So please...love me do
Love me do

The evening turns to early morning and Terri stumbles down the stairs.

"What time is it?" she mumbles.

"Just past four," comes the reply.

"Are they..."

"Yes. They're still at it."

"I can't believe it." She rubs her eyes. "What about you? Do you have everything you need?"

"I'm as ready as I can be. Somehow, though, I suspect that the morning run will be taking a backseat this morning."

"Clockwork, David. He never misses." She yawns. "I'm going back to bed."

David sits and watches the minutes tick away. The morning light is trying to peek in through the kitchen window. He strains to hear any sounds coming from Noah's direction but, save for the morning birdsong, his ears are met with silence. He gets up to stretch his legs and wanders into the kitchen where an exhausted Noah sits, placidly asleep, in his chair. David cannot help but notice the satisfied smile that lingers on his lips. He glances over his shoulder at the keyboard on the table. The last thing Noah has written still glows upward from the screen. It is the final line from Sinatra's rendition of 'Fly Me to the Moon'.

In other words, I love you

"Zel, it's me."

Mansbridge's early morning call finds Belinski already at his desk, preparing an update for a meeting with Cuddy later in the day.

"Ethan. Good morning. How are you making out with the doctors?"

"That's what I'm calling about. I've checked every connection in every which way and from every angle. And believe it or not, I've even resorted to some old-fashioned methods. I've spoken to all three docs on the phone."

"And?"

"And you're not going to believe what I've discovered."

The sweet sounds of slumber reverberate in Gineli's ears, and he is quick to trumpet the alert.

"Guys…what's going on? Wake up!"

"What the hell are you takin' about for Chrissakes? I'm sharp as a tack over here." Lemaire is indignant.

"Same," mumbles Templeton.

"Yeah right," grumbles Lemaire. "You're alert alright. You been snoring like a bear in a cave for the last half hour."

"Teamwork, fellas," cautions Ginelli, suddenly the voice of reason in the group.

Inside the house, David is shocked as Noah pushes back from the table, disappears into the basement, and returns in shorts and a tee shirt. In a flash, he is at the back door.

"Here he comes guys. He's on the move," whispers Ginelli as the door opens and a figure steps out. "Looks like he's coming your way, Guy."

"I got him." Lemaire peers out through the open car window. "Holy shit. He's goin' for a run. And he looks like he's in friggin' good shape. How the hell am I gonna keep up with this guy?"

"Hold on," Ginelli yells into the mic, "there's two of them."

"Two?" shouts Templeton. "How can there be two?"

"Yeah, I got the second guy. He's getting' on a bike, for Chrissakes."

Lemaire dashes from his vehicle and bee lines for David. He makes a grab for his arm and knocks him sideways. David caroms off of a juniper bush and the bike crashes at his feet. Shocked by the attack, and fearing the worst, he abandons the bike and runs off as fast as his unfit legs will allow. He dashes through a neighboring yard and tumbles out, disoriented, into the lane on the other side. Fairly sure that he has lost his pursuer; he heads off at a trot in what he thinks is the direction of the crescent. He knows that it is imperative that he locate Noah as quickly as possible.

Ginelli makes it to the front street in time to drag Lemaire to his feet. As neither man knows which way their suspect, or suspects, have gone, they decide to spit up with the younger afoot and the elder heading for his car.

"Best laid friggin' plans, for Chrissakes," mutters Lemaire as he scampers across the lawn. Then louder, "we better find this son of a bitch, Beto, or our asses are in a friggin' sling." He bounds for his car in a surprising display of athleticism.

The streetlights are still on, and a light fog has rolled in off of the prairie. David slows his pace and tries to gather his bearings. Traffic, on this Saturday morning, has yet to materialize, and the few sounds that reach his ears seem to come from no particular direction. He curses at himself for letting Noah out of his sight a second time and his labored breathing does nothing to ease his sense of panic.

He takes a gamble and chooses a path which cuts between two houses. As he reaches its end, he comes to a stop. He recognizes the mansions and the tree lined canopy of Wellington Crescent. And his blood chills.

Her muffled pleas reach his ears and he fears he is too late. Ten yards away, he can see her legs, protruding out from behind a giant elm. The slashes through her sweatpants are soaking up blood and one of her running shoes lies, lifeless, in the grass.

But she is obviously still alive. He races toward her, fearful that Noah will quickly finish the task before he can reason with him. He storms out from behind the tree, arms waving and confronts the assailant. His heart lodges in his throat.

"Blessing!" He screams. He stands, dumbfounded.

Lawrence Blessing kneels behind a young woman. Her arms and legs are bound, and she is covered in slashes. Her captive has one hand over her mouth and, in the other, he has a knife, which he holds menacingly at her throat.

"Just back off, Whittier. This doesn't concern you."

"You!" He splutters. "It's you, goddam it." He takes a step forward.

"Don't dare!" Blessing spits. "Another movement and I'll slit her throat from ear to ear."

David's words stick in his mouth. He struggles to control his emotions and his legs barely support him. And his bladder feels like it's about to give out. He holds his ground.

"What the hell…why?" he manages to say.

"You'd never understand," comes the reply, "but this one is actually your fault."

"My fault?" David says incredulously. "How the devil…"

The woman squirms and Blessing pulls back on her hair. The knife draws a trickle of blood from her neck, and she goes limp. Blessing returns his glare to David.

"You and your little talks." He sneers. "Before you showed up, I could tell Noah anything. He'd just sit there while I told him all about my little… hobby. Stray dogs, rabbits…whatever I could catch. I'd carve them up and then tell him every delicious detail.

Even the first two murders." A little smile of remembrance. "And he'd just sit there and listen. Wouldn't move a muscle."

"But why…"

Blessing ignores the interruption.

"The last one…oh she was nice. I told Noah how I cut her legs…the sweet sound the flesh makes when the blade slides through it." He shoots David a look so malicious that he feels chills down his back. "Well, he jumped me. He tried to hit me. After all I've done for him."

David begins to hope against hope that he might somehow talk Blessing out of it. That he can reason with him. Stretch out the conversation.

"You must know that you can't get away with this. I'm a witness for god's sake. Do you think I won't say anything?"

Blessing gives him a look that drips with condescension. "Got that covered, too, Whittier. See that backpack." He points to the ground a few feet away. "Inside, I have a knife. And guess whose fingerprints are on that knife? Stafford's a very sound sleeper. So… when I'm done here, I dip that knife in this little beauty's blood," he shakes the woman by the hair and she bursts into tears, "and leave it on the ground."

"But I'll tell them what really happened. You can't expect…"

"No, Whittier. It's you who can't expect. They won't believe you. They'll believe the evidence. And all the evidence points to Noah Stafford."

Blessing lets his words sink in for a moment. And then adds.

"Fata meis" He glares at an unresponsive David. "Don't they teach Latin in British public schools anymore, Whittier?" He sneers. "Fate is in my hands." He looks at his victim. "Especially yours, darlin'."

Then he grabs the woman by the forehead and pulls backward. She looks David in her eyes and through her tears, pleads with him.

"For god's sake, do something. He's going to kill me. Please… help me."

David takes in the reflection of light from the streetlamp as it bounces off the cold steel of the knife. His feet are rooted to the ground, paralyzed by his own fear. Another moment in time overwhelms him and he responds to the alarm going off in his head. Lunging forward, he reaches for the knife. With one hand across Blessing's face, and the other around the wrist holding the weapon, he shakes violently, hoping to dislodge it. The two men struggle, each vying for the upper hand. The woman manages to crawl across the grass and starts to scream. David finally gets on top and raises his fist. The punch, however, is never delivered, and he feels the knife rip through the cartilage between his ribs and into the soft tissue of his heart. He gulps a lungful of air and then, feeling the strength ebb from his body, rolls onto the ground. His final words, real or imagined, are 'Christiane... I love you.'

Blessing turns his attention to the woman, screaming beside him. He scrambles to his feet and, as she writhes back and forth in an effort to free herself, he kicks her in the stomach. Then he raises the knife and holds it to her throat.

"The fun's over, lady. Your time has..."

With an explosive thud, a body crashes into her assailant and Blessing is thrown to the ground. The knife flies from his hand and Noah grabs him with both arms. While the woman screams, he squeezes with all his might and refuses to let go. The two men remain for some minutes, locked arm in arm until a voice silences their grunts.

"Get your friggin' hands off him." He looks at Noah. "And *you*, too, for Chrissakes." He glares at Blessing. Then he blurts, "which one of you is Stafford?"

Blessing leaps to his feet. "That's him, officer," he shouts breathlessly. "Be careful. He's a freak. He tried to kill that girl."

"No, no, no, no!" The woman screams. "Not him." She yells, looking at Noah. Then she points at Blessing. "Him! That fucker tried to kill me." And she erupts into tears.

Blessing stands there, sucking in air, and looking about for an escape. But he has no intention of running. And he knows it's over. He looks at Noah, kneeling on the ground, panting.

"You would have made the perfect patsy, pal. It was the brilliant setup." He looks at David's lifeless body lying on the ground. "Until that asshole showed up."

Ginelli and Templeton arrive to assist and, before long, the sound of police sirens echo in the distance.

CHAPTER
Seventeen

Lawrence Blessing has waived his right to legal assistance. Now that he has been discovered, he no longer cares about his freedom. His attention has turned to self aggrandizement. He will finally have his chance to reveal the enormity of his intellect. To show just how clever he has been. His ego demands it. He sits at the table, alone, a fitting end to a solitary existence. And, just like one of his idols, John Lennon, who once wrote, 'no one, I think is in my tree', he is awash in a sea of his own superiority.

Belinski sits across the table, accompanied by his partner, and a third member of their team, Inspector Ethan Mansbridge, and he grapples with the notion that this seemingly insignificant man could be responsible for such evil.

"What a waste," he says to no one in particular. Then, more formally, "Lawrence Blessing, are you aware of the charges against you?"

Blessing smiles, as if some exotic parlor game is about to begin. "Of course, I am detective. I think you'll find that I'm aware of most things of importance."

Gone is the anxious tone of the nurse who pleaded with him to maintain silence about his so-called habit. The tenor of the man sitting opposite is confident, sure of himself. Belinski can't help but wonder if this, too, is an act, or the true nature of the killer.

"For the record, Lawrence Blessing, are you responsible for the murders of Angela Wentworth, Rosamie Pagliani, Jennifer Grant and David Whittier?"

"Well, detective. The first three I can give you an enthusiastic affirmative. To the fourth one, Whittier, I would have to answer an emphatic no. Technically, he attacked me. My response was purely self defense. I would have been happy to let him walk away."

Belinski swallows like he's eating rotten fish. A random thought runs through him that he'd rather engage with a hundred Vasilios Bouras's than one Lawrence Blessing. Part of him wants to end the interview on the spot. Leave the answers to a court of law. But he knows that it's important to get everything on the record. He presses on. And he cuts to the heart of the matter.

"So, Lawrence. You wanted to be a doctor."

Blessing is irritated. He's waited such a long time and he doesn't want his dance cut short by a cop who doesn't have the capacity to appreciate his accomplishments.

"Let me keep it simple for you, detective. I didn't want to be a doctor. I *was* a doctor. A resident." He tosses a look of derision towards Mansbridge, as if hoping that he has at least one audience member who might be worth impressing.

"I wanted to be a surgeon." Blessing sits a little taller in his chair.

"Alright. You wanted to be a surgeon. Glad we got that straight."

"Just imagine it" Again he directs his comments to Mansbridge. "A perfect marriage of vocation and avocation. Having the ability to save lives…or not… literally in the palm of your hand." His gaze is distant. "That delicious feeling of scalpel slicing through flesh. The smell of the blood." He licks his lips. "My dream, occupation and passion all rolled into one."

"So, what went wrong?" Belinski does not stray from his line.

"Wrong, detective? Let's not be so black and white. It is never right or wrong. Shades, detective. Hues. Nuances if you will." Blessing looks at Belinski, waiting for him to rephrase the question more to his liking. He's met with a silent stare.

"Fine. I have a certain proclivity. And I like to indulge myself from time to time. One night I was on a break. And believe me, detective, they don't give you many. So, I found myself down in the morgue." He smiles at the recollection. "Alone." He glares as if the inference should be obvious. "I slid out a cadaver on the trolley and I started cutting. I'd done it before. Call it a pastime." He smiles at Mansbridge. "Well, I was pretty engrossed in what I was doing, and I didn't notice that I was being watched." He flashes a look of disdain.

"Dr. McCracken." Belinski prompts.

"She was in charge of the morgue. And she caught me red handed." A glance to Mansbridge. "Pun intended. I pleaded with her not to turn me in." He looks at Belinski. "You would have appreciated the dialogue, detective." He adopts a tone that Belinski recognizes from their previous conversation on the grounds of the hospital. "But she would have none of it. She was on the phone to my supervising physician before I got back to the ward."

"Which leads us to Dr. Mehta."

"The bitch wouldn't even listen to me. Sent me packing immediately."

"So, to round out the story, you appealed to the College of Physicians and Surgeons, but your expulsion was upheld."

"Palasades." Blessing continues the story. "What a piece of work. She thinks that the sun rises and sets out of her…well, she ruled against me as we all can surmise."

"So, you wanted to get back at the world."

"Not the world, detective. Just the ones who betrayed me."

"And three innocent women are dead. To satisfy your need to get back at the ones who hurt your feelings."

"For justice." He intones. "Iustitia."

Belinski ignores the word which had plagued him for so long.

"But there was more to it, Lawrence. You left us clues. You wanted to show just how clever you were." Belinski pokes at his suspects soft spots.

"Isn't that just typical," Blessing pushes back. "Why do cops think that criminals are trying to outsmart them? As if that would be hard to do." He looks at Lemaire. "What's a cop, anyway, but a school yard bully who's graduated to a gun and a badge" He sneers. "They weren't for you, detective. The clues were for the so-called brainy bunch."

Belinski looks at his colleagues. Whether it was prearranged or simply an audible, he nods and Mansbridge takes over.

"I'm Inspector Mansbridge, WPD. I'd like you to fill in a few details. Seeing as you've brought it up, let's start with the message you left at each of the crime scenes."

Blessing perks up, clearly happy to have the person whom he feels might be most appreciative of his cleverness, directing the conversation.

"I graduated at the top of every class I was ever enrolled in, Inspector. Grade school, high school. I had a perfect grade point average my entire undergrad years. *They* recruited *me*. Do you know how rare that is for a Med school?"

"So, when they rejected you, you felt you needed to demonstrate that they'd made a mistake. That someone as bright as you would be a benefit to the profession."

"Do you know that studies have shown that thirty percent of all doctors are narcissistic sociopaths? What's one more going to hurt? And one of such promise."

He leans forward and pleads with his eyes. "I was smarter than any of them. What gave them the right to toss me out? To take away my dreams."

"So, you wanted to show them just who they were dealing with…in a matter of speaking."

"Exactly. They call themselves intellects. I left them signals. In Latin. But I doubt they ever had any idea that they were being threatened." He scoffs "But I knew."

"And that gave you comfort." He takes a moment. "But I have to be honest with you Lawrence. You weren't the only one who understood the message." Mansbridge nudges.

"Oh, but you're wrong there, Inspector. I came to realize that there simply wasn't any way that they could have deciphered my little threat." He sighs. "But I do admit that I enjoyed teasing them. After Wentworth, I realized that I was in a league of my own. That nobody could ever figure it all out."

Mansbridge holds Blessing's eye for a moment and then nods in Belinski's direction. "He did."

Just for a moment, Blessing, for all his braggadocio, is silent, as if the floor is shifting slightly under his chair.

Mansbridge takes the opportunity to shift gears.

"But why a fourth murder, Lawrence?" His tone is softer, almost friendly.

Blessing is glad for the change of direction. Happy to have the spotlight back on himself, he resumes. "Stafford had been changing. I can't describe it except to say that he had suddenly become more aware of the things going on around him. Over the years, I'd told him everything. All my secrets. He was my father confessor…well my audience at any rate. And I began to worry that, if he kept progressing, he might spill his guts."

"You'd told him about the murders?"

"Of course. But I'd also been setting him up. Just in case. Think about it. The first murder…I was sent home with him. There was some kind of bug at the hospital. He was a basket, and his aging parents couldn't cope. I did Wentworth while he was out for his run."

"So even then, you were looking at him as a scapegoat."

"I have an ability to see the big picture. To think ahead."

"And the others?"

"Precisely the same procedure with Grant. I knew that Stafford had gone home. And I knew where he lived. It was child's play to linger until he left the house. And history was repeated as it were."

"I see," says Mansbridge like a keen student to his mentor. "But I'm curious, Lawrence. Why the mutilation" Why did you have to cut the face in the way you did?"

"You like that. I'm glad." He preens like a peacock. "I was spelling it out. Literally. I turned the smile into a U. Understand? It's both practical and metaphoric at the same time. 'U' signifying it could have been you. And 'u' as in replace the 'I' with a 'u'. How much clearer could I have been?" He leans back proudly.

Mansbridge knows the team has all it needs.

"But the one in Selkirk. You really fucked that one up. You got the address wrong?" His tone is darker, more provocative.

"One mistake, Inspector. I'm sure you've made a few errors in your life."

"Still," Mansbridge squeezes, "it wasn't the perfect crime. You're nothing but a wacko with an axe to grind. Just another pathetic loser."

He lets his words hang in the air for a moment, then, satisfied that he's made his point, he stands up and walks from the room, leaving a deflated Blessing sitting, alone, at the table.

Belinski rises and calls for a guard and he, too, heads for the door. Lemaire, close on his heals hesitates, and then, turning to Blessing, who is sitting with his head in his hands, he says.

"Iustitia! Ya freak. Shove that where the sun don't shine, for Chrissakes." And he slams the door.

There was no funeral. No memorial service to celebrate a life well lived and, in the end, the name of David Wittier slipped quietly into anonymity. And if he was aware of the measure of success he had achieved, that awareness has disappeared with the closing of the last chapter of his life.

Weeks have passed since his total and complete discharge from the Selkirk Mental Health Centre and Noah, laptop resting nearby, sits at the familiar kitchen table. The therapy, instrumental to his recovery, has been put on hold, as an entirely new manner of 'treatment' fills the moments. Several times a day, he and Andrew log on and wile away the hours immersed in each others company. And Noah's improvement has been exponential. And although the prognosis for speech is unknown, his ability to communicate ideas is no longer limited to the thoughts and expressions of others. And, much as the savant possesses 'islands of genius', he has already begun to write. Poetry and even the odd short story fly from his fingers and onto the screen in front of him, much to the delight of his audience of two.

And as for Terri, she is thrilled to be appropriated to the role which she has, for so many years, been preparing. Part cheerleader, part loving sister, she has retired from the jewelry business and welcomes the opportunity to watch over the world of her brother. And not a day has gone by that she doesn't offer a silent prayer of thanks to David for everything he did for Noah and her. *With love there is hope. With hope there is life. With life there is happiness.*

The trees have turned and there is a hint of frost in the air. It has taken longer that he would have preferred but the apartment is empty and the new head of security at Biekler Industries has dropped the last of his boxes on the porch. His son, Joey, who has been dodging and weaving through the piles of leaves which dot the front yard, calls out.

"Hey dad, wanna toss the football around?"

"Love to, champ. Just want to talk with your mom for a bit."

She is standing on the porch, watching the scene, and he hugs her and swings her around in a circle. And he knows that what ever words might come out of his mouth will be completely inadequate to describe what he feels. He'd rather enjoy the moment than talk anyway.

Anne lands on her feet and sums up what he feels in one simple expression. "This feels right," she says as they stand, arm in arm, and watch as Joey is tackled by an imaginary opponent.

"So, how are the new partners making out?"

Belinski laughs. "Well, I had coffee with them yesterday. And I'm not there was a winner, but it was a conversational battle royale like no other. I wished them well and told them that if they ever needed anything…they should call Mansbridge."

Anne smiles and nudges her husband with her hip.

"Oh, and by the way," Belinski continues as he reaches into his jacket pocket. "Speaking of Ethan." He holds up an envelope. "Wedding invitation. He and his partner are getting married."

"I'm glad for them." Then Anne gives him one final nudge. "You're being beckoned."

Belinski leaps down from the step. He dashes out into the lawn and says, "Alright, champ. All yours."

Joey dodges one final would-be tackler. "Ok, dad," he shouts. "Go long."

Acknowledgements

This book could never have been written without the encouragement and support of my wife, Cheryl, who listened, guided, and provided suggestions which I found to be invaluable. Her insight into the writing process, coupled with her ability to say, 'it's good', in such a way as to leave no doubt in my mind whether a particular line or phrase was acceptable or rubbish, is a talent unto itself. She has been essential to this book's completion and to every moment of every day of my life.

As to the legal and procedural protocols regarding the varying situations in which my characters find themselves, whether in the interview room or the courtroom, receiving cautions or charges, I can honestly say, with full disclosure, that I have, greatfully, no firsthand experience. Fortunately, I have a daughter whose career path has turned out to be most beneficial and I express my gratitude to Tracey Pniowsky, LLB, for her assistance in these matters.

I would also like to thank the soon to be Dr. Markus Harwood-Jones. Academic, author, artist, social activist and one of the most unique and special people among us. Our talks and discussions have been a source of both information and inspiration. I have so much love and respect for him and am proud to call him my grandson.

My gratitude extends to my sister and brother-in-law, Bonnie and John Buhler, the real-life version of my characters, the Bieklers. I shamelessly lifted some of the lines they have shared with audiences over their many years of philanthropy. I just couldn't write it any better. What I did say about the Bieklers in the story, I stand by in real life. They are among the finest people around. And, as an aside, it is their home which adorns the cover of this book.

For background on Ethan Mansbridge's military career, I turned to LCol (retired) Cameron Buchanon, whose experience and guidance is most appreciated. It helped in my understanding of the character and, time willing, has provided a protagonist for the next story.

To the countless professionals doing such outstanding work in the field of Autism Spectrum Disorder, thank you for your dedication. Although one of my protagonists, Noah Stafford, did not, in actual fact, have ASD, I borrowed heavily on their research in order to bring him to life. The more I read, the closer I got to know him.

Finally, to that rag tag group of misfits who, for no other reason other than chance, grew up in the old neighborhood, this book is for you. Though some of you are no longer with us, and others have moved on to other places, what we shared in those times together, in the streets and the fields, helped shape who we would become. And while we are no longer who we were, who we are now, is the sequela of those early days. *Praesens est ex praeteritis*, eh? In your honor, I have named many of my characters after those very streets we roamed together and, although time and circumstance have seen us go our separate ways, the bonds we built then remain unbroken. It isn't hard to close my eyes and feel your presence… swinging for the fences, hiding, seeking. Goin' long.